THE MOON IN THE LINING OF HER SKIN

Kiran Manral is an Indian author, podcaster, columnist and mentor. She has published books across genres in both fiction and non-fiction. She lives in Mumbai.

Happy reading!

THE MOON IN THE LINING OF HER SKIN

KIRAN MANRAL

hachette
INDIA

First published in 2024 by Hachette India
(Registered name: Hachette Book Publishing India Pvt. Ltd)
An Hachette UK company
www.hachetteindia.com

1

Print ISBN 978-93-5731-816-7
Ebook ISBN 978-93-5731-449-7

Hachette Book Publishing India Pvt. Ltd
4th & 5th Floors, Corporate Centre,
Plot No. 94, Sector 44, Gurugram 122003, India

Typeset in ITC Galliard Pro 11/16
by R. Ajith Kumar, New Delhi

Printed and bound in India
by Manipal Technologies Limited

FSC
www.fsc.org
MIX
Paper | Supporting responsible forestry
FSC™ C043100

'As if you were on fire from within.
The moon lives in the lining of your skin.'

– PABLO NERUDA

Prologue

'Shall I come wearing the visage of a lost world?
How shall I dress when descending into your clay?'

– RIYAZ LATIF

IN THE BEGINNING WAS THE INFERNO, THE BLAZE that lit up the heavens and seeded the hells. Gases collided, atoms danced, the void was set ablaze, and from nothing emerged something, fuelling the furnaces of the universe, the multiverses.

In the beginning, there was nothing and then there was everything: time, matter, space, atoms, molecules, vacuum, infinity. From nothing came everything, and everything would go back into nothingness. Before the beginning, when there was nothing, we were there. When there will be nothingness again, we will be there. In the spaces between the beginning and the end, there will be us. We are the eternals, the ones born of the void, the ones who will go back into the void, the ones who are the void. We are the emptiness from which everything began. An emptiness so vast and overreaching that all of humankind's efforts have not yet begun to comprehend it.

We first emerged from the fires of creation, from the explosion that set the universes into motion. We rode on pieces of rock and debris hurtling through the void, we swirled in the distances between our suns, we cooled down, we heated up, we found hidden corners of the universe that would allow us to survive, between earth and mud. We were here. No one saw us, but we were here, scattered across the ethers, creatures of wind and air. A Petri dish on a planet.

From the stars came the stuff that germinated this planet. Us, born of fire, made of flame. We left no ash when we burnt. When the world was moulding itself, we were watching and waiting. We watched as creatures crawled out of the swamps, formed themselves from the mud, unformed themselves, formed again, were wiped out by the debris hurtling through a violent universe in its cradle. We have lived before, we will live again. We are everything that is unending and everything that will never begin. We are what was there, before the single cells formed in the primordial oceans. We are the life tied to this planet, life that found no form, no shape, that inhabits the rocks beneath the surface, that rides the zephyrs and nor'westerlies. We were smoke and ash, molten and fluid, with nothing to define us except perhaps the urge to be.

Our kind don't die like humans, like animals, like plants; we keep forming over and over again, over thousands of years. We have seen Rodinia, Pannotia, Pangea, Gondwana.

We are made of all that the earth brought together unto itself, before it spun into what it is today. We have seen the mother ocean, the beginning and end of all life in this part of the solar system. We have seen continents take birth, break away, boundaries between land and sea erase and grow again. We have seen all the earths and all the worlds and all that lies between the two, all that humankind cannot see, cannot ken. Not yet. We were created by the one who created it all, only he can destroy us. We are indestructible. We are forever and ever. We walk amongst humans, we can take their form without the flesh, with their flesh, and sometimes we take over them. And then we never let them die, because their death would be the end of us in flesh too. But die they must, and we must live on. That is our curse and blessing.

Noor

'There are darknesses in life and there are lights, and you are one of the lights, the light of all lights.'

– BRAM STOKER, *Dracula*

I WOULD RUN AWAY, YET AGAIN, TONIGHT. THE whispers had begun, soft susurrations on the edge of my consciousness now, soon they would grow into a roar in my head, dinning out every thought. They were warning me, they who were watching out for me, those of my kind whom I had forsaken to become this creature neither human nor divine. No longer angel and far from human. Run now, Noor, they told me, whispering gentle warnings, tiptoeing first into my dreams, apologetic and hesitant, then breaking down doors to storm into my waking thoughts: they are coming for you, the hounds of hell will be released yet again, and they will hunt you down. My brothers and sisters, who were the unfallen, who watched out for me, whom I had abandoned in my insanity to taste what being human meant.

Mankind didn't know what it was tampering with when it began digging down to the centre of the earth, from the bed of the ocean, in Russia, in Qatar, in Oklahoma, in Canada, in Bavaria, in Mexico. Man wanted to open up the earth, for they knew more about space than about what lay within the planet they lived on the surface of. Humans should have known, should have heeded the cries of the damned that echoed through the miles of rock, begging to be let out, back on to the surface, breaching the Moho, the last delineated barriers between mankind and the damned, barriers that the volcanoes had already erased wherever they erupted. They were just making it easier for them to emerge through the thousands of miles of rock and crust; it took them no effort when they found one, they slithered out in seconds and covered thousands of kilometres on the surface in one short run. I knew, we knew, we ran away from them. No matter how many tunnels one closed up, they found new pathways drilled into the earth that led straight to hell. All the levels of hell. And from them emerged the hounds, drooling and slavering, sniffing down the surface for traces of the fragrance of roses that always emanated from me, driven by their charioteer, the one whose name would never be mentioned for fear of summoning him. From these holes in the earth emerged the evil that should be confined within, they had no route to emerge on to the surface.

The hounds of hell, they had no mercy, there was no pleading my case with them. To look them in the eye was to die instantly if you were human, and it was a mercy to die instantly if you were human. They could suck your soul out through your eyes if you locked gazes with them, blasting holes into your ocular sockets as they devoured the only thing precious about you – your soul. If you could see them with the human eye, they would shock you into senselessness. I could see them as they were. They had a hundred heads, each with slobbering jaws, dripping acidic drool that etched grooves in the earth as they strode it, each jaw with rows of sharp fangs ready to rip flesh from a soul. The one who commanded them did not care about the human destruction left in their wake. Humans were but collateral damage when it came to collecting fallen angels. I was one. They had my scent, they would sniff me down from the four corners of the earth, no matter where I hid, unless I managed to throw them off my scent. I could not camouflage it, I was fragrant like a thousand roses, a fragrance that heralded my coming, a fragrance that trailed as I walked away. It was a fragrance that humans were confounded by, humans lost judgement and coherence when too close to me. I could tempt them to do what I chose at that particular moment, whether to feed me or to consort with me.

They were simply doing what they had been tasked with, having been commanded to drag me to the netherworlds. A fallen angel could not be allowed to roam the earth for so many years – I had lost count of how many centuries it had been, millennia from the time of my descent. One loses track of time when one has lived so long in undying flesh. I had escaped them each time they came, every few years or a few months, or whenever it was that they remembered I was still on the loose, a fallen angel who could only be permitted to be a demon, never allowed to be a human, never ever allowed to forget that she could never be human.

When I first fell, I fell into the land where the Tigris joined the Euphrates, where all was golden, crops swayed in the fields, rivers fed the lands, and cities were ruled by benevolence and grace. I would never rise into the light again. I was there when the great king had his code engraved on the tablets that modern man had yet to fully comprehend. I lived in the house of a merchant who had taken a fancy to me much to the despair of his many wives. I outlived him and then moved to the palace as handmaiden to the noblewomen, then to the temple as a sacred consort, and then, as the generations moved on and I stayed unchanged, moving to another temple in another city as a high priestess.

I kept moving. I had done it all, all that I had been sent to keep humans away from, to warn them about, to keep them on the path of virtuousness. I had succumbed to the temptations of the flesh, of the carnal, of the vicissitudes of emotions. I had wanted to know joy and sorrow, bliss and pain. I had sunk into the sin I had been sent to warn the people about. I was there when legendary armies pillaged and sacked the cities, driving the people into despair and ruin. I fled from the devastation on feet that were slow and human, fled to the east. I had walked the surface for centuries, through high mountains and arid land where the sun was relentless and the cold scathing, where men were scavengers, building homes in walls of stones covered with cloth, living off the shrubs that grew around, raising their own livestock, drinking the clear water of streams and breathing the crisp clear air of the high mountains. As I fled to safe havens, the others of my kind fled too, scattering to the four winds, fleeing from that which pursued them, pursued me, rising from the bowels of the earth ever so often, through the tunnels to hell, these abominations invisible to humans. Visible only to those they hunted, their horror was punishment enough for daring to want immortality and the flesh. I fled again, hoping that the further I went the more difficult it would be to track my scent. But distances mattered nothing to the hounds. They just began emerging through hell-holes closer to where I was; the ground sank into broiling magma and they slithered out, sniffing the breeze for me, for the others like me who had fallen, still fleeing them. How many had they collected yet, how many of us had managed to escape, how many more had fallen, I didn't know. I was alone, and tired, and terrified. My light was fading more and more as time passed by.

It was messy and tiresome, the demands and limitations of this human body. You had to eat, drink, urinate and defecate. You were subsumed by the extremes of temperature, the flesh rebelled against the heat, it shrivelled against the cold. When it was time to run, I cursed these feet, no matter how quick I was in human terms, I was limited by how fast my legs could carry me. This is what I'd chosen when I had dropped from light into flesh, forsaking the ethereal for the corporeal, choosing flesh and blood of the human body, its joys, its pains, its desires, its pleasures. But not its fear of death. I could not die. I would not die. Death was not a privilege allowed to us who chose to fall. I would spend eternity in the hell they put me in.

I was still glorious if I chose to unfurl myself in my full radiance, but where on this earth could I dare do that without a human chancing to see me; humans were everywhere on the surface, wherever one looked. Even in places where you thought you wouldn't see a human for miles, one would suddenly emerge – a traveller, an explorer, a journeyman – and they would carry the tale of the woman who unfurled her light for miles in the midst of darkness wherever they went. The ones they told it to, they would hunt you and try to destroy you. It unsettled humans, a glory they could not explain, match or control. At first, they would worship you, then when the pleasures of worship paled, they would try to pull you down, either with words or actions, to their levels of ordinariness. When both worship and denigration didn't satisfy them, they would try to destroy you.

Shining in a sack of coal got you picked out, I had learnt to dim my light on the surface. Sometimes, dangerous things picked you out, things that wanted to take your shine for their own, that sucked out all that made you radiant and ground it into their darkness where nothing redeemed them, not even shards of stolen light. My radiance was so bright it could blind the human eye. I had dimmed over the years, as fragments of my light dissipated into those I had taken the purest light from; the kernel of light that lay unawakened in most humans, coiled at the base of their spines. I had been created from light, of light, and wherever I went the darkness would be waiting to claim me as its own. So, I dimmed my light.

I was light within flesh, muscle and tissue covered with skin. I was light without the shadow, the one darkness had staked a claim on, when light had abandoned me. I abandoned the path of the light, even though it still shone through me, shimmering through my veins, skeins of moonlight glittering in a riverine estuary seen through my skin. But the light really hadn't abandoned me, although I had chosen skin over light. That was the only explanation as to why the hounds hadn't been able to drag me down to the hells. And that they did not know my true name. No one did, except the one who had named me. The name given to me when I had been created had cadences too complex for the mortal tongue, it came from a language not meant for mankind or demon to use, from the language of those who were of the light, from the light. I had no right to use it, now that I had fallen from the light, but it still called me at times, a soft murmuring within my head that warned me, that told me I needed to run again, away from where they had tracked me down.

My light, silver and rippling, a blaze once, faint remnants of all that was still heavenly in me, a faint glimmer now compared to the brilliant radiance I used to be: but still too powerful for them to drag me against my will. But I was in human skin, and human skin was vulnerable, I was vulnerable, I felt pain, I felt fear, I felt all the things I didn't when I had been just fire and light. Skin had weakened me. The hounds sensed that, they fed on fear, they leached the courage from one, easier to just give oneself up for the taking. How long can I keep running? As long as it takes, I told myself. As long as it takes.

Tonight, I would run again. They had emerged on the surface, I could sense that, the whispers in my ears had become screams. Their growling would burst through the skies, a sonic boom echoing through the ethers, shaking the window panes, rattling the roof. A howling only I would hear, sounds no human ear could. It would only be my blood that ran cold in these veins that criss-crossed my body. Only my eyes that would see the horror they were as they strode magnificently across the earth in huge bounding leaps that covered kilometres in a matter of minutes.

I had come here to this house, in this sleepy mofussil town in the Doaba, the patch of land fringed between two rivers, verdant and fertile, one bitterly cold night many years ago. I thrived where there was a confluence of waters, where waters enclosed land, I sought it out. The night I fell from the skies was black, and mournful voices were calling out the names of the dead, and the frost seeped into your veins, turning skin to ice, when to step out was to risk losing a limb. I was barefoot and bleeding, and had no idea why I had been dropped here in this lane, in this strange town, where the winters were cruel and the summers were worse. Of that night I don't remember much. I don't remember anything of where I had been before that night, of being chased down by the hounds. I remember trying to desperately flee the tent with the nomads in the vast outback of rugged mountains and bare land. They had kindly given me shelter and food. I had watched in despair as they were eviscerated into nothingness before my eyes, as the slavering jaws bent down to collect me. A flash of white light searing the skies and nothingness, and the falling, an infinite falling through layer after layer, piercing each with a rip that tore the invisible fabric dividing the various dimensions that separated all the worlds, landing with a thud on what seemed to be a road in an unfamiliar place, a road fringed with low homes in an unfamiliar town.

The homes were all barricaded against the icy cold, some had lights lit within. The wind sliced my skin with icy fingernails, piercing my unwrapped throat, stabbing my eardrums, freezing my thoughts. I was bleeding, and I had fallen from great heights, and I was running from what would still be chasing me, playing cat and mouse with me; the acrid, sulphurous stench of the hell they had come from in my nostrils as the portals between the worlds were still ripped open. I looked desperately for escape, for refuge. Ringing the doorbell, the voice came into my ears, a familiar voice, one that I knew I should know but my mind was blank at that moment, with no memories.

If you asked me now as to why I had picked that particular house of all the houses in the row of houses on the street,

I would be hard pressed to answer. Perhaps it was because theirs was the only house down the length of the street with all lights on and the curtains not drawn to keep the casual stroller down the street from peering in. The people within, they waited for the doorbell to ring, for someone to need them as much as they needed someone. As I dragged myself down the street, shivering in the inadequate clothes I had on, the blood freezing in my open wounds, I sensed an unquestioning welcome awaiting me here.

I pushed open the gate, my breathing heavy and laboured. The hinge creaked, alerting those within that someone had entered. Perhaps that was why the creaking hinge hadn't been oiled, the creak was necessary, the creak was the sentinel. If there were dogs, they did not bark. A light came on above the door, lighting up the porch, and the door was thrown open without the precaution of a safety chain. An elderly lady stood there, looking me over. She wore a bulky hand-knitted fraying sweater, thick woollen socks under her moccasins, her hands tucked into the pockets of the sweater, a muffler wrapped around her face and neck. Within this packaging, her face was tiny, crumpled and curious.

'Who are you?' she asked. She seemed unperturbed to find a young woman on her porch, bleeding from gashes all over her body, barefoot and bedraggled, clad in clothes completely inadequate for the weather.

'Help me,' I pleaded in a voice too exhausted for coherence.

She beckoned me closer with a gesture as imperious as

it was graceful. An unbidden thought came to my mind, through the chill and the pain, perhaps she had been a dancer when she was younger, her muscle memory still retained the grace and economy of movement. As I came into the circumference of the yellow light spilled by the bulb, she caught a glimpse of the wounds on me, gasped and called for her husband.

'Sunoji,' she called, her voice redolent with the unmistakeable tone of command that had the Sunoji from within scurry out hastily, wrapping a shawl around himself, bracing for the cold that would inevitably hit him when he stepped out onto the porch. He was a kindly man too, that I could see. His eyes were warm and gentle. He had once worn a turban, I knew, and he had given it up when he had married this woman. She had come across the Radcliffe Line, a young girl, buried beneath corpses in a train full of carnage, someone she didn't know had grabbed her when the mobs were butchering her family and fled to the railway station, stowing her under a seat. She had sat there terrified as mobs stormed the train compartment and butchered all those within, sparing no one, failing to notice her huddled, shivering between dead feet, sitting soaked in the blood of those killed. She had grown up an orphan, taken in by a kindly home. They had married each other for love. They had lived together all these years with love, they had raised children and they had created a home with love.

What I needed now to heal me, to keep me safe, was a house that had been lived in with love. I could feel my light struggling to emerge, to reach out to the love that enveloped them, to draw from it, to seek the strength it needed, I needed. I would be safe here, the voice in my head told me, that strangely familiar voice that was looking out for me when everyone, even my kind, had withdrawn in fear. I put my hand out and she held it. The silvery threads reconnected, after all those years. I had met her before, in another life, in another skin, from another time, when I had been travelling through mountains bare and stark, hostile and treacherous, I had walked across rivers of ice and valleys of stone and soil, I found shelter where I could, and I had walked, walked and walked. She started, and peered at my face curiously.

'Who are you?' she asked. 'Why do I feel I know you?' I had lived so many lives now, had so many lovers, touched so many lives, that I would never know when I met them again in new skin. They would know me though, they would feel the light in me reaching out to the light I'd left behind in them as I'd taken what I'd wanted from them.

I fell to the ground in a dead faint. I didn't know what happened after that, but I know they took me in, tended to my wounds, nourished me back to health. It took weeks before I could stand again, before my wounds healed. They never asked me what had compelled me to step out on that freezing night. They didn't know what it was that I had been fleeing from that night, and why I'd knocked on their door. I never did tell them, it would terrify them, that what had chased me could return sometime, anytime, and take them as well as me. They didn't ask me where I came from and when I planned to leave, what my name was, who my parents were. And so, I stayed on in their home, like a guest who had overstayed her welcome, becoming day by day part of the household, filling up their need for a living creature to alleviate their loneliness, like one took in a stray to care for, and in return be needed. I was safe for a while, a few days, a few weeks, a few months I didn't know. She grew fond of me, the waif who had landed up on her doorstep, in the thick of the darkest days of winter, when even ghosts refused to wander the streets and breaths congealed into ice before one could even exhale. She called me Noor, after the child she had been and lost before she became the woman she was. She had a new name now, she gifted me her old one, the one that had been discarded when she was torn from her family in the melee of the Partition of these countries.

I was Noor now. I was light. She didn't know that when she gave me her name, the name she had abandoned, she had given me a new power. She had named me for the light I was.

When the susurrations began that night, I was ready. The fire rose up the walls of their room and engulfed them in a quick searing embrace before they could wake and register what was happening. I was humane with those I chose to sacrifice, sacrificing only those who were ready to go; if there was no one around who needed to end, I ran. I may have fallen but I was of the light. I first made sure they slept, never to wake, thanks to a generous meal I had cooked, served piping hot from the stove, ladled with ghee and crushed sedatives, sedatives I had carefully sourced from the lady's own stash of sleeping pills. She couldn't sleep without them, the pain was excruciating, it was a matter of months now. The man had been more prosaic, if he had any unfulfilled desires of his youth, he had tucked them away in the grind of providing for the woman he had married, the children they had birthed. She had clumps of cells rotting her body from within, she would be dead in a few months anyway, I knew, even if she had been diagnosed and they began treatment. He was already sliding into the blessed oblivion of forgetting, where he would soon forget everything, even his own name. Death was inevitable. I only hastened it. They would have faced the wrath of what chased me had they lived, had they faced what no human should have to face. I was doing them a kindness, I told myself. I was ending them when they were still happy. I stroked their heads as the fumes asphyxiated them and drew their energy into me, diminished energy, but enough to get me some more time in this skin before I needed more light.

Her thoughts, as she died, were still confused. 'Noor,' she whimpered. 'It was always you, wasn't it, the one who put me on the train? How can it be? How can you still be the same after all these years?' That had been a different life, a different me. She remembered. I had all but forgotten.

I smiled. Of course, it was me, I had plucked her from the carnage of her home and family, and fled with her to the railway station where I put her on the train, bidding her to hide beneath the seat until they reached. I always came back to those who had touched me. She owed me her life, and I was here to take hers, that was how it worked. I was led to them by the skeins that connected us, I just needed to follow the silvery lead, etheric and unseen to the mortal eye. Their fate was sealed when their skin touched mine, even in passing, even if they didn't realize it back then.

It had burnt down perfectly, old and crumbling as it was, brick, mortar and wood, almost like divine providence was guiding the lick, flare and spread of the flames. I left the house from the main door, giving it time till I reached a fair distance away, before I allowed the flames to rip through all the rooms unfettered. The blaze lit up the night. I grabbed the bag I had packed earlier with all the money and valuables I could find in the house and a few clothes for good measure. I ran down the road, the cover of darkness my cloak, the bus waiting for me at the bus stand, the driver unquestioning, the conductor unquestioning, like they had been expecting me. Perhaps they had. I would disembark from this bus where it ended and take another one, disembark where it ended and find myself shelter. This is what I did, this is how I survived in this world which wasn't meant for me, me in the skin. Skin which was so different from the light.

Those sleeping within had no chance, they would say later. There were two charred bodies found when the flames had been doused, they wondered why they didn't find a third body, mine. I was too far to be tracked down by the time the ashes were cold and they began sifting through the debris. No survivors. One missing person. That was if anyone remembered me and noticed I was missing. I made sure to erase myself from most memories. If asked to describe me, they would find it difficult to put the details together to make an image of me. I had never been photographed, I can never be photographed. No one would notice me unless I wanted them to notice me, and no one would remember me unless I wanted them to remember me, and now, in this time, in this place, I had wanted to slip through unnoticed, unremembered, a wraith on the fringe of peripheral memory, a gust of breeze that blew past their lives, ruffling nothing but their thoughts on the surface of their consciousness. I was the woman without a shadow, the woman within whom light shone through unhindered, I was the woman darkness chased to make her its own. I had once been an angel, made of light. I had fallen, I was that abomination, neither divine nor demonic, scuttling to find shelter in a world that had given her skin but not protection.

It was the fag end of a hot scorcher of a summer, things burnt easily in summer, bone dry and a tinder-box, all it needed was a spark to set the flames roaring. Summer in this part of the world was a continuum of long, never-ending days, where the night peeked in, embarrassed to interrupt the communion between the earth and the sun, locked in a long, intimate embrace. Autumn, which would follow, kissing everything red and orange, was the glorious retreat of summer, the Northern hemisphere whispering goodbye to the lingering sun, while the South opened itself up to being taken by it, the darkness of lengthening night, minute by minute, day by day, reclaiming dominion, cold north winds sweeping in from the vast expanses of the Siberian tundra, across the arid stretch of the Tibetan plateau to where the Himalayas stood sentinel between their freezing grasp and us, sneaking in fingers of ice through the gaps between rock and air. I had always loved winter. The cold, the sleet, the dreariness, the grey skies, the grey days that shifted imperceptibly into nights so black that even our shadows deserted us, when the stars were hidden by the fog and mist that swirled above the streets, making the street lamps pale and indistinct blurs, hiding sidewalks and cloaking homes, making the ordinary mysterious.

I would leave, only to begin all over again. It was unending, the lives I would live and the lives I would end, to live the lives I needed to live.

Rani

'Here is the world. Beautiful and terrible things will happen. Don't be afraid.'

– FREDERICK BUECHNER

I HAVE BEEN MARRIED THIRTY YEARS TODAY. THIRTY years too little. Thirty years too much. It all depended on how you looked at it. Some days I was grateful I was here, safe within the four walls of a home, still alive, still breathing. On other days, the infinite what-ifs of my life came back to haunt me: what if I had not gone where I had gone, what if I could have been a wife in the true sense of the term, what if I had a child or two and spent my life caring for them and raising them... What-if was a path I tried not to go down too often. My life had taken a detour years ago, and I no longer knew or wanted to know where that path would have taken me. I had once traversed it on a daily basis when I had been newly married. What-ifs were a dead end. One turned around midway and returned to the here and now and what was and what is and what will be. I had travelled often enough on the ship of my ghost life, but I had never quite waved it goodbye from the shore.

Today was my thirtieth wedding anniversary and my husband had forgotten it – it would have worried me had he remembered! So lost was he in his own world, a world that I was no part of. He had other things, other people to occupy his mind. I didn't blame him, it was all my fault. We didn't celebrate anniversaries, we didn't celebrate birthdays, we didn't celebrate anything anymore. Perhaps the daily quotidian of staying alive to see a new dawn was celebration enough for us.

I was peripheral to him now, and perhaps that was how it was in most marriages, one partner existed as white noise in the other's focus of attention. Sometimes I wondered if he even saw me anymore, or whether to him I was now just that cup of tea placed on the table, dinner heated up and served in casseroles on the dining table, the eggs fried just thus, sunny side up so the yolk runs golden, and the bread toasted hot and buttered fresh at the breakfast table as he reached out for it, his eyes on the newspaper. I did not mind the lack of attention and the lack of love it implied, for it kept me safe. His attention and love would get me punished, a punishment that would involve pain and suffering of the kind that would not show on my body but agonize me into madness, welters within my body, unseen to the world, a shrapnel of pain searing my head. I had all the attention I didn't want, every second of the day, for days on end, until it left me. It. He. Him. Majnu. That which must not be named. That for which I had no name. That which had claimed me for its own and would never relinquish me.

I was what was called the possessed. What had possessed me was an entity I could not define. He was smoke and fire, air and ash. He stayed with me every second he chose to and disappeared for days, weeks, months on end, precious stretches of time I could be free only to brace myself for his inevitable return. A lover no one could see. A lover only I could feel, hear, sense, touch and never ever hope to escape. A lover so insanely jealous that a kind word from my husband would have him flagellate me until it felt that the skin on my back had split open and was bleeding all over the floor. But there would be nothing to see, nothing to touch, everything was as it should be, smooth-skinned, even. How do you ask for help when there are no signs of what afflicts you to show? Who would believe you? Would they not call you mad and incarcerate you in an asylum? Perhaps that was what I was, insane, totally insane, cloaked beneath the externality of bourgeois respectability.

Rani, this is what it is, I reminded myself over and over, in the times when I had my mind back to myself. You, who were so steeped in misplaced pride in yourself, now have nothing, absolutely nothing to lean on. It has all been taken from you, stripped away after a moment's unseemly rage. And now you live trapped in a marriage that is a straitjacket, trapped as the plaything of something that has taken you over for years and years. What use was your pride to you, except to earn you the wrath of those who felt threatened by it, by their own inadequacy in the face of it? But I was greedy for life and the hope that someday I would be free of it. Some days, when I was free of it, my hand would reach out to the kitchen knife, the sharp one I took for the meat, and I would sit at the dining table and contemplate the veins of my wrists, knowing I needed to slice them diagonally, and fail to put the knife to them. The professor's sleeping pills were at the side of the bed, a bottle I picked up when I dusted the side table and kept back, afraid that if I held it for a moment longer, I would be tempted to empty the contents into my mouth. The poison we used for the rats lay under the kitchen sink; it would be a moment's work to drink it all up. But I resisted. What if I would never be free of it even after death, what if death would just mean being bound to it for eternity? The cat purred, his coat as black as night, as he wove his way against my legs and down the stairs to the basement where he lived. His saucer was empty of milk, I'd barely just put it out. I was responsible for it, I had to live.

The harpies of my youth, those who sat wrapped in shawls on the string charpais in the courtyards of their homes soaking in the sun on winter afternoons, their moustached lips quivering in condemnation as I passed their doors, had marked me with their beady eyes. Nothing good will ever come of that girl, they said to each other in tones not so low that I would not hear, she will bring disgrace and ruin upon her family with her wantonness. Being wanton meant not wanting to shrink, I did not want to shrink. I revelled in the attention I got. Little did I know it was dangerous, attention was good and bad, and the bad often outweighed the good.

Their words, like all unkind words uttered to pierce the heart, reached my mother's ears, they came to her through the filtered reiterations of unfounded gossip, and brought tears to her eyes. Don't shine too much, she told me, your youth and beauty are not the gift you think they are, they are a curse. Dim your light, wear muted colours, tie up your hair, get the stitches of your kameez taken out so they don't quite cling to your body, cover your chest with your dupatta, a woman's modesty is in covering her bosom with as much cloth as she can. She had over the years, shrunk into herself, first when she got married and then as each child emerged out of her, sucking out her essence, until there was nothing left of her, except a shell and the fierceness of maternal love that kept her going.

I was disdainful of the harpies then, I told myself then that they were jealous of what I had and what they had long lost. Now I knew better. They had not been jealous, they had merely been prescient, warning me to not attract attention, to not flaunt my beauty, my youth. They had been beautiful, vain and proud too in their youth, before time had raked his claws through them all, humbling the beautiful and bestowing grace upon the ugly.

Attention attracted evil. Evil brought doom. These were all old wives' tales, concocted to keep disobedient young women in line. Nothing would happen to me, I was young, I was strong, I was God's chosen child, the sun laughed upon me, the moon blessed me, I shone. Nothing could touch me. It was the hubris of youth, the illusion of infallibility. We all have it, the ones who are blessed to emerge from the finest mould that the creator had made, like I had. I was blessed with what the Gods had gifted me, a lissom body, a complexion that was milk and cream, features so sharp they could slice an approaching palm, eyes shaped like almonds, deep and haunting, lips pink, full and enticing. I had taken the best of both my parents and made it my own. I was the chosen one.

And then I called evil upon myself. It began with a bracelet at Bilkis Bi's stall, the old crone who sat with her trinkets spread on a makeshift stall, just outside the steps of the old marketplace. I had wanted a bracelet of green stone from her stall. Jade, I told myself, carved jade, but then rationalized that it couldn't have been the real stone, not here in this little stall. It would be worth nothing, she would be happy to rid herself of it, I thought, but it was precious to her. She told me it was not meant for me, not for sale. The ends were two dragons roaring flames into each other's mouths, and where the light caught their carved scales, the surface shimmered like molten metal. Golden inserts punctuated their bodies. It was old, I could feel the weight of the years on it, infusing it with the strength of time that had seeped into it.

I put it on my wrist, fascinated by the green against my pale skin, the luminescent veins running through it sparkling in the light of the dropping sun. It then spoke to me, calling my name in a voice so soft and silvery I thought I was imagining it. This was mine, it had to be mine, it was claiming me for itself. I could feel it tightening its grip around my wrist, closing in, welding itself to my skin, with a rough dry heat that seared flesh, making it crackle. The crone suddenly noticed I had put it on. She gasped, a rough garbled cussing in a language I could not comprehend, and grabbed my wrist, pulling it off with a rough strength I would not have thought she possessed. Her hands felt like the inside of a tandoor, searing hot, scarring skin to a crisp.

'That's not meant for you,' she had said, taking it off and tucking it carefully into a pocket concealed in the voluminous folds of her petticoat. 'Take anything else that you want. I'll give you a discount.'

'But I want that one and nothing else,' I had said petulantly with the arrogance of never having been refused anything I wanted from anyone all my life.

She shook her head in denial, her rheumy eyes narrowing as she looked at me, her face, wrinkled and shrivelled as it was, expressionless. She was assessing me. A red-hot rage boiled up inside me, rage I'd never quite learnt how to control. I lashed out and threw all the trinkets displayed on the trestle table down to the ground and kicked hard at the bamboo pole holding up the cloth shading her precarious stall. I regretted it the moment I'd done it, but what was done was done, and I was too immature to realize that there was immense power contained in a contrite apology. The precariously arranged stall collapsed instantly, scattering all her wares onto the grey brown mud on the unpaved ground. I watched, anger still red hot behind my eyeballs, as some of the trinkets got trampled underfoot by the passing crowd. Some stopped and cast a curious glance at what had happened and carried on unperturbed. Others stopped to help, because she was, after all, a familiar face on this pathway. The other stall owners left their wares unsupervised and rushed to help her.

I was the oldest of four daughters, I'd learnt early to be the chief of the pack and the pack now was the gang of four of us friends in our first-year degree college. Backing down and apologizing would have resulted in a loss of face in front of them, or so I'd thought then. I was barely seventeen. That moment of rage, unfounded as it was, had been my undoing, it had pushed my life on to a track far removed from what I had expected to live out.

'You shouldn't have done that, Rani,' Rupinder told me ruefully. 'It was not a nice thing to do.' Such cutting censure coming from someone as gentle as Rupinder who never raised her voice, not even to scream in fear when a cow chased us down a road one strange morning with no provocation and none of us even wearing red.

'You mind your own business,' I had replied, turned away, uncaring of the censorious eyes of those passing by, branding me a harridan, some surely to carry the tales of this behaviour to my parents.

Rupinder was the kind one in our gang of four, with her large watery eyes and visible downy moustache above her upper lip that she would not remove. She was the only one who would dare stand up to my rage and temper tantrums without getting fazed. She was also the only one I was really scared of, perhaps because she was the only one who wasn't scared of me. She bent down and began helping the old lady gather all that I had scattered on the muddy ground, picking up the amulets with reverence, wiping them with her dupatta, uncaring of the mud dirtying it, and placing them gently on the trestle makeshift table the old crone had begun setting up again.

I turned back, the rage still bristling within me, and kicked it down again, hauling Rupinder up from the ground. 'Let's go,' I remember saying to her, 'Why are you wasting your time helping this old witch? Serves her right.'

The crone turned to me, taking in a deep long breath and then speaking in a voice that made me tremble with fear.

'Your beauty and your pride will be your downfall,' she intoned, standing in the midst of the debris, the whites of her eyes turning black as she looked at me for a long scary moment. 'You will lose everything, including yourself.' Around us everything was unchanged; the sun shone on the crowded path, the dappled light filtering through the tree canopy that fringed it, people walked past us, around us, the noises of the marketplace loud and raucous. I felt a chill settle over me, a sudden sensation of being dipped into a tub full of ice water on a winter morning, the thin frozen sheet on the surface cracking as I was dunked in.

Had I thrown a needless tantrum just for a bracelet that was probably just plastic? But it wasn't. It was precious, I had deduced now, judging from how carefully she tucked it into her skirt, and how intricately it had been carved with dragons and inset with gold bands. Perhaps I wouldn't have been able to afford it, and her not wanting to sell it to me was a face saver in disguise. The stall was almost set up again, a few trinkets remained scattered on the ground. A woman came up, her back towards me and bent low to pick up whatever trinkets remained on the ground. Her movements were gentle and deliberate, almost like a meditation. She glowed, she glowed like I had never seen any human being glow before, soft light flowed out of her in waves, her skin was veined with streaks of silver light that flashed iridescent for a brief second, a blink, before it turned normal again, making me wonder if I had imagined her like that, lit up from within, like the signboard at movie theatres.

Her voice, as she spoke with the crone, was mellow and refined, her accent and the language they spoke with each other alien to my ears. Another country, another time, another civilization, another time. I had never heard the language before. Perhaps she was from the same place the crone came from, a country far beyond the borders of ours, ringed by mountains and arid, rugged territory that was rife with conflict, weapons and bloodshed. She looked up at me, and in that instant, I lost all the misplaced pride I had in my appearance, for I had never seen a woman so exquisitely beautiful. I had the inexplicable urge to take her in my arms and smother her with kisses and to run my hands all over her body, an urge I had never ever felt before. I wrenched my eyes away and my breath caught in my throat. Her eyes were grey green pools of pain and darkness I wanted to drown in. Cat's eyes, they were called cat's eyes by unkind people who said nasty things about those who had light eyes. Her eyes changed colour even as I looked into them transfixed: green, grey, opaline, tourmaline, the sharp green of the jade of the bracelet, a dull pewter.

The crone took the bracelet out from her skirt pocket and gave it to the woman, she slid it on, and it tightened around her wrist, moulding itself to her skin. She saw my glance on the bracelet and sighed, smiling a smile that was milk and honey and all the desire I had never known or felt in all my years. It was hers, that is why the crone had not given it to me.

'Did you want this?' she said, putting her hand out, the bracelet glinting in the evening sun, lighting up the mysterious worlds within the jade's translucency. I knew I could have it if she chose to give it to me. I took her hand without thinking, feeling a warmth flow into me from her body, the silver cocoon of light that seemed to be a living, pulsating thing around her enveloped me as well, drawing me into an embrace where nothing mattered: not the world, not the bracelet, not what anyone watching would think of me. There was only this strange desire to crush her lips with mine, suck at her breasts, lie on top of her like a man and take her, just take her.

There was something hypnotic about this woman, and it terrified me. I stood, rooted to the spot, unable to move, seeing my hand reaching out to hers and the light from her flowing into me, binding us together with a connection I could not break free from.

'Noor, stop this wickedness right now this moment, she's a child,' the crone yelled, her tone imperious. She whacked us with her staff where our hands held, breaking the flow of the light. The cocoon of light withdrew itself and with it was gone the insanity that had suddenly overcome me like the sun dropping, behind a mountain range. We broke eye contact, her hand jerked away from mine – was there guilt in that sudden withdrawal of contact, of skin on skin? I came back to the here and now. We had been standing apart, my hand on her bracelet, for what seemed to be no longer than a fraction of a second, wondering if I had really felt that way about a woman or had I been imagining it. Was I suffering a sunstroke?

'Noor.' Her name echoed in my head. I said it out loud, tasting it on my tongue, the salty sweet musk of it.

She laughed and pouted back at the crone. 'Why won't you allow me some fun?' she said. 'It would be a lovely change.'

'Not her, she's a child, she still has to learn her lessons,' the crone muttered and then muttered away some more in the language I did not understand. The spell was broken.

The sun was already slanting through the lower branches of the trees fringing the path to the marketplace, as dusk neared. We had been out all day, much after college had ended, wandering around aimlessly. Decent girls didn't wander around, they went straight home after college ended. I was indecent, was it any wonder that the harpies called me disreputable, and tales of my supposed transgressions had spread far and wide? The boys followed me hoping to get lucky, no matter how much I scolded or insulted them.

The shadows we cast on the uneven, muddy ground had lengthened to eerie proportions. I looked at the four of us, standing against the rays of the setting sun, and at our shadows on the ground. I started in shock. There were four of us, but only two shadows. Where Noor's shadow should have been, there was only an orb of pulsating brightness, shifting shape, glowing, pale white, sparkling with iridescence. I realized I had thoughtlessly put my hand into the light that surrounded her to touch the bracelet. I looked disbelievingly at my hand, my wrist still glowed, a glow that faded as I looked on, almost radioactive in the dull light. Bilkis Bi absorbed the sunrays like a black hole, she had no light around her, nor did she cast any shadows. A chilling realization crept up my spine, and I walked away as quickly as my feet could take me, dragging a worried Rupinder behind me.

'Let's go home,' she said. 'You are not yourself today. You are behaving strangely.'

I didn't know who or what I had become on that day.

'Come quickly, let's get away,' I whispered to her. 'There's something quite not okay with these two.'

She followed me on reluctant feet, whispering back, 'What is not okay? Tell me, tell me...'

I waited until we were a fair distance away and got ourselves some hot jalebis with milk. 'They had no shadows, those two women, both the old lady and the young one who put the bracelet on her hand, Noor. The rays of the sun passed right through them.'

She blinked in disbelief. 'How is that even possible?'

'That's what I saw,' I told her. 'They had no shadows.'

There was silence between us for the rest of the walk towards our homes. We did not know what to discuss about what we had just seen, discussing it would validate it. We had seen today a woman who glowed and a woman who had no shadow. Rupinder turned off where the lane leading to her home branched off from the main road, and I continued walking alone. The regular louts hanging around the by-lanes made their usual vulgar comments, weighing their chances of getting lucky if they followed me. It was only fear of my father that kept them away, I knew. Someday, when he retired from his position, they would have no fear. I hoped my sisters and I would be far away from this lane then. I lived further off, where the houses thinned, the lanes lengthened and darkness had already taken over the paths leading to what we called home, now a speck of light in the distance, the bulb outside the main door set into the wall of the bricked-up compound. Nights had begun falling early these days, summer had passed us by and winter was circling us, we were long past the equinox, the day the nights began to rule this hemisphere of the earth.

I saw her when I turned off the main road into the paths that went towards my house, past deserted old workshops, where the shadows dappled the streets with lives of their own. She was standing against a crumbling wall, lighting up the small circumference of the path and the wall around her, like a glow-worm would. I had just left her behind at the marketplace barely a few minutes ago – how was she waiting for me, how did she know where I lived, how had she reached here without crossing my path, what was this sorcery?

The fragrance of roses enveloped me before she came up to me, a fragrance I would forever associate with her for the rest of my life. 'Rani,' she whispered, coming up to me, her voice a silvery tinkle that reverberated through every part of my body, putting her hand out to take mine, waiting for my acquiescence before touching me again. I did not realize then that touching her would change me in so many ways.

'Come with me, I know you want to. Let's run away from this town.'

I didn't know that it was an important decision I was making, but I made it. I put my hand out automatically to take hers. She grasped mine with a strange strength that belied her slight built. 'You know, don't you?' she said, looking into my eyes with her eyes, now flashing tourmalines in the fading streetlight. 'That you were never meant for this, this life of human nothingness, getting married, having children, becoming a slave to domesticity. You were meant for so much more. You have the light in you now, I have gifted you some of my light. But my light is not stronger than her curse, which will keep you alive but will not save you completely from what is to come.'

Her hand soldered itself to mine, a strange static bound us together, I could not unclasp myself even if I tried, I knew. Nor did I want to. Who was she, this woman, and why was she suddenly everywhere I went today? What was her connection with me? Why did she arouse such strange sensations within me, sensations I knew I should not feel for another woman, sensations that were never to be spoken of, acted upon? She drew me to her, the light warming me up all over, within me, without me. At that moment I would have gone anywhere with her, not knowing who she was or where she would take me or whether she would put me into the flesh trade after selling my virginity to the highest bidder. I'd heard about these women, these pimps, who conned young girls and took them to countries where they were reduced to nothing but sex slaves. I'd heard stories of the girls who had escaped and returned to homes they weren't welcome in anymore, broken shells, the abuse they had suffered eviscerating all that was human and hopeful within them.

'Come… where…?' I asked her, confused. This was not me. I was the sassy confident one, she had shaken me to smithereens of uncertainty.

She laughed. 'Just come, you'll be safe with me. You'll be happy. Her curse won't touch you while I'm with you. Come quick, it is almost nightfall. It will fall on you the moment the last rays of the sun withdraw from the surface of the earth here.'

Her other hand traced a line from my forehead to my lips and rested there for a moment. Her lips came to meet mine and stayed there for a long while, probing, caressing, exploring. She smelt of roses, an entire garden of roses. I would have followed her to the ends of the earth and happily fallen off them if she had asked me to. What was this light, this cocoon that enclosed her, a shimmering pulsating embrace pulling me into its ambit? A dog barked somewhere, voices floated in from the distance, we broke apart. I looked at her disoriented, wondering what was happening to me.

'Come,' she said, her hand still grasping mine. I looked down and saw her hand glow, the veins silver, the moonlight traceable under her skin. A shiver crawled down my spine. 'Who are you?' I asked. 'What are you?'

'I am all you desire and all you need, I am the light,' she replied, her voice echoing in my head long after she stopped speaking.

I stepped back, terrified, terrified of what she was, what I couldn't explain and of what I was feeling for her. The connection between the two of us broke abruptly with a snap. She shrugged and released my hand. It felt like a blindfold had been lifted from my eyes. She stood in front of me, ordinary and unremarkable, no glow, no shine, an everyday woman in her late twenties, not any different from most of the women around. Just a woman I had never met before today, never seen, never known. Just a woman I had kissed right now with more passion than I would ever be able to summon for anyone else for the rest of my life. I didn't know that, of course, back then. I know that now. Then I had just walked away in confusion, little knowing that the single moment of touch had bound us together, strands of a tenuous silvery connection I would never be able to break all my life.

She would come back into my life years later, and she would take what she hadn't back then. She stayed in my mind, even after all these years. Noor. Who she was, how did she know that crone, Bilkis Bi, I would never find out. What I did know now, after all these years, was that Bilkis Bi's curse, hurled at me when I had thrown her stall down, had descended upon me almost immediately.

Noor had been trying to save me from what was to come, she had seen Bilkis Bi's curse hovering over me when she had uttered it at that moment, a black screeching shade of a falcon circling me, waiting to swoop down on me when day turned into night. It did after she had walked away and I was alone, walking down the dark path beside the canal to where our home was twinkling in the distance. It lifted me up and threw me into what I could only call a blackness, an infinity of never-ending blackness. I was there for I don't know how long, suspended, neither dead or alive, unable to move, terrified, marvelling at this place I was in, which made even the possibility that I was dead seem welcoming. I was there because they couldn't decide what to do with me, the black falcon that had swooped down upon me, and the one who had hurled the curse on me. And then a sudden searing hot burst of light, like the radiance of a thousand suns cracking the darkness into a never-ending whiteness, and I fell through a white nothingness, bleak, metallic-smelling nothingness, feeling the earth rise up to cushion me as I fell soft as a feather upon it. Cold, broken bones. Lying on a rough surface, gravel, a road. The roar of a car, many cars, the rumble of a truck, the approach of a vehicle, headlights picking me up as I lay, headlights sweeping past me, unwilling to get into the trammel of police reports and first responders. A screech of tyres. Voices. Hands lifting me up, handling me roughly, putting me into what seemed like the backseat of a car.

Is she dead? someone asked, a man.

No, she's breathing, another replied.

How far is the hospital from here, a woman asked.

An hour or so, the first voice replied.

We can't wait for the ambulance, the woman said, *we have to take her there.* Roses, I was lying in a garden surrounded by rose bushes, the air was suffused with the cloyingly sweet scent of thousands of roses. Then there was silence, and I felt the cocoon of light envelope me again, this time it gave me strength.

'Noor,' I felt myself say, rather than heard.

The hand stroked my forehead, gossamer touch of life.

'You're going to be fine. You'll live,' she whispered, a whisper that went into my brain, racing through neural pathways that were shutting down and forcing them open again. Then she was gone. I felt it. She was watching over me. She had been watching over me, she had got me out of the black abyss.

I would live. I would survive this. I will find her again. Then the abyss again, a Stygian blackness that I knew I had to find my way across if I wanted to die or even live. I did. I had been gone for days I was told later, weeks, I had no sense of time where I was. With no memory, no explanation of where I'd been, my bones broken, my mind foggy, my words disoriented. When I returned home from the hospital a few days later, the whole neighbourhood came out to watch me enter the lane where the vehicle could not enter. The lane where I had last kissed Noor before I'd been picked up. No one came up to me, to us, to commiserate, to express their sympathies, to offer courage and strength. They watched us, like one would watch circus animals, the stench of voyeurism in their presence. I could hear their thoughts, imagining unspeakable horrors of what they thought had befallen me. The most horrific that they could imagine was that I had been abducted by louts and raped, then flung on the highway once they had been done with me. That I was unviolated, something confirmed by even the doctors at the hospital, didn't fit in with their theories. They made up new ones. I had run off with a boy, they told each other, and he had abandoned me on the highway when he realized I hadn't carried along any jewellery. One whispered that she had seen me embracing a woman in the lane, like lovers. The others laughed at her, these things didn't happen in our small towns, she should stop making up false stories they told her. She didn't repeat it again.

Like vultures, their thoughts circled over their heads at a distance.

'Keep your head up and your back straight,' my mother said to me in an undertone. 'You don't have to be ashamed of anything.' I walked with difficulty, my limbs were disjointed, not obeying my commands. I couldn't remember anything from the days I had gone missing. Someone, something had picked me up and then thrown me down, that was all that I could remember, which was of no help to determine whom a complaint needed to be filed against.

I was sent off to my maternal aunt's home in the big city where I would be taken care of, in much the same manner as a stray dog would be cared for. Not too far away, a few hours, ride on the state transport bus. Only till the whispers died down, they told me, my parents.

'I have three other daughters to think of,' he said. 'I'll call you back home soon.' I waited for the call that never came, and soon became elongated indefinitely as months passed by living with relatives who treated one like a contagion. Scraps of food, fewer scraps of affection and nothing more, coupled with a newfound strange repulsion my aunt and her family displayed towards me, as the whispers about me reached their ears. The fact that I was unviolated meant nothing; I had been abducted and that was violation enough.

I left her house within a few months, finding myself a job at a local college in the administrative department. The principal was kind enough to offer me a room in her home as a boarder, charging me bare minimum as rent, just a token to help me keep my pride in the face of adversity. It was unforeseen generosity I was in no position to refuse. I became her right-hand girl in college, someone who attended to all her requirements, helped her with her administrative tasks through the day, and at night I took myself to my books to give the exam I had missed the previous year.

Little did I know that the worst was yet to come. There was nothing visibly wrong with me. I was still as gloriously beautiful as I had been barely a few months before my world was turned upside down and inside out. I had thick, soft, brown hair that I parted sternly in the centre and plaited every morning, giving no leeway for stray tendrils to escape, to find their way into the fantasies of any who might be looking on at me. My skin was pale and freckled at the bridge of my nose; I no longer plied myself with *malai* and haldi like Maa did to all us sisters every morning keep our complexions clear and milky. My eyes were still the same deep pebbles as they always had been, but they were dull now. Something vital had been extinguished in me, it made my eyes dead and my smile a rictus grin. I had forgotten when I last laughed full-throated. It probably had been the morning when I had upturned that crone's stall. I hadn't laughed after that. She had probably laughed at me every day since. If she knew what had become of me, she would have laughed some more.

I lived in that room up on the roof for a year, two years, I lost count of the days, months and years until the day I looked at myself in the mirror and saw myself no longer a girl but a woman, a woman ripe in the prime of her life, untouched, unkissed by a man. I never went back home, I was never called back. I called my mother once a week, my sisters were married off quickly to the first proposal that came along for each. My father passed away a month after my third sister's wedding. My mother cried every time she spoke to me but didn't call me home. I was the black sheep of the family, better in absentia. A year later, my mother passed away. My sisters were content in their lives, lives they did not want the shadow of a sister with a tainted past hovering over. Also, an unmarried beautiful sister was dangerous to invite home; husbands were often tempted to treat a sister like they would their wife, down to expecting the same privileges of the body. They were only too happy to forget I had ever existed, they were all married now, content in their households. I had no contact with them anymore, nor they with me. Strange how they seemed only too happy to be rid of me. I bore my solitude like a sigil on a banner. I was the only one responsible for me.

Being alone was terrifying, but I was coming to accept that perhaps this was what was destined for me. But there was worse to follow, horror that I had never imagined possible, had never seen, had only heard whispers of back in my childhood about what I never knew.

It all began after a visit to where they told me prayers would be answered, ruins of what were once magnificent structures, now ancient crumbling stone and masonry, creeping vines and moss growing on them, and leading down from the surface, stairways to a warren of passages beneath the earth, lit up by candles and votives, people flocking in hordes to tie on their supplications to forces they didn't understand, and frankly, neither did I. The stones in the mausoleum sang songs that I wondered if others could hear, the moss on their surfaces told stories that unfurled like a kinetoscope projecting on to the bare wall, images that shifted and changed with the light. The crumbling walls, the stones loosened by the years, the wind, the rain, stood sentinel over what could not be contained within.

I had written out my little petition as I'd been advised, and taken it down to where they were, those who they told me had the power to grant it and all the infinite petitions that came to them every week. I'd asked for a lover who was brave enough to claim me for his own, despite my circumstances. I should have chosen my words more carefully. I should have mentioned a man, I should have asked for a human, I should have specified I wanted a husband. My petition had been granted almost immediately, in a way I would have never imagined had I ever been told of it.

Don't wear perfume, don't leave your hair loose, dim your light. They are covetous, these who bestow blessings or choose to play tricks. No one told me of the many rules I needed to adhere to before I went there, they only told me of the blessings I could get. I dressed up as I always did, with care and pride in my appearance. I applied the attar of roses to my wrists and the nape of my neck as I always did. The scent of roses made me happy, reminding me of a moment in my life when I had felt inexplicable desire burning me up within. No one had cared enough to warn me to tie my hair up when my hastily tied hair fell loose as I bent to remove a pebble from my sandal. It was then that it hit me with a force so strong it threw me off my feet, dropping me to the ground in a dead faint. The wind so scalding hot I felt I was being dipped in a cauldron of boiling oil. Kind passers-by stopped, splashed water on my face, mistaking my faint for that of a heat-stroke, the droplets of water they splashed evaporated as they hit my skin, I was in a stupor, responding to nothing. Strangers took me to the nearest clinic, where they found a number in my wallet, on the ID card I was carrying, and dialled it. The college principal sent her maid and her driver with the car to take me home and called the doctor home to see me. He prescribed paracetamol and a blood test if the fever didn't abate after a couple of days. For three days I burned up from within, a fever that no paracetamol nor sponging with cold water would alleviate, a heat that escaped as gusts of smoke when I sighed or breathed. I could feel it in my head, something, someone, a presence that had wrapped me around itself.

The fever did not abate. The delirium had me wandering lands I knew did not exist on this earth, marks came upon my body, marks of love, marks of violence, marks made on flesh by a creature that was air and smoke, a creature not of the flesh but with the desire for flesh, mine. He spoke to me honeyed words of love and beauty, making me quiver with uncontrollable desire that he could not assuage. He exerted his command over me with unspeakable violence, wounds I bore on my flesh, wounds that were not of the flesh, wounds invisible to the human eye, I bore them within me, in places that were covered by my clothes. There was shame in bearing wounds that I could not explain, wounds that did not bleed, could not be sutured, could not be healed by medicine.

After a week of the fever not abating, my landlady's cook took me to a baba located prosaically on an extension floor built over a coaching class for IAS aspirants in the warrens of the marketplace. He was most unlike what I'd imagined one dealing in the occult would look like. If anything, he looked like a middleman, a broker, one who got recalcitrant files into government offices through wheedling, bribery and the like. Leather-faced, squat and balding, he was dressed in a grey safari suit, shiny with use and wash, a fraying collar that bore its years with dignity, and a pair of dark Ray-Ban glasses in the dim room. A broker he seemed for sure, albeit who dealt with the spiritual realm rather than the physical, corporal and the material. Was he really what he claimed he was, I wondered, or a fraud? I would try anything to rid myself of these bruises all over my body, bruises no one could see, scratches that appeared out of nowhere, blue-black abrasions on my torso where I was punched repeatedly by an entity I couldn't see, the same entity that could caress me as gently as a reverential lover and bring me to a quivering orgasm within seconds when it chose to.

'*Beta*, sit down,' he commanded, his matter brusque and yet reassuring, before lapsing into a long, long silence. The cook whom I only knew as Mrs Khurana, a hearty and loud middle-aged woman with a penchant for the most lurid floral prints on nylon fabrics for her salwar kurtas, gestured wildly at me to keep silent when I began to ask what I was supposed to do. He suddenly began muttering something incomprehensible and gestured, a gesture that was neither a wave nor a command, just a sudden vague gesture that resulted in what seemed to be an explosion all around me. A whiff of smoke emerged from my nostrils and darted around, much like an errant child refusing to behave in a toy store. The baba reached out swiftly for one so bulky, and grabbed whatever it was in his left hand, funnelling it into what seemed like an empty Old Monk bottle, quickly screwing the cap back on.

'I've confined it for now,' he told me. 'Take this bottle and keep it hidden. And get married as soon as you can. It will leave you if you are spiritually and emotionally attached to a human male. Don't ever open it. Not even if you feel tempted to when you hear his voice. Once you are married, get rid of it immediately, throw it away, into a river, into a trash pile, down a mountainside, bury it deep somewhere where no human will ever dig and find it, and release it. Do this as quickly as you can once you get married.'

Surely he was joking, these did not exist. Did they not end when we ended religion, when we became just citizens without religion? When the state became our religion.

The bruises on my body were real, the whispers in my head were real. Whatever it was that had taken to me was real enough, even if I couldn't see it. I could feel it, and if getting married was the only way to rid myself of it, I would do so. I took the bottle home with me with as much care as one would hold a newborn, keeping it carefully in my little trunk, a little tin trunk my mother had gotten me when I was leaving home, carefully packed with a few clothes, some pickles, some warm clothes and some money she had saved away from my father's eyes.

I went through the things in the trunk that I had brought with me from home, the memories of a youth hastily abandoned, a mother's dupatta, fraying and the familiar fragrance I associated with her now faded, the molecules dissipated in so many years. I had spent all these years away from home and spent all those years in the hope that I would return home. Living in transit was unsettling, one was constantly ready to up and move at a second's notice. I picked up a diary, one that I had stopped updating from the date of the event, unable to read back to myself, the person I used to be.

It was then that the photograph fell onto the bed almost providentially, showing me someone I had left behind, a me almost unrecognizable now. A me I could never be again. It was then that I saw him in the photograph and remembered about him, the boy who had loved me with a strange passion back then, and was probably still in love with the idea of me, a ghostly memory stored in his heart, a memory that he would force-fit into the reality of now if I returned to him. I had taken this photograph with me when I left home and went to the city. It stayed in my diary, along with all the phone numbers of friends past. Some of them I knew I would never call again. When such devastation befalls one, the world around falls away instantly; when one becomes the centrifuge of something inexplicable, people step away gingerly from the fallout.

In the photograph, he stood strapping, tall, reclusive, in the last row, his eyes on me, standing three persons away to his left. I had been aware of his gaze and ignored it, as I had always done, all through the years. I wondered where the rest of my classmates were. I called a number, spoke to a long-lost friend, asked about him, called another friend, called a third, got a phone number for him, and called him. He was unmarried yet, they told me; he would marry me, I knew. Men were sentimental like that when it came to first loves, while women weren't. I didn't even know if he would answer the call, whether he would be at office. He was. I remembered the flood of relief I felt on hearing his voice. His voice was the strangeness of the familiarity of his memories and the unfamiliarity of mine.

'How have you been?' he asked, there was nothing more to ask, and nothing less. There were questions with answers and answers with no questions and the skein of time, memory and what we chose to remember and forget ravelling through them all.

'I've been well.' And with that it was done. I would get married to him. It came on me with a certainty I could not explain. And once I was married, I would throw the bottle away into a landfill, or a river or a lake, where it could never be retrieved from. He had no choice in the matter, I had made up my mind.

I had not called him in all the years I had been away. He had moved to another town, not too far from the town we had both grown up in, had a government job, government living quarters, a small living room, a bedroom, a kitchen, an attached outhouse, a man Friday to manage his day-to-day for him.

'I'm coming to you,' I had said. 'I will board the next bus out to your town. I'm coming to you.'

There was none of the unnecessary whys and what happened that would make one reconsider and turn back, tucking the impulsive decision back into the closet of unfulfilled hopes, where it remains beating out of tune, a heart of its own, slowing down its rhythm as the years passed. I knew I would have turned back had there been the slightest hesitation on his part to have me come to him.

'Come, I will be waiting,' he replied and that was that. He was sitting on the bench at the lone tea stall next to the exit of the bus stand, a glass of tea gone cold in his hand, scanning every blue and white state transport bus that arrived. His eyes melted into dampness when they met mine. He stood up and waited, uncertain of how to respond to my presence. It reached out to me with the speed and sharpness of a whiplash, the curious love he still felt for me that was still unchanged over all these years, me who had never loved him back, never thought of him with anything more than a pleasant affection, flattered by his unstated devotion, so obvious to everyone but him. And me.

I had changed, I knew, from his memory of me. But his expression when his eyes met mine reassured me that nothing had changed his feelings for me, feelings I had taken for granted as a privilege to my beauty but now needed in order to find refuge from that which plagued me. He hadn't changed though, I realized, when I set eyes on him again at that dusty, noisy bus depot, the crowds milling back and forth, the honking of the buses as they swept in and out, imperious in their purpose. His eyes still sought me out in a crowd, ignoring the damage the years had wrought on me, stripping the roses from my cheeks and twinkle from my eyes, until I'd become unrecognizable to myself. He looked straight at me and stepped forward as I'd stepped off the bus at the bus stand that evening all those years ago.

I had wiped my face with a damp handkerchief before stepping off the bus in a vain misplaced attempt to remove the soot and dust of the long journey off myself. It hardly made any difference to my appearance. No one would notice a grubby woman, her beauty, if any, camouflaged beneath the dupatta that covered her head, a modesty I now imposed upon myself more for convenience than any sense of societal propriety, my body hidden beneath an oversized salwar kurta in a drab beige colour, handed down to me in a charitable gesture, one that I had not gotten altered to fit me because the extra girth it gave me was comforting. I had learnt now to beat down my beauty into acceptability. Shining brighter than the rest marked you out for envy, for punishment. And I knew the consequences of living too bright: you attracted terrible things towards you, unwanted attention from humans, unwanted possession by the others.

I walked up to him, holding on to my tiny tin trunk containing nothing more than a few clothes, an empty bottle of Old Monk and all my hope for release from what it was that had taken over me.

'Rani,' he said, his voice rough with a sore throat or a surfeit of emotions, his hand reaching out for mine, unthinking of what eyes might be watching us might think. The years had added to his shoulders, he was no longer the lanky boy I'd last seen back in college all those years ago, a lifetime ago, before it had all unravelled. His face had filled out, his jaw was chunkier, his eyes had dark depths in them that the passage of the years had placed there, bit by bit. He had grown into a handsome, mature man while I had withered over the years. The energy that had made me radiant had disappeared, and what was left was a pervasive sadness and a resolute anger that ate away at me like drops of acid, hollowing me out from within. But this was my attempt at a second chance at life, perhaps someone who loved me would teach me to love myself again, to want to live again.

I held on to his hand like it was a rope tossed to me over a bridge I was falling off, my nails digging into his flesh. He did not seek release.

'You came,' I whispered.

'Of course, I did,' he replied, this man who had always used his words with care back when he was a boy. I, on the other hand, had been impetuous and carefree back then, uncaring of where my words fell or who brushed against them or who inhaled them. By the time I had learnt that words had power and needed to be uttered with care and measure, I had been scarred beyond measure, my body with bruises no one could see, my soul with the darkness that would never leave me.

'How are you?' I asked, not asking what I wanted to. He took the bag from my hands in a gentle, supplicant gesture, almost like he was asking permission to take care of my things. It brought tears to my eyes. No one had shown me such tenderness in years, not after my mother.

'Where should I take you?' he asked.

'To your home,' I replied, fully understanding the implications of what I was saying. His face froze for a moment, then confusion rippled over his stolid features, an exquisite interplay of conflicting emotions, tender and yet passionate and roughshod at the same time.

'Have you eaten? Let's eat first.'

The tears began trickling down my face. He sat me down on the bench at the tea stall first and fed me a hearty breakfast of steaming hot aloo puri, washed down with tea. The salt from my tears rolling down my face, mingled with the spice of the *sabji*. It isn't food that fills the stomach, it is being fed with love.

He then took me straight to a temple not too far away. 'If you want me to take you to my home, I will take you there only as my wife.'

I nodded. He didn't ask about what had happened to me in the years between my leaving town and calling him. For that I was grateful. We then went home, man and wife, a hurriedly bought red and gold dupatta draped on my head over the faded second-hand salwar kameez I was wearing, the photograph clicked at the photo studio down the road the only proof of our marriage I had should anyone ask. No one would ever do so in all the years that we would live together as man and wife. It would never occur to anyone to ask questions, we fitted together like we'd always been man and wife.

The bottle I kept in a cupboard, forgetting that I should throw it away. It simmered there, waiting virulently, pulsating with the threat and the promise of the power it contained, waiting for the spell that bound it within to fade, to lose its strength, to allow it to escape. That I forgot about it was my greatest mistake. That I remembered too late what I had forgotten was what would trap me again into something that I would never be able to rid myself of for years and years.

Then my husband, in his ignorance and curiosity, did what he shouldn't have. He had opened the bottle, sniffed it curiously. 'Why do you have an empty bottle in the cupboard behind your clothes?' he had called out.

He had let it out only to let it come sweeping back right into me.

Gulab

'But he who dares not grasp the thorn
Should never crave the rose.'

– ANNE BRONTE

IT WAS TIME TO MOVE AGAIN, I KNEW. TEJA WAS getting restless again, he was as restless as a troupe of monkeys wrecking mayhem on a tin roof. I was tired of the uncertainty of picking myself up and moving overnight, never being able to ever make a house a home, forever poised on the brink of unsettled even as one settled. Teja, as he was known, or Tejinder as his father named him, after his father in turn, was a good man, I always thought of myself as a good girl, an obedient mouse. I knew the exact moment I became a monkey from a mouse, a feral one at that.

My bedridden, blind grandmother was incapable of protecting me from my father, caring for her through the day and getting abused by my father every night was not what life should be for any girl, and I saw no relief in sight. My father would never get me married off, for who would then care for his mother and his mother showed no signs of dying. There was nothing to it, after all he fed me and owned me. I didn't know any different; morality had not percolated down to me from a dead mother, a delusional grandmother and an evil father. I kept quiet. I looked at other fathers playing with their daughters, walking them with love to school every morning, taking them to the movies, feeding them at the restaurants down in the main market and wondered if they too had learnt to stifle their screams. If they too learnt to accept pain as part of growing up. That they expected to be beaten up and tortured every night. Other kids played hopscotch and hide-and-seek with their friends, I played hide-and-seek to escape my father's wrath after lights were out. But he always found me. My light, faint, blue, never quite went out.

I did not know that other fathers did not inflict pain on their children every single day, until there was no resistance, no emotion, no pain. That they did not stub out their lit cigarettes on the skin of their daughter's bodies, that they did not cane their daughters until their backs were full of thin raised welters.

It didn't help that he was a police inspector. Whom did one complain to when your own parent was the keeper of law and justice in your small town, and who would believe you when he was the most proper, respectful, upright person in the whole town?

The only way out was to escape. I would escape, go to the big city, find a nice boy, get married and have two children whom I would never beat up. I could always beat up my husband I told myself, if the urge to punch something was overwhelming.

It gathered slowly within me, the dream of escaping, insinuating itself into my every waking moment. I could escape. I began saving money, packing a bag. I put in the tin box that held my dead mother's jewellery in it, it wasn't much, a few earrings, a chain, four bangles. There had been more jewellery, that I knew. My father had sold most of it to fund his debauchery. These I had ferreted away, hidden within my things. They were mine by right, my mother had worn them as a bride, she would have wanted me to have them. I barely remembered my mother, all I could remember was the fragrance of roses, a fragrance that still brought tears to my eyes. I could not remember the woman they said was my mother, although I saw photographs of her in the house. I looked very unlike them both, my mother and my father.

'You are not of his blood,' my grandmother told me one foggy evening, when I had burst into tears beside her bed. 'Your mother found you in a barn and brought you home, a newborn. We don't know who gave birth to you and abandoned you there.' Like that explained everything. Would being of his blood not have had him use me for whipping practice?

My father laughed at her words. 'She's lost her mind, don't pay heed to her.'

He was a handsome man, built tall and strong, a ruddy

complexion that got ruddier when he was drunk. Soft-spoken and polite to the world, rough and harsh with those whom he took in for the crimes they committed. He mourned to the world, refused to consider getting remarried, even though proposals kept coming in by the droves for him. After all, I would be married off soon, and he would be alone. It was a good marriage for the many spinsters languishing unmarried in a town where the men went off to the big city to find work and returned with big-city brides and no desire to settle down with any of the local women.

After my mother died, my grandmother fell from the roof and broke her spine in three places. It was an accident. She'd gone to dry the *badis*, the sun dried vegetable and lentil nuggets, on the roof – there had been no reason for her to go to the edge of the slope. She was now bedridden for the rest of her days, a vegetable, cared for by a help who slept in the outhouse, leaving me vulnerable and alone to whatever horrors my father might inflict on me at night. The cataracts in her eyes were never removed, so that she lay there with milky white vision.

Did Gopa Buaji, as I called her, the lady who worked in the house through the day, a middle-aged widow as sturdy and broad as a tree, know what went on in the wee hours of the night, when the night owls hooted and flitted from tree to tree and the fruit bats fluttered through open windows and then glided out apologetically? Did my screams not reach the outhouse where she lived with her young son, or did she choose not to hear them, just as she chose not to notice the bruises on my body? I didn't know. Or perhaps it was selective deafness, she heard me quite clearly when I was being insolent with her and would reach out to land me one tight slap when no one was around. Perhaps screams travelled at a slower frequency than rude retorts.

The one time I gathered the nerve to begin telling her about what my father was doing to me, she went outside to wash clothes with a tub of hot water which would get cold before she dipped the first garment in. It was winter, but the sun was out, and she didn't want to lose the little warmth there was. The clothes would be strung on the lines behind the kitchen and be dry by evening if the sun held. It was not a topic I brought up again. Perhaps she had her own reasons for holding her silence, although she could be heard loud and clear down in the main market when her son returned home with his report card.

My father would kill me too, I knew, if I dared. Also, it was the burden of knowing that I was placing on her, she who had no other place to live or source of income. Knowing would make her homeless in the dead of winter. He had already killed my mother and tried to kill my grandmother. Strange man, did he not realize he'd taught me himself that it was no sin to kill one's own?

I shot him with his own service pistol as he staggered home, inebriated, in the dark of the night. I heard him park his vehicle on the main road, down below our lane; the path coming up to the house was steep, a drop on one side, a mountain on the other. I had been waiting. I knew when to wrench the pistol from his holster, how to disengage the safety catch, to check if the chamber was loaded, and how to aim and fire. He had taught me how to, one crazed night when I was still a child. I still remembered. It was a clean shot. I was quite proud of my skills. I guess he would regret it now, but it was too late. He would be quite dead soon enough to be troubled by any regrets.

No one emerged from their houses to check what was happening. It was a cold night, windows were shut, good folk were hunkered down into their *razai*s with the heaters on and this was the hour that those not of the surface of the earth roamed the earth. No one was keen to make an acquaintance with them. The blood spurted from him over my face, my head, my clothes, warm in the cold night. He collapsed almost in slow motion to the ground. For a long moment I stood over him, waiting and watching. I kicked him off the edge and knew there would be no sound of his body hitting bottom, he would crash through the canopy of trees deep enough to kill him if he hadn't already been dead. I should have taken the cash from his wallet, I told myself moments after I'd kicked him off. I could have added to my woefully thin stash of notes. And his ring. And the gun. How was I ever going to survive if I couldn't make practical decisions even while killing someone?

It had taken me a year to gather the money and the courage. I should have done what I did years ago. He lay somewhere broken and mangled from the fall, deep in the forest, carrion for the vultures and the hyenas, his flesh rotting off his bones, becoming the mulch of the undergrowth, covered by frost and sinking deeper and deeper into the ground. He would never be found. I would never be traced. I wondered what had happened of my grandmother with the unemotionality of one thinking about someone at a distance. Perhaps she had died. Perhaps she was still alive, at the mercy of the neighbours. I didn't care. I had left, I had to find my own destiny. I hadn't gone back to check, though I would soon, I told myself. I would return to claim what was mine.

Some nights I woke up screaming, with sweat pouring down my body even in the dead of winter, as he crawled back rotting into my room, into my bed, the stench of the bog on him. Other nights, I yelled at him to move on in the afterlife and find someone else to harass. I was only trying to put the light out, he would whine, apologetically. The light scared me, he wailed. Bloody wuss in death, for all his swagger and bravado in life.

When I got off the train at the big-city station, the first thing I noticed was the crowd, the incessant surge of people that pressed against you like the strength of the horde surrounding you, sucking you in, making you one of them, a strength I had always wanted all my life, but had found only when I ran away. The second thing that hit me was the smell, city smell. From the crisp, clean air of my hometown in the hills to this toxic air soup of fuel fumes, dust, sweat, was almost a physical assault. I had only seen such surging crowds in the annual melas back home where everyone from the adjoining villages gathered to watch the plays being staged, where the crush and push was part of the charm of going to the fair, as was to buy trinkets with the little money I had saved up from here and there. Bangles, hair clips, cotton candy, I was pleased with little, I had no courage to wish for more.

When I decided to run away, I stopped spending even on those little luxuries. Sadly, I had no clue what I was to do once I ran away. You always need a plan, they say, my plan ended at the point when I climbed into the train. What was I to do in a big city where I knew no one, I didn't know. Where was I to live, how was I to feed myself, I knew nothing. I trusted the fates to watch over me. I sat on the railway platform with my little bundle of things, worn and faded salwar kameez that had no place in city life, a warm shawl that had been my mother's, my mother's gold bangles, chain and earrings that I had carefully placed in a pouch and stitched into the inner seam of my bra, concealed by the fold and fall of the dupatta around me. Little did I know that cities were not kind to seventeen-year-old girls with nothing and no one to protect them. I would learn soon enough that the bra was no place to hide jewellery, the bra was the first place the city groped you in. Not that I had much to be grope worthy, some louts might take offence at finding nothing much after all that effort.

I waited at the platform as the crowds thinned and night fell, wondering where I could go, not daring to step out into the city and the unknown it held. Outside the station, I could see bedlam, a crush of vehicles, honking, pedestrians, the coolies yelling for passage as they lumbered past, with suitcases stacked on their heads.

'Who are you waiting for, little girl?' a crone with paan-stained teeth and a face lined with deep creases asked me. She had been selling amulets and trinkets just outside the main exit and had noticed me sitting on the bench for hours. She looked at me like she knew just what I'd done. The last time I'd felt so guilty was when my class teacher had caught me filching someone else's fancy pen. Same thing, both crimes, filching a pen, killing my father.

I shook my head in fear.

She hobbled closer, a bag slung on her shoulder, a staff propping her up from collapsing into the grey cemented flooring. 'You don't have to be frightened of me,' she said, smiling not very reassuringly. 'Tell me, who are you waiting for?'

I fidgeted with my fingers and my toes, looking down at my feet, drawing my little bag closer to myself, putting a protective arm around it, shivering from the cold, uncomfortable at her attention and her questions, terrified of her. She looked like she could be a million years old and then some more, and had lived every minute of it. Her face was a web of wrinkles, striated like the rings of a tree trunk, her body bent into a hairpin, her hair a mass of white that was unsuccessfully confined into a tiny bun, with tendrils standing out in every direction.

'There are scarier creatures than me outside,' she cackled, noting my hesitancy. 'Humans who are really monsters, who can harm you in ways you couldn't even imagine. I want to help you.'

I had heard of the old women who took young girls in with kindness and then sold them to brothels. These were apocryphal tales that had trickled down from those who had gone to the city without the consent of their parents, stories that were held out as warnings for the girls who dared to dream of escape and held them tethered in place, within the restrictions of the home and the patriarchy that transferred them from the care of one male to another. I wondered if she would put me into a brothel, I wondered what a brothel was like and whether it would dim my light. She looked at me with kindness, a kindness that felt like she had gotten into my soul and saw it all, the agony, the pain and the desperation. She offered me a handful of peanuts from her pocket. They were probably laced and would knock me out, but it would be good to be knocked out in this unbearable cold. She popped one into her mouth and chewed it with as much deep rumination as Gaura, my cow back home.

She settled herself next to me, tucking one foot under the other, placing her bundle on the seat beside her. The only other occupants of the adjoining bench were a family of three – a father, a mother and a young girl – who sat in silence, waiting for the time to pass as they waited for whatever it was they were waiting for, a train, a decision, a pickup, death. The crowds had thinned out, it was the dark of the night, an hour when humans sleep and the undead prowl.

'I know it all,' she whispered, leaning towards me. 'I know what you've been through and why you ran away. You killed him. You did the right thing. But you will not survive alone in this city, it will tear you to pieces. Don't come with me if I scare you. I will send a man to care for you. He will have hair that is long and the eyes of an eagle. He doesn't know it, but I will send him to you.'

I gasped. I turned to look at her. She was already fading, as I blinked there was a shimmer where she had been. A figment of my imagination. A real person. A ghost. I did not know. I picked up my bag and ran out of the railway station, terrified. The peanuts were still in my hand, unthinkingly I popped them into my mouth. I was hungry, and even if they were given to me by a ghost, they were solid enough. Never ever turn down food. I was hungry.

The ticket checker had already come twice, asking me if I had a place to go. He could take me somewhere else, he said, moving closer, his intent unmistakeable. I had got up and gone to sit next to the family, who were still seated and silent. Perhaps they were in mourning. He moved away in confusion, but he would be back, I knew. I had to get away before he did.

I had been marked and my purposelessness noted. The louts from the railway station circled me like vultures over fresh carrion as soon as I stepped out. Four of them, of varying heights and builds, each characterized by the impunity that builds like a patina from a lifetime of doing deeds considered to be out of the moral purview of good behaviour.

The burliest of the four walked up to me and put a hand on my shoulder, a touch that sent icicles of revulsion down my spine. I shrugged to rid myself of its weight and turned around. Another of the group blocked my path. The first man put both hands out and held me in my spot. I tried to scream, but my throat was paralysed with fear. Around us the crowds milled back and forth, and no one stopped, not even for a moment, to intervene. I looked around desperately for a policeman, there was none to be found at that moment. Trust them to make themselves scarce when needed. 'Come quietly without making a fuss and you won't get hurt,' the man said, reeking of stale alcohol. I shrank back, wishing I'd carried my father's gun with me. I hadn't thought I would need it, I'd thrown it down into the ravine after him, after I'd kicked his body off the edge of the road. Destroy the evidence, the television serials had taught me. I had destroyed the body and the weapon, I had no witnesses, I was safe. But I was not. I was stupid.

'Leave me alone,' I whispered. He laughed, a laugh that indicated he had no intention of doing so. It was a laugh I had heard in countless Hindi movies, just when the villain pounces on the heroine with evil intentions of deflowering her. I'd just never heard it in real life before.

A voice spoke out from behind me, a voice with an authority to it that made me turn around in surprise even as

I was being bundled off, kicking and screaming, in the thick of a crowd, with no one stopping to intervene, except for a couple of curious onlookers with no trains to catch. The men stopped. Hands released me, they disappeared, a swift shuffling of footsteps on concrete in the other direction as I turned, expecting a man in a policeman's uniform to be standing there. Instead, there was Teja. I didn't know he was Teja then, of course, all I knew was that I was staring at the most imposing man I had seen in all my life, a man with hair down to his shoulders, an unruly mop of hair that was bleached copper from the sun. It cried out for shampoo and deep conditioning. Long hair, eagle eyes, she had said. I tick marked both.

'Come with me,' he said, picking up my bag, and walking towards a lane that branched off from the chaos of the railway station. I had no option but to follow him.

'Go with the man with long hair, I will send him to you,' she had told me, that old woman in the waiting room, the one who had been real or the one I had imagined. I followed him without a word. He had long hair, didn't he? I would have followed him anywhere, to the ends of the earth, even if he took me there on a battered motorcycle that made enough noise to wake up the dead in the *kabrastans* and cemeteries we passed on the way. It didn't seem like I had too many options right now.

'Hold on tight,' he said when I climbed on behind him, and I did, feeling his muscles under his thin shirt, and I realized I did not fear his touch. Now that I'd killed once, I knew that there was nothing to stop me from killing again if I needed to. It was easy, once you got past the nuisance of guilt and morality. After all, people would die anyway, one was just preponing the inevitable. I didn't tell Teja all these thoughts of course, not now, not ever. I was just thankful that luck had thrown him in my path or was it vice versa, or perhaps, it was really that old crone who had done so. Strangely, I trusted him. And not just because she had told me to go with him. He seemed to be a person one could trust, more importantly, a man a young girl with no one to turn to could trust.

The ride was short and the destination we went to was a single roomed tenement in a crowded locality, where the houses were cardboard shoe boxes stacked one on the other, cheek by jowl, sharing common walls, with steep, narrow and deceptive stairways taking you up the floors into what seemed like a never-ending expanse of rooms that unfolded mysteriously with seemingly no logic as to how they multiplied on the limited base they sprung from.

He parked at the end of a narrow lane and beckoned for me to follow him. Houses tumbled around us, as did night sounds, sounds that were hushed through the day and needed the darkness of night to emerge. He stopped in front of a ramshackle construction that looked like it was taped together, by scotch tape and goodwill, standing upright by the sheer force of the prayers of the residents. We began climbing stairs that were so narrow, steep and treacherous that I put both hands against the walls that enclosed the stairway like a tunnel to keep my balance. What kind of a man took a girl he had just met home, and what kind of a girl went with him. Ah well, he couldn't be worse than my father, I told myself. And I couldn't be worse than what I already was.

His home, when we reached there, was a modest one, but neat and clean. A tube light lit it up into friendliness and life, chasing away the dark shadows that wandered on the walls, a single bed was arranged against the wall opposite the window, a small cupboard against the wall opposite the door. Two *muda*s placed perfunctorily below the small grilled window. No curtains on the window, no attempts at prettifying the space or keeping the outside out, the window I realized faced a wall almost at touching distance, there was nothing to be seen or to see. A door opposite the main door opened onto what seemed like the kitchen, and from there, probably the bathroom. The fan had no dust on it, the corners were clear of cobwebs. This was a man who took pleasure in the cleanliness of his surroundings, that I could tell. He was fastidious about the place he lived in, for all that he was slouchy and laid back in his general demeanour. Or perhaps he had someone who lived with him, doing the cleaning for him. A sliver of jealousy shot through me, why would I imagine he had no one he was attached to, him a grown man. He probably had hired house help, I told myself. Or if he did the cleaning himself, I was lucky. I would need to do no work. Because, I had already decided, I was staying put here with him until I had a plan.

'You can go freshen up in there,' he said, pointing towards the door opposite. I went through. The kitchen, if it could be called that, was barely bigger than a cupboard with a concrete floor and a black stone platform. The bathroom was clean too, a door within revealed an attached toilet. There were no feminine accoutrements to vanity, I noted. A functional soap, toothbrush, toothpaste and shaving tackle. This was a bachelor's home. There was no woman who lived here. I was the first woman who had entered it, this I knew for sure although I could not explain how. The entire house was smaller than my room back home, yet it felt safe in a way I could not explain. Here I was safe, with this man. Safer than I had been with my father.

When I emerged, he sat me down on the divan and sat on a *muda* opposite me, within touching distance of me if he chose, looking at me for a long minute before asking me the questions he hadn't so far.

'Where is your home? Why did you run away?'

Because I killed my father, my father who had been torturing me for years, I thought. I kept silent. And if you keep up with these endless questions, I might kill you too, I thought. I continued to keep silent.

'Are people looking for you back home?'

I shook my head to indicate a no. No one would be looking out for me. No one cared enough. The only one who might have was dead.

'Did you rob anything before running away?'

I had only taken what was mine, my mother's ornaments and money I had saved up. That wasn't stealing, I thought to myself, that was taking what was mine. I shook my head in the negative again. He might take me for a speech-impaired person if I didn't speak up soon.

'How old are you? Do you have any identity card? Show it to me.' I didn't. I had forgotten to carry it along. Or I had consciously decided not to. I had no identity now. I shook my head yet again in the negative. I would get dizzy with all the head shaking.

'What did you think would happen when you reached Delhi, where did you plan to go?'

I shrugged. I hadn't really thought about it. If I had thought so far ahead, I would never have gathered the courage to run. Courage is one of the most elusive things we have, when it comes to us, we must gather it to our hearts, barricade it with firm intention, and ration it out to ourselves in careful doses, lest we spend it all at once and then end up spending the remainder of our lives in abject terror at anything and everything that we come across. I had spent all my courage all at once when I'd shot my father in the back of his head and caught the train to Delhi. I now had to build it up again.

'Do you speak?' he asked finally, his face crumpling with concern, looking into my face with eyes that felt they would bore right into me.

'Yes, I do,' I said. 'I can speak. I can hear.' He sighed in relief. He hadn't heard me scream yet, perhaps he wouldn't sigh in quite so much relief if he had. I could puncture eardrums when in full voice.

'The old lady told me to go get you and to take you home,' he said, running a tired hand across his forehead. 'I don't know what made me listen to her. I don't need any complication in my life right now. I don't need an extra person in my life right now. But you can stay here for a few days. A week.'

I nodded, in gratitude. I would stay longer. He took my wrist and stared in wonder at the veins, running blue light under the thin skin.

'Did I imagine it or did I see your veins glowing?'

I shrugged. It had always been like this but I dimmed it hastily. It wouldn't do to have him suspicious of me, like those who glimpsed the shine became. Like my father had. Damn these men, they wouldn't let a woman shine in peace.

'You imagined it.'

He sighed.

'I'm sorry. I once knew someone who shone through her skin.' He didn't elaborate more, but my curiosity was piqued. Who could it be who had the exact same malaise I had. My father kept me confined to the house when he spotted me shining, it wouldn't do for people to ask questions. I was young then, I hadn't learnt to dim my shine. He'd tried to kill me, and then killed my mother when she'd stepped in to stop him. Then my grandmother, when she threatened to tell the world about what he had done. But he couldn't bring himself to kill me. I had no such reservations, I realized. And no regrets once I'd killed him.

I had now learnt how to dim the light at will. I shone only when I knew I would be unseen, but sometimes when I was terrified or angry, it shone through, unhindered, giving me courage and strength. And as I grew, it became stronger in me, the light. I had never seen anyone else with it. Perhaps it was true what my father said, I was an abomination. That my mother had picked up the child of a *chudail* from the barn and brought it home. That he needed to exorcise what was evil from within me, and the only way he could do it was by breaking my body until I could no longer shine. But that was what made me unbreakable, the light. It was useful, this light that coursed through my veins. Especially when the lights went out, and the paths were dark. I scared glow-worms away.

I had limited options, Teja told me. He could give me a place to stay for a few days until I found my bearings. His voice was honest and concerned. If that made me uncomfortable, I could stay for a couple of days in a gurudwara while he tried to find me a position as a full-time domestic worker in one of the big houses. I could go to the hostel for destitute women and stay there a few days until I figured out my next steps. But beds were scarce there, and it was probably safer in the street than in some of those homes he said. I nodded.

'I will stay here,' I told him.

'Are you educated?'

I could read, both English and Hindi. I had taught

myself on borrowed books and salvaged newspapers from the big house when they discarded them after my father had stopped my schooling. He was educated, I could tell. He threw in English words into his Hindi with the disdain of those for whom they were common parlance and not hard taught.

'What work can you do?' It was a valid question. I could keep house and cook, I replied. Skills enough to get by. Other skills I would learn on the way. I asked him a question of my own in return.

'Why are you helping me? What is in it for you?'

Men did not help without reason or lust.

'Why should I not help you?'

'Because you don't know me.'

'What is your name?'

My mind was a blank, I could remember everything except my name. All I could remember was the careening body of my father as he fell down straight like a stone until I could no longer see him in the darkness of the shadows that prowled the ravines, that would have pounced on his remains, dismembering him, tearing out his entrails and gnawing flesh off bone, leaving bits and pieces of him until the sodden earth sucked him up and turned him into mulch.

'I can't remember my name,' I replied as honestly as I could. 'I can remember everything else but I can't remember my name.' Perhaps I didn't want to remember my name. Perhaps I didn't want to remember anything that could take me back to where I came from.

'I will name you. And you will tell me everything else about yourself that you can remember.' The authority in his voice was astounding. I was too taken aback to protest, and yes, I would need a name in this world, given I could no longer remember what mine was, what name I had given when I'd booked that ticket on that train and whether that name was mine to begin with or something I had stolen from the recesses of a distant memory.

'What should I name you?' he asked, looking deep into my eyes. His eyes were copper and bronze and caramel and gold. The glint from a stray ray of sun on the sand. The eyes of a hawk, she had said, the crone. He had the hooked nose to match, that she hadn't mentioned. He was peering deep into my soul and sifting through the painful and the joyous and doing away with what caused me pain to remember. I could feel him in my head. I knew I wouldn't have to tell him anything, he already knew, somehow. This man, this beautiful man whom the crone at the railway station had sent to me, was in my head like a tidal wave, careening through everything in his way, wiping out whatever caused pain to remember. A vacuum cleaner for the mind, that's what he was. I put my hand to my ears, trying to shoo him out. That was the problem with men, always trying to get into one without permission, body, heart or brain.

What was my name? I couldn't remember. My name caused me pain. It brought back painful memories of my name being called out by my father, when he stomped through the door and the hallway, the alcohol lacing his voice and adding sharp edges to it. My name was painful to recall. My mind had chosen to forget it, I would remember when I was ready to remember, when I had healed enough.

I picked on the frayed hem of my kameez, the one with the huge ugly roses all over with it, it wasn't something I'd chosen for myself. How had I expected to slip away unnoticed wearing this abomination, I wondered. Surely everyone I'd encountered had suffered retinal damage from the ugliness of the print and would pick me out in a line up with zero hesitation.

'It was her,' they would say, pointing at me, 'I've had rose-shaped floaters in my eyes since.'

He smiled. He dressed well, that I had noticed. He had on a blue and red checked shirt with faded denims that fitted him well on the hips, sneakers that were original and not the duplicate knock-offs that all the boys back in the hill town I came from wore. He wore clothes he had bought for himself, not clothes scavenged off charity. I felt strangely inadequate in front of him, I had never worried about what I wore earlier, as long I had been warm enough. Now I felt embarrassed of the faded old salwar kameez I wore, my socks with holes in them and the sweater darned with differing-coloured wools. His gaze didn't notice all this, it stayed on my face, with a certain caressing appraisal in it. He looked at the roses scattered all over my kameez, defiantly red against the sallow green of the background, gleaming monstrously on the cheap synthetic silk of the fabric.

'You are Gulab. You are like a rose, delicate, so *naazook*, it feels that I could crush you if I held you tight.' He was welcome to try, I thought to myself. And then, thought, no, what if I really broke. He was, after all, twice my size. And then some more. 'You are a *gulab ki kali*.' He'd probably watched too many old movies with these corny lines, but my breath still caught in my throat. No one had ever spoken to me like that. I wanted him to hold me tight, I wanted him to crush me. I wanted him to do things to me that I knew would give me pleasure I had never known. I quivered, plucking at the frayed hem, separating each thread from the other, my voice suddenly stuck in my throat. He noticed the quiver and sat quietly on the stool opposite me, looking at me with a gaze that was appreciative but not rapacious.

'You are too lovely to be let out alone and unguarded into the street. Those men at the railway station would have torn you to bits and sold you to the first available brothel.' He laughed, a rough jagged bark. 'Do you even know what a brothel is?'

I could guess. 'A place where bad things happen.'

'I am Tejinder Singh. My friends call me Teja, I live here alone.' He put out a hand, a formal gesture I'd only seen in movies. I took it gingerly, it dwarfed mine. His mind was out of my head now. He shook my hand tenderly, almost afraid he might break my bones if he applied any pressure. My eyes filled up with tears, no one had touched me with such gentleness ever.

'What do I call you?'

'Your man.' His answer was matter of fact, leaving no

room for me to protest. Did I have a choice in the matter? If I did, I chose not to exercise it. This was what would keep me off the streets for a while until I figured out my next step. The streets were not a place I wanted to be at. '*Koi bachcha wachcha nahin chahiye*,' he had said the first time he had fucked me, after waiting politely for my consent for a week, asking me if I would allow him to have sex with me. The condoms were his responsibility, I told him. Did I want to get married to him? Not for now, the sex and the roof over my head were enough. I was being practical, a man like him was not for marriage. Not that I was a girl for marriage. And what would I get married to, a man who scurried around from town to city to village, lying low for months before emerging again to repeat the process like a rat.

That was three years ago, we were still together. I was almost twenty now, the three years since I'd left the village had done me good. It had straightened my shoulders and made my gaze direct and piercing. The city did that to you. He had done that to me. He had become my man, and by extension, I was his woman. It had kept me safe, I was no longer carrion for vultures.

We hadn't discussed where he came from or where I came from, or what had made me run away. Nor what my name could be and if anyone was looking for me. He waited, it would come back to me, he told me, my name.

'If it doesn't come back to you, you are another person now. That name is not yours anymore, you don't belong to that name anymore.' I was happy to be rid of it. After all, there was another name that I knew was mine, but I just hadn't been called it yet. I would know when I was.

He came from a small town in the north west of the country, sitting almost on the border between India and Pakistan, a border so porous that people and contraband passed to and fro despite barbed wire, border guards and patrolling. He'd been a medal-winning student in his college, with ambitions of sitting for the civil services exams when he found himself on the wrong side of the syndicate through the simple expedient of being in the wrong place at the wrong time. Caught in the middle of a crossfire between gangs, becoming a witness for the police, and the mob's eyes on him had made him run away with only the clothes on his back. Being on the hit list of two warring gangs wasn't conducive to leading a settled life ever since. He'd run all the way to Delhi where he'd been surviving on his wits and his fists since, the anonymity of the big city suited him. And then he became a hitman. He did a job, moved, across states, from small towns into the anonymity of the big cities, not staying for more than a couple of weeks, a month at the very most in a single location. It had been almost a decade now, of moving and moving, the restlessness had seeped into his blood. The crone watched over him.

'No matter where I go, she finds me, I don't know how. She makes sure I survive. Gets me jobs.'

'What's her name?'

'Bilkis Bi.' I felt I should have known the name, known

the crone. I would know her soon enough. I could still feel her eyes on me, black stones bouncing off rock.

He told me this, after a week, after we became lovers, after I began trusting him enough to tell him why I'd run from home with nothing but a few hundred rupees and my mother's little stash of gold. I'd offered to sell some of the gold to pay him for rent and food. He could read my mind, he could get into my head, in my memories, sifting around like one would sift through mounds of sand, searching for shells, trinkets, the occasional lost coin, there was no point in pretending with him, in hiding anything, in faking what I thought or felt. He took the two gold bangles I was handing over to him as payment for my stay and food, and gently put them on my wrists, his touch warm against my skin.

'Wear them, they look good on your wrists,' he had said, lazily tracing the blue veins that ran beneath my skin from the crook of my elbow to my inner wrists, my light surged within, blue and restless to show itself, to seep into him.

He was unlike any other man I had ever known. He towered over most other men, long of limb and broad of shoulder. His hair had hung wavy and thick, a forest of unmentionable desires, right to his shoulders, lightened by the sun and lack of care or vanity. His chiselled features were angular and broody until he broke into that rare smile, one that lit up the world around him for miles. When he smiled, you forgave him anything, you would do anything for him, you would spend your life trying to evoke that smile from him, a smile that would light up the deepest recesses of your dark and troubled soul with its childlike radiance. He wasn't what one would call conventionally handsome, but he made people stop mid-sentence when he entered a room and wonder exactly what it was about him that drew their attention. Later, I would realize it was a complete lack of self-awareness that tended to intimidate most people and terrify others. A jagged scar along one cheek ensured he could never be called handsome, I would never learn where he got the scar from, he wouldn't tell me that even when I lay naked against him, tracing him out with my fingertips, my tongue, leaving small kisses against it, the little deaths having scooped our souls and our reticence inside out for a moment. After all, we were still strangers. I had barely known him then a couple of weeks, and it was time to move again. I would move with him to the ends of the earth. For now. Tomorrow, I did not know what I would do.

He was taciturn most times, only loquacious when he'd poured some alcohol into his system. After he was around three to four pegs down, he would make me sit next to him and tell me, in excruciating detail, the woman he had lost when he had run away. He had never found her again, he never would, he mourned.

He was too young then, barely eighteen, a boy in college. She was older. Exactly how much older, he did not know, he couldn't tell, he had never asked. 'Sometimes she felt like she was a million years old. At others she felt like a young girl.' She had initiated him into the world of physical pleasures, it was the norm, older women showed young boys how they needed to pleasure a woman and drew their pleasure from them, there was no taboo in it. It was how it was, and he'd done the unthinkable and fallen in love with her. There was no space for love in what should have been a relationship based purely on lust. It was rather silly, to hear him ramble on like he was giving me some Shirin Farhad–Laila Majnu story, him with his gash on his cheek and knife in his waistband.

He knew nothing else about her except her name, that too only her first name. 'Noor.' He said it reverentially, a sigh escaping him as the roundel of the 'r' left his tongue. She had taken him to places he had never been in, both in the small town he lived in and in the body he was in. She shone, he said. 'Like you do. When I was next to her, I felt like nothing could ever harm me.' He had nothing to offer her but his obsession with her, and she wanted nothing from him but his body, as she took from the others she took on as lovers. He knew about that and had accepted it.

'She told me that I was not to do anything stupid like fall in love with her, but...' Of course, he fell in love with her. Men do stupid things like that. And so do women, of course. Which is why I had fallen in love with him. It would pass, I'd told myself initially and I would get on with my life. Give it a week, a month, it was like the flu, it hit hard and made you miserable. Then one morning, it was gone. Three years and I was still here.

I resented the woman who still had the power to make him sigh over a decade after he had moved out of her life.

He still sometimes called out her name when he came in me, shuddering at his climax.

'Noora, Noora...' I would poke him in the stomach. 'It's me, Gulab.' That would shrivel him up quick enough.

I hated her, the one he imagined I was when he shut his eyes.

He would then describe her to me, her face as full and round as the moon, her skin lit from within and glowing with an unseemly fire that he had never seen in any other woman, her eyes grey in some recountings and green at others and all the colours of the sea and lakes, her brows arched and high, her cheeks flushed a deep pink when she came. Her hair had thick curls that barely stayed restrained by the thick bun she tied it in, or the long plait down her back that swung sinuously, hitting one rounded buttock then the other as she walked, making his palms yearn to cup them and squeeze them. Her body curves that could derail a man's thinking. Sometimes he would get graphic in his description of her body and then realize I was listening to his ramblings and stop embarrassedly.

He was a good man to me. He was also a man on the run and exhausted with the running, a man who lived on making the hits that he was hired for. 'I have a zero-fail record,' he boasted, 'No one stays alive after I shoot them.' He had a bag where he kept what he needed for when he had to go on a job. I was not allowed to touch it. I was told where I needed to go next, and he would find me. It would all be arranged by those who hired him. I was an encumbrance I knew, but one he had taken on willingly. How could I have his child when both of us were killers? The genes we would pass on were unthinkable. I ensured no sperm spilled into me without the raincoat of a condom.

'How many have you killed till now?' I had asked once.

'I've never counted,' he had replied and left it at that.

The neighbourhood we lived in now was one that was not just decrepit but infested with unsavoury elements. On the floor below was a woman who entertained clients in the time her husband was out to work. Everyone knew about it except her husband, or perhaps he did and chose to turn a blind eye. I cooked meals in the day to the sounds of flesh smacking against flesh and animal sounds of mating. On the ground floor was a family that dealt in contraband that they distributed through a network of street kids. It was a fine neighbourhood to raise kids in, I thought to myself.

'Whatever they offer you, don't take it,' he warned me. 'Never take it, even just to try it.'

I assured him I wouldn't. 'Don't step out when I'm not around. Lock the door and stay inside. Don't let anyone come in, even if they beg and plead.' They would have to break down the door to get in.

'Someday we'll take a proper house, you and me, far, far away. I'll stop this business.' It was strange he called it a business, this killing of other human beings. I was no one to be judgemental. I'd killed too. We'd been here a few months now. Time to move.

We would be together as long as I was useful to him,

I knew that. I kept his house, I cooked food, and I was available, a body whenever he desired to slake his lust. We kept moving, and here we were, in this one-horse town in the land of the five rivers and the doabs, the border a touching distance away, the district a different one. Right now, there was no time to dwell upon what we would be, or could be, marriage and children. He was not very far from where he had run from, a few hours away by bus, perhaps he was running back to where he had started out all those years ago. The lovesick fool, was he hoping to run into Noora? There was no reason why we were here, we could have easily gone the other side, towards the badlands of the plains, where the gangs roamed wild and the police, too terrified, let them.

I noticed her in the marketplace one morning when I had stepped out to pick up vegetables. She shone, no, I was being ridiculous: I had never seen anyone else with the kind of shine I had when I chose not to dim it, a faint vein of light running like electricity, white and blue, under my skin. But yes, there was a glow around her that drew every eye towards her like a magnet, it was pale, the feeble yellow of a winter sun. She was aware of it, she tried to diminish herself, she was wearing dull grey, unleavened by any design or embroidery, her dupatta draped modestly around her, a drape that if anything, only accentuated how glorious she was. Surely, she was a queen, I thought to myself, no ordinary woman would shine like that. I found myself being pulled towards her, despite myself. A *chumbak*, that's what she was. A human magnet.

Unthinkingly, I fell into step behind her at a discreet distance. It was the end of summer, the heat was dry and blistering in the late afternoon. It would be pleasant in a little while, and autumn would set in soon enough bringing with it the sudden crispness of cold air coming in from the frozen north, beyond the high plateau, beyond the mountains that had formed when the earths collided, from where the sky danced with magnetic lights and the land was frozen. I followed her through the market to what I supposed was her home, where an elderly man opened the door to her. I asked around, grocery store owners in neighbourhoods were always generous in supplying information, even when they did not know you, if you were young and pretty and smiled appealingly. I even widened my eyes and fluttered my eyelashes if needed, it always worked, even with the most crabby old curmudgeons.

They were husband and wife I learnt, he was a retired babu and now taught at the local college to spend his time fruitfully. She was much younger than her husband, they told me, at least by twenty or thirty years. And she looked much younger, almost like his daughter. Her husband had shrunk and wrinkled and turned into an old man and she had only grown more beautiful by the day. She didn't interact with anyone from the neighbourhood or call anyone over. The families around had tried to set up a friendship when they moved here ten years ago and then decided to maintain a distance from her when she refused to age like everyone around. Surely, she was drinking blood on full moon nights, which is why her face was unlined and she had no children. Maybe, she sacrificed her unborn to dark forces. Tongues wagged about her, and they had no hesitation in wagging to me, a stranger.

That there were *daayan*s I knew for a fact. There had been one living on the outskirts of our town, beyond where we lived. I had never seen her, she had left right before I was born and no one knew what had happened of her. She had lived in a small wooden hut on the outskirts of the town where the trees ended and the mountains went brown, a house they say she had built with her own bare hands, stripping trees from the ground, raising stones from the mountains, invoking spirits to help her. She lived with only her dog for company. People kept their distance from her, young men were fascinated with her when they came upon her sitting on a stoop in the middle of the nowhere leading into the forest and would be swept off their feet by her beauty. Those who were foolish enough to follow her to her home would return home after spending the night with her, drained men, burning with a high fever only to die in a couple of days, consumed by a fire within them that no hakim or *vaid* could figure out the cause of. The villagers had tried to burn her house down, the whispers went, many, many years ago, back when my father was still a young man but it refused to catch fire despite the kerosene they flung and the kindling they heaped against the wall. She balled the fire back and threw it back at them, a fire that skittered through the forests and caught the tops of the trees and the dry grass in the undergrowth, razing to the skies. No one had ventured near her hut again. She shone like a fury, they said, when she was angry, a blazing field of crackling light surrounded her and burnt up all that came in her way. And then one day, she disappeared, with her hut. She was never seen again. I would have loved to make her acquaintance. Perhaps she would have some explanation about the light in my veins. Apart, of course, from it being a useful mutation in times of voltage fluctuations.

Surely, this woman was not a *daayan*. She was much younger than her husband, old men invariably find themselves young wives when their loins refuse to perform to their command. The next day I came across her in the marketplace, I followed her again. She went into a store that sold salwar suit materials, embroidered and plain, to be tailored to size and vanity. She fascinated me, a fascination I could not explain, it drew me to her. It was the glow I guessed, I'd never seen another human glow like she did. Was she the Noora of Teja's youth? I had to find out, and then ensure they would never meet if she was.

I stood at the counter opposite her, watching her in the reflection. She had old eyes that had seen the passage of time, eyes that had suffered and found no solace. When one looked into them one realized she was beyond the count of time. Old eyes in a young face. I was curious when I stood next to her and examined her; her skin was still plump and smooth, the creep of crumpled skin had not begun its indentations on the surface, the flesh had not begun falling off the bone, there were no tell-tale stains around her hairline of dye injudiciously applied, nor of white roots to confess to a vanity covering of the grey. High cheekbones, an aquiline nose, a jaw that was chiselled like a sculptor had done his life's best work on it. Diamonds sparkled in her ears, in her nostril and on her fingers and wrists. She suddenly turned towards me in the cloth store where we both stood, looking at the bales of fabric on display, the suit sets draped on headless mannequins, tightened at the back with clothesline clips to create the illusion of being worn by a female body. Perhaps she had noticed me staring at her. I could see the pupils of her eyes, black dots, we were that close. Why was she looking at me so intently? I jumped, guilty of staring, of following, of asking about her. If I were a boy, it could be obsession, but I couldn't explain my fascination.

'Which one should I buy?' I asked her, embarrassed. 'The yellow or the blue?'

She smiled a slow languorous smile that was at once electric and erotic, then held both against me, taking a long hard look at me, a gaze that was a caress that made me quiver under its strength.

'Both would look lovely on you,' she said, her voice mellow, her accent indeterminate, not high-born but trained in dropping the hard edges of the rustic, 'but the red you are wearing suits you the best.'

She wore a salwar kameez that had been tailored to fit her, not bought off the shelves. It had expensive embroidery at the yoke and on the sleeves, embroidery that was bought in patches at other markets. It was pale blue. The colour someone who wanted to be left alone wore. I wore red, I dared people to cross my path now.

'Take the yellow,' she said, after a moment's pause, 'there's time enough to wear blue.' Her words were heavy.

I paid for the yellow and thanked her for her advice. 'Why did you tell me there's time enough to wear the blue?'

'You'll know what I mean when you're older. Blue will be a colour that you will either hate or love once it comes to pass.' She would have looked lovelier in pink, I thought to myself. The roses were still in her cheeks, her eyes deep and black, and paradoxically warm.

She smiled politely, picked up her parcel from the counter and made to move out of the shop. Then changed her mind and turned back towards me.

'What is your name?' she asked.

'Gulab,' I replied. It was what Teja had named me the night he had met me and I had stayed Gulab. 'Gulab Devi Singh.' The Devi Singh, tacked on in due course, was indeterminate enough to not pin me down to a specific place, a specific community.

I now even had an identity card with this name – anything could be managed if you could pay or intimidate the people who got things done. She looked at me from head to toe. Did she suspect I was lying and that was not my name?

'That is a lovely name, and you are fresh like a rose, a red rose. Do you live close by, Gulab?'

I told her I lived down the lane.

'What does your father do?' I had the answer to that ready: I had lost both my parents years ago, and my brother and I had just moved here because my brother now had a job here.

'What about the rest of your family? Surely you two aren't completely alone?'

We were, I told her, we had been abandoned by the extended family because no one wanted to take on the onus of raising us.

'So, the two of you have no one here?' she asked.

'No one,' I replied, truthfully. We did have no one, no collective fold of the family to gather us into their bosom, to watch out for us, to ensure we were fed, clothed and sheltered. And perhaps that was all for the good, the collective fold of family could be stifling.

I could see in her eyes not sympathy but something more calculative. It seemed like a weighing up and an assessment. She linked her arm in mine and insisted on paying for the suit material I'd picked. I liked her already. I was easily bought; a suit material, a roof over my head, little kindnesses could buy me over.

'Think of it as a gift from someone who also has nobody. Why don't you drop in sometime? Or come home with me now, for some chai? We rarely get any visitors, you know.'

I demurred half-heartedly and then followed her without a murmur when she insisted. We entered her gate, a modest iron one anchored to the walls which had two lights firmly inset into the pillars holding the gate up. She clicked it shut firmly behind us as we went in, scanning the leafy lane with a quick sweeping gaze. It was late in the balmy September afternoon, not a soul was to be seen out at this time, even the street dogs were somnolent in the best shady spots they could find. A dog barked ferociously from somewhere in the immediate vicinity but was not to be seen. I started and looked around some more, expecting it to emerge from the undergrowth fringing the compound wall and tear me apart with sharp fangs. And then it did, a huge black creature with eyes shining red like coals on a flame.

'Don't worry,' she said. 'Shera is very gentle.'

Shera looked at me and growled, a low rumble that seemed like it was coming from beneath the earth and pulled back his lips. I felt my limbs grow cold and remained rooted to the spot. Shera ambled up to me and sniffed me, but when she gestured at him to back down he growled and ran into the rear of the compound. The gooseflesh on my limbs refused to subside. His teeth looked like he had been filing them on stone for extra sharpness. He could have taken out a chunk of each my calves without even bothering to exert the full tectonic strength of his jaws.

She turned the key in the door and threw it open. The rooms were large and well maintained, the furniture an accumulation of years, with no regard to decor or style, each item chosen for beauty or perhaps sentimentality. I could tell with a single glance around the room that some of the items in there were very valuable. I wondered how much I could filch without her noticing. Don't blame me,

I'd learnt how to be nimble-fingered in order to survive all these years. I had begun by nicking small notes from Teja's wallet itself. After all, a girl had to look out for herself.

'Sit down,' she said, gesturing towards an antique carved couch, which I intuitively knew was very expensive. 'What will you have? Some tea, or something cold, Pepsi, *sharbat*?' Was she royalty, by any chance? She did behave like it. Perhaps there were some tiaras and diadems tucked away in the attic, and some rich brocades in the wardrobes, waiting for me to get to them and sell them off in the second-hand market.

I replied that I was good with anything, whatever was convenient for her to make, I didn't want to inconvenience her. Not yet at least. Perhaps I would, later.

'No inconvenience at all, I will be making some tea for my husband if he has woken up from his nap, I will make some for you too,' she said. Her eyes looked deep into mine. What was it about her that was fascinating me so, I wondered. I hadn't even asked her what her name was. Professorni, that's what everyone addressed her as. Ridiculous that they should call her by what her husband did for a living. Did they ever do the reverse, call the husband by what the wife did?

'I'll just be back,' she said and went off into an inner room. For so large a home, it was strange that there was no house help. Or perhaps it was their day off. Most homes in this area had staff that lived in day and night with the residents. I could hear her footsteps go up the stairs with a speed that was almost a run, then some hushed voices float down from the room above. I wandered around the room, looking at the various curios and photographs in the frames arranged on the sideboards, hung on the walls. They were all similar, the husband and wife, either individually or clicked together, a procession of photographs that showed the years and the decades pass but only for the husband, the wife remained untouched by time's scythe. I picked a frame up in my hands, it looked like one of the most recent ones. I had no photograph with Teja, I realized. Three years together and no photograph together.

'That was clicked last month,' she said, having come back into the room even though no footsteps had heralded her entering the room. She picked up another in which her husband was very young and so was she, with a red and gold dupatta draped around her head. 'This is from our wedding day.'

She hadn't aged a minute. What sorcery was this? I'd read about vampires who didn't age even for hundreds of years, but she had no fear of sunlight and the brightness of day like that kind was supposed to have. She would have been fried to a crisp on the sidewalk the other day had she been one.

'How...' I didn't know what the polite way would be to ask how was it that she remained unchanged while her husband gradually sank into a dignified middle age.

She looked at me, almost as if she could read my thoughts and then chose not to answer them. The diamonds in her ears sparkled as a ray from the setting sun came in through a window and caught them full on. I wondered how much they were worth, those earrings, that ring on her finger with a diamond so huge it was probably one of those they called solitaires and worth a small fortune, and the ones set into the pendant at her neck, the small stone in her nostril. How could I nick them was my next thought. I had to accept it. I was now a petty thief. Add that to my newfound list of skills. Murder, robbery, evading the authorities.

'Do sit, Gulab, my husband will be out any moment. He's most curious to see who I have brought home. I rarely bring visitors home, you are an exception. I'll get the tea ready. He likes it strong and sweet, what about you?'

I assured her yet again that I had no specific preferences. She left the room as the husband walked in, his gait, his expression, his entire bearing the opposite of hers. While she was light and nimble on her feet, almost like she was zipping through the house on wheels, he was ponderous and heavy, each step he took resounding through the floor with an echo. 'Hello, hello, hello, hello,' he boomed. 'Hello,' I said, applying the brakes to his litany of unnecessary hellos. He looked startled. Perhaps no one had ever thought to reply to his hellos.

He was grey and his hair had thinned on the crown, showing scalp beneath. He must have been broad boned and muscular in his youth, he had the structure of one who was built for the mud and sweat of the wrestling ring, but fate and circumstance had shifted him towards the drudgery of babudom. He must have been quite good looking back in his time, but now in his late sixties or early seventies, he had let himself go with the graceless spread of one unconcerned about appearances. His face was leathered with sun from the long walks to the college he taught at now over the past few years, walks that allowed him the luxury to think undisturbed and uninterrupted by the prosaic tedium of mundane conversations that he would gladly cross the road to avoid. It was an affliction of the elderly, the lack of enthusiasm for social interaction that swiftly accelerated until it became a relentless aloneness, waiting for death.

I folded my hands in greeting. He nodded and asked me to sit down, asking politely about my home and family, clucking sympathetically when I told him I was orphaned and lived with my older brother. 'That's brave of the two of you,' he said. 'What does your brother do?'

He kills people. He's a hitman, a gun for hire. And he's not my brother. We fuck. What did one say to a question like this? He's looking for a job, I replied. It was the truth. He was always looking out for jobs.

She came in with a tray bearing three cups of tea and a plate with biscuits. She sat down on the sofa next to him and handed me a cup, our fingers touched for a brief, brief second, it flowed into me from me, from me to her, the light. I wasn't imagining it, she shone. Like I did when I chose to. The Professor gulped his tea down and excused himself; it was time for his evening walk, he said.

'Do have some,' she said, pushing the plate of biscuits towards me. Her eyes were on me, calm and unruffled.

'What do you miss the most about your parents?' she asked.

I thought for a moment, a long hard moment where multiple thoughts jostled in my head shrieking to be voiced. 'Perhaps the feeling of belonging to someone.' It was the truth. There was nothing else I missed, but the sense of home, of people whom I could turn to and know they were there for me, no matter what.

A strange undecipherable expression passed over her face. It wasn't empathy, but a strange, feral expression that was scary in the brief moment it played over her features, making her face go from beautiful to absolutely terrifying for a split second before it went back to be placidly beautiful. I felt the gooseflesh rise on my arms for a brief moment before it subsided. And then she shone again, so radiant I felt my soul reach out and embrace hers, waves of warmth and light reaching out from her to me, making me bask in them.

'Sometimes you don't want to belong to someone who wants you to belong to them. Anyway.' She put her hand on mine. 'You belong to me now.'

And I was powerless to take my hand out from under hers.

Rani

'A crown of kisses to the queen of dreams.'

– ALBERT CAMUS

PERHAPS I SHOULD HAVE EXPECTED IT, A LIFE THAT was comfortable enough to keep food in my stomach and a roof over my head and not much more. This was what I had signed up for, hadn't I, when I chose to hitch myself to this man.

He took me around the country in a dazzling whirl of important and mofussil postings. We lived with a retinue of staff, I had dinners and lunches to be organized, a social calendar that was too full for my liking, an obligation I carried out punctiliously but with no joy. When news came that his parents had passed away in quick succession a few years after we were married, he'd sold off his share of the property. He would have nothing of the life he'd left behind in that town which only held unpleasant memories for me. With the money he'd received from the sale, he'd given half to his only sister who had not been part of the will and with the other half, he bought this sedate one-storeyed house in this sleepy town for us to live in after he retired. He was meticulous like that, he planned. I lived for the day, there was no other way for me to do so, I never knew when it would return to claim me, which sleep I would be woken up from feeling the weight of a body on me, the heat of air surrounding me, the pressure of something I couldn't explain within me.

He'd taken some pieces of his mother's jewellery for me, the ones she had mentioned were meant for his wife, the others went to his sister. I wore them with joy. The rest I kept in the bank locker – there was nowhere to wear them to now, we went nowhere.

'She would have been fond of you,' he said, 'had my father allowed her to meet you.'

I had nodded, perhaps she would have, perhaps she wouldn't have. But I knew that I would never have been accepted as the daughter-in-law of a family with honour in a small town when I had so publicly lost mine all those years ago. We went nowhere now and met no one, not together as a couple at least. He was embarrassed when I was next to him, I knew that. It was unseemly how I had remained the same as I had been all those years ago. It was unnatural.

His sister and her children visited us occasionally, bringing with her jars of pickles and homemade delicacies he enjoyed eating. She would stay a few days, and then return to her home in the town we had left behind. I enjoyed her visits; Rajjo brought to our lives the whiff of normalcy, with her expansiveness and unfettered love for her brother which she reluctantly at first, but then unreservedly showered on me too. I became a younger sister whom she generously took under her wing. Her children, two rambunctious boys, didn't let my husband feel the lack of children in his life.

Now that we had finally settled in the house he had bought back then, I realized it was enough for the two of us, and more. His parental home and land gave us enough to keep aside for a lifestyle that was comfortable enough far beyond what a humble government servant would make. I was happy to just be allowed to live in relative small-town obscurity where no one kowtowed to him or looked at me with curiosity, this woman who did not age, because they didn't know how old I actually was.

'We might as well live in comfort, Rani,' he'd told me. 'It's not like we have to worry about getting a child educated or getting married off.'

There was no rancour in his voice when he said that, he'd never had any rancour about us not having children, about me not letting him have my body as was his right as a married man. I couldn't bear the touch of a man on my skin. What owned me would never allow it, it would sear me with lashes of fire that would raise welts on my skin invisible to the human eye. Staying chaste was the only way I could live. It kept me ageless, it poured into me the agelessness it possessed, I was its plaything, it would toy with me whenever it chose to. When it didn't need me it would end me, that I knew. Until it needed me it would keep me alive and just as I was when it first took me, when I was in my mid-twenties, flush with youth and sensuality.

We had kept a low profile, I had been sure to not do anything that would call attention to us, it had allowed us to live undisturbed in this little *kothi* in one of the lanes off the main street, in a town that had sprung up out of nothingness, bordering the state capital, soon becoming a throbbing metropolis of its own, albeit without the swagger and power that the capital was infused with. The roads were broad, the squat one-storeyed homes were giving way to tall residential complexes with fancy amenities packaged and sold as dreams.

The house I filled with grand furniture, heavy brocade curtains, and all the beauty I could fill it… the joy of beholding beauty, claiming it for one's own. Perhaps it was the same joy that the one which had claimed me for its own derived when it had taken over me, what had prevented the years from claiming me for their own, prevented time from driving its scythe through me.

'Some people don't age quickly at all, you're one of them. I'm a lucky man!' he had said one morning over breakfast, when I'd wished him a happy birthday. He had turned sixty that day. I would turn sixty a few months later. 'Men my age envy me. They don't realize how awkward I feel to look like your father when we step out together.'

I realized with a start perhaps this was why he had stopped accepting invitations to socialize, from colleagues, from neighbours, why he wouldn't accompany me anymore to the marketplace on Sunday mornings, although it had been our routine for years. I was that awkward thing to him, a wife who would not age, a wife who made him acutely aware of how the years had taken him down and wrestled him to the ground. Little by little, inch by inch, he had been diminishing right in front of my eyes and I hadn't even realized it. His stature diminished with the stoop the years brought to broad shoulders of youth narrowing them to a rounded curve, the lack of physical exercise except for his evening walk, telling on how his muscles had shrunk. The notch on the belt went one higher each year as his body shrank beneath his clothes, he wore his pants higher now. His reflexes were slower, his words more measured than they had been previously, the gaps between his sentences longer. If he had been taciturn earlier, the years had made him even more so. Somewhere, along the path, love had disappeared and what remained between us was acceptance, a strained acceptance of what it was to live together, and not be husband and wife of the flesh.

Nonetheless, I had been a good wife. I had woken him in the morning with a cup of tea and a smile, I'd had a hearty breakfast ready by the time he'd bathed and dressed for college, I'd kept a neat and tidy home, managed his social duties, been a good hostess and a pleasant guest, frugal in my spending, modestly elegant in my appearance. I'd cooked a hearty meal for him every night, and he had never known lack on the dining table. The loneliness was aching though, I longed for touch. Human touch. When I touched Gulab, I could feel the longing sear through every nerve, every synapse of my body, I didn't care that it was unseemly, what I felt. I always knew what I was, I had learnt that the day I had held hands with Noor and felt her light enter me. It shone through me still, her light. It would never leave me, I knew, until I met her again and returned it to her. It was mine now, for safekeeping, and had been so all these years. It was her light that had kept me alive, despite what had claimed me for his own. He couldn't defeat it. He could never take me over completely. Now this girl had it, that light, I saw it in her, felt the light in me reach out and touch it running through her veins when she stood next to me in the store, that sudden whiff of roses as she passed, a fragrance imprinted in my mind. Perhaps, she was my escape route, perhaps I could still live a normal life, I could pass on what possessed me to her. She had told me, I could. She had said she would send a rose to me. The fragrance of roses still haunted me after all these years. Perhaps Gulab was the rose I had been waiting for.

'Why did you invite that girl home?' he had asked me after she'd left the house. 'It is not like you to invite anyone home at all. You've only been too happy to have no visitors at all.'

I had no answer for why I had done so. Or perhaps I did have an answer, only perhaps it was not an answer I could tell him. I had noticed her staring at me, following me, the light drew her to me and it drew me to her. She shone too, perhaps she just didn't know it yet, and I needed to know where she had got it from, or from whom. Perhaps, I could still find Noor. She was the only one I had seen in all these years who shone brilliantly, a light she had been generous enough to share with me, a stranger.

'I just felt sorry for her, no parents and just an older brother.'

He gave me a long hard look, one that said much more than his words did.

'I've never known you to have sympathy for anyone or anything. This is a first.'

But he would be a gracious host whenever she visited, that I knew. He would welcome Gulab, have polite conversation with her, talk with her about her parents, her home, her dreams, her ambitions. We would have a meal I would cook with the choicest ingredients, *kesar* to add that tinge to the rice, the best cuts of mutton in the biryani I would make, cashew nuts fried and sprinkled on the topmost layer, the deep-fried onions, browned to a crisp on the surface. The *kheer* with creamy milk, cashews, raisins. The peas and the fried paneer floating in a rich tomato gravy, the puris puffed and fried fresh just before the meal, I would feed her a good meal. You made a person indebted to you when you fed them a meal, they were obligated to return, to deepen the relationship, to pay back for the food in ways other than food.

She would return again, I needed to observe her, to chat longer with her, to learn about her life, find out where she got the light from, the pale blue light that skipped and danced just below her skin, streaks of light moving swiftly through her veins. I encouraged her dropping in again and again, unannounced.

'You know,' my husband said the next morning over breakfast, 'It is strange but I get the sense of an impending bereavement.'

He had always been a sensitive soul, camouflaged in the bear like body he had been saddled with. I held my silence and buttered his toast before handing it over to him. He continued, after a brief silence. 'Teaching at college no longer gives me any joy as it used to. Perhaps I should stop and stay at home. We don't really need the money, we have enough and more to live a comfortable life.'

'You will get bored at home,' I replied, placing the buttered toast on his plate.

He harrumphed in reply and went off to college, where he would return from only at the end of the day in time for evening tea, or if he got engrossed in a book in the library when the library closed for the day, at around 7 p.m.

Gulab dropped in, unannounced that evening, around tea time. She was exquisite, the more I looked at her, the more I fell in love with her, it came from her too, a faint fragrance of roses. Perhaps the name was apt, she was a rose.

'I'm leaving town,' she said. 'I just came to say goodbye to you.'

She had the light. She had been touched by an angel, she had, I had, that was the only explanation for the light within her. She didn't know it, I didn't know if she did. I did. It was time to let it take Gulab and free me of the burden I had been carrying.

I put my arm around her and took her into the house. Is this how they took lambs to the sacrifice, with intense love?

Gulab

'It's the emptiest and yet the fullest of all human messages: Good-bye.'

– KURT VONNEGUT, *Bluebeard*

TEJA HADN'T QUITE BEEN HIMSELF SINCE WE MOVED here and now after a couple of weeks of laying low, he'd become even more fidgety and unnerved by heaven knows what. I knew what he would say before he said it, his voice flat and matter of fact.

'We need to move again,' he said, looking out the window for the umpteenth time on a bright Saturday afternoon. The view outside was not remarkable enough for such repeated attention, it was an array of flat rooftops, with clothes drying, satellite dishes, and water tanks. The occasional group of women sitting on a charpoy in distant courtyards and gossiping the late afternoon away before the sun sank beyond the horizon of rooftops, young boys and girls making sheep's eyes at each other across the divide of boundary walls and small ledges, some emboldened enough to jump across, and in others, earnest students trying to cram for forthcoming exams.

'How much more are we going to move? I'm tired of moving. We need to settle now, someplace.' Settling was for tea leaves and people. Humankind, after all, developed only after they found fertile river plains and formed settlements. I was quite done with the hunter gatherer life, and oftentimes I wasn't sure if I was the hunter or the prey.

He nodded. He knew I was right, I was right most times, and he had stopped resisting his innate masculine tendency to try and prove me wrong. He was sensible like that. He got up and went across to the window and rested his head against the frame. Outside, the mundanity of small-town life chittered on.

'Where can we move to so we don't need to ever move again?'

Small towns offered no anonymity, big cities were better, we could sink into the morass of crowds where no one cared for the other, neighbours merely shared walls and not lives, and no one cared for anything but their own survival. We could drop off the surface of the civilized world, move out to where no one bothered anyone, a landscape so remote and hostile that people survived if they could or died if they couldn't. We would leave immediately, he told me, the dragnet was closing in on him, he'd already received warnings from the few well-wishers he was still in contact with from his home town. The ones tracking him had caught wind of where he had moved and were closing in on him. He had a day or two before they caught up with him. There was a price on his head, there would be no questions asked and no mercy given. That was how it was. We needed to leave tonight, and there was to be no argument about it. I knew better than to argue with him. He also knew better than to argue with me, so I decided where it would be we would go. We would go where I came from, because he couldn't go to where he came from. And there would be no one there to object to us. My father was dead. That I was quite sure of. My grandmother if she was still alive was as good as dead. It would be a comfortable existence.

'We can go to my home,' I told him. 'I'm ready to return now. We can stay there in our house, undisturbed and no one will bother us. It is mine. There is no one else with the right to it, and it is so far off, no one will find us there. If anyone else is living there in the house, I need you to help me throw them out. We'll tell everyone who asks that we are husband and wife, you don't have to get married to me if you don't want to.'

'I don't want to,' he replied with an honesty that stung. 'I love you, but I don't want to get married.'

'I'm not asking you to.' He was flattering himself. I was not about to sign up for seven lives with a hitman. One who himself was on a couple of hit lists. It would be good while it lasted, I had told myself. Then we would go our separate ways. But my period had been delayed. And I needed to stay put in one place for a while.

'Do you remember your name now?'

I did, but I was Gulab now. I had shed that name and that life, emerged from it shining and whole. 'It doesn't matter. Those who live there will remember it for me.'

And that was the end of that conversation. I was thankful that he didn't ask me for my name, the real one, the one I had grown up with. Names were burdens when they bore the weight of unresolved trauma, I no longer had any urge to bear the weight of my past, anymore. I'd kicked it off the side of the road along with the corpse of my father.

It wasn't far, a bus ride of a few hours away, I knew. I wondered who lived in the house now, if the elements had claimed it, whether my grandmother was alive or dead. I would know when I reached there.

'Pack up, we can leave immediately.'

We lived so we could move at a moment's notice. A few clothes, that was it. And of course, what did one really need, just enough cloth to cover one's mortality at the end. I needed to say goodbye to the Professorni, I told him. She was the only person I needed to meet before I left. I couldn't explain why, she meant nothing to me and everything. She was suddenly so important to me, so important that my breath caught in my throat every time I thought of her, that there was this strange tug in my chest that seemed to connect me with her, that she felt like part of me in a way no one else in the universe had so far. Not even him, Teja, he whom I loved so much with every atom in my body, with every fragment of my soul, that I had followed him unquestioningly across the country, from town to town, city to city. I would go meet her this afternoon, we could move directly after I had done so. No one would track us down to my house on the heights of a mountain town, it was completely off the grid. He agreed, albeit reluctantly. A house on the outskirts of a mountain town would be safe, no one would come hunting for him there. Across the borders of states, the police grew lax. He cut his long hair short, a crop that was barely a millimetre from his scalp. It was a penchant he had, changing his hairstyle with every move, growing it out, cutting it short, growing a beard, going clean-shaven. There was not much else he could do with his face, his nose already marked him out before he could even announce his name.

'I'll take our bags and wait at the bus stand,' he said, 'You go meet her and come there directly. Make it quick. We don't want to reach there too late at night, it will be cold and difficult to find our way to your house in the darkness.' We would reach late at night anyway now, give or take an hour or two. He was completely rotten at estimating time and distance, everyday stuff, though he could perfectly calculate the trajectory of a bullet considering wind factor, velocity and motion.

I would be there in time for evening tea, it was the weekend, they would have their evening tea by 4 p.m. without fail. I knew their routine by now. If I reached a few minutes before, I would be invited to sit with them and have a cup too. She would go into the kitchen to fetch another cup, while he would have his head in whatever book it was that he had been reading when I interrupted. Shera didn't bark when I entered the gate anymore, he recognized me by now, and apart from a couple of welcoming yips went back to whatever was occupying him, a dead rat, a dog outside the gate, a vendor hawking something of absolutely no dietary interest to Shera. The man who took him for his second walk of the day would come by 4.30 p.m. The Professor would have his cup of tea and step out for his evening walk if he was home.

At precisely ten minutes to 4, I rang the bell at the gate of the bungalow. The barking began instantaneously but Shera didn't come out to investigate, perhaps he had been tied up. The Professorni emerged from the front door and beckoned me to come in, I pushed the gate, it was unlocked. For a home that supposedly had so much wealth to be plundered that they would leave the gate unlocked and the dog tied up was something that niggled at me. I put my misgivings to a side and entered the small grounds, the gravel path leading up to the front porch making my steps uncoordinated. The barking became short yips and then ceased altogether. The dog had decided I was not worth his alertness and had moved on to other distractions.

'You've come right in time for tea, I hope you will join us for some?' Of course, I would, that's what I had come for, hadn't I? To have some tea, say goodbye and check if there was really a treasure in the trunks down in the basement that I could nick. I nodded and stepped in, going straight to the living room. It was an easy familiarity that bordered on the insolent, but then I was no longer concerned with what people thought of me. I knew I was a murderer, and that was insolence enough.

'I'm leaving town,' I told her, 'We're going home, back to our hometown. I just came to say goodbye.' She looked into my eyes, a gaze that inverted my stomach and made me feel hollow and gutted. I liked her. Would I be able to steal from her? I waited. The moment of morality and conscience would pass, I knew, and it did. I wondered how I could knock her out with minimal damage. Perhaps the ugly ceramic vase on the sideboard?

'I will miss you,' she replied, the thin silver edging to her dupatta glinting in the slanted rays of the late afternoon sun that found their way through the window. Outside, the evening birds had started to sing their songs of departure back to their nests.

She gestured towards the living room where the Professor sat at the dining table, deep into a thick leather-bound tome, his spectacles perched precariously at the tip of his nose. The tea tray was on the table already, two cups poured out, the teapot with its hand-knitted pink tea-cosy comfortably demure. I had timed my entry impeccably.

'I'll just get one more cup for you,' she said, turning around and padding into the kitchen.

The Professor sipped from his cup distractedly and excused himself for his evening walk. I was alone in this house with her. I was tense with anticipation, of what I did not know.

'Has he gone for his walk already?' she said, coming into the room, with a cup and some snacks. 'Such an antisocial character he is.' There was no reproach in her voice, just a tinkling amusement.

She finished her tea, I waited. It was inexplicable how one couldn't take one's eyes off her. She was increasingly beautiful by the day; today her skin glowed like she was lit by a flame from within. We made mundane conversation about my hometown, about the house on the ridge, about going there with Teja who was, I confessed now, not my brother, not my husband, but just a man I had taken up with when I'd run from home. She smiled, no judgement in her gaze. I had the unnerving feeling as she looked into my eyes that she knew what I wasn't telling her, all the things I had hidden within me, the years of torture at the hands of my father, pushing him off the side of a road, running off to the railway station carrying only a bag with three pairs of clothes and a few hundred rupees, the old crone, meeting Teja at the railway station, and all that happened after that. She looked into my eyes, and I knew that she knew all the secrets I hadn't told anyone. And the new ones I now had.

She reached out and caressed my face, it was a touch that now sent shivers down my spine, terrifying me. It wasn't the touch of the light, it was the caress of something so black and dark that I was frozen to my chair, unable to move, a terror taking control of my body, making me unable to move, to escape, to protect myself from what was to come. From what I knew, I don't know how, was to come.

'So beautiful, so angelic.' Her voice was not hers anymore, but strange, hoarse, masculine. I looked up with a start. It was her and yet not her. Her touch was different, it was searing hot, a flame tracing its path across my skin. She was in my head, going through my memories, one at a time, sorting out the skeins, playing with them, making my ears ring until I began screaming.

'Have some more biscuits,' she said. I blinked. There were no screams, except for those in my head. I picked up a biscuit. No. Something beyond me made me pick up the biscuit, my hands moved of their own volition. I bit the biscuit, tasting ashes in my mouth, the smell of burnt flesh in my nose, acrid, raw, making me gag.

'Come,' she beckoned. 'It is time you met him.' I didn't understand what she meant, but I moved to her command like a marionette, jerkily, strings of what controlled me invisible to the eye. She moved towards the top of the stairs that led to the basement. The door swung open, there was a faintly musty smell that came from the closed basement. Shadows played catch in the basement below. A lone bulb dangled from a wire in the middle of the room. She went down the steps, I followed her. There was nothing in the musty basement but an old trunk, rusting on its hinges, a trunk that seemed like it hadn't been opened for years, the lock rusted as well from disuse.

She handed me a key. I opened the lock and swung the lid open. She picked up an empty bottle that was within and handed it to me. I looked at it amused – why was she handing me an empty bottle? I unscrewed the lid unthinkingly, knowing it was my undoing. And then I heard myself screaming as if from a distance. The creature within the bottle looked up at me. Its eyes were fire, its breath was smoke. It smiled at me, a slow, deliberate smile, one that cracked what made its face into a thousand crevices below which what seemed to be lava gushed and moved, molten and red hot. It dissolved into air. The air in the room was scalding hot, I could feel my skin singeing under the heat, a heat that was unlike anything I had ever experienced before, not even when red hot coals from the *angeethi* had fallen onto my foot, the scars of which I still bore all these years later.

'You shouldn't have come here today,' she whispered at my shoulder, the Professorni. She sounded frightened, weary, standing right at my elbow, looking dispassionately at the creature. 'You should have just left when you had the chance.'

It flew out of the bottle, the creature of smoke and fire, a being with no substance, swirling around the Professorni in a miasmal embrace, and then turned towards me. The air was heavily fetid and sulphurous, gagging me. It put a hand on my shoulder and I could feel it in my head, poking around, prodding around, a pain that seared my temples. I screamed. I felt the room slowly turn around me. It came face to face with me, looked into my eyes and smiled, a smile that twisted my gut. Its eyes were flame, its breath was flame, and it was framed by a nimbus of flame, singeing everything around it, sparks that flared everything it touched into tongues of fire. And then it poured itself into me, I could feel my body jerking as the blast of heat funnelled itself through me.

I spilled on to the floor. I tried to claw myself up through the acridity of the air around, which had suddenly become a morass of sludge weighing me down. The Professorni stood over me, not reaching down to help me, her body rigid.

She took my hand and pricked it with a swift movement. A drop of my blood fell into the trunk where it sizzled for the briefest moment and then turned into vapour. I felt my heart constricting, like a pair of iron hands were crushing it and the breath whooshed out of my body.

I heard her in my head, a voice that did not come through her lips, her tongue, her larynx. It was heavy with grief and regret, laced with helplessness.

'I'm sorry, Gulab, I wish I didn't have to do this to you. I wish it didn't have to be you. I liked you, I really did. But it is the only way I can free myself from it. You silly girl, you silly, silly girl, why did you not just go away, why did you come back to say goodbye?'

I was not a silly girl, I wanted to tell her that, but the words formed in my head and stayed on my tongue, unspoken. I was a girl who was a survivor, I would survive anything, I would survive this. My thoughts went black, the room went black. Now there was only blackness whirling around me, inside me, a blackness so deep I didn't exist anymore and the only thing I could feel before the nothingness took over was the sudden eagerness of red hot flames all around me, whispering to each other in a language I could not understand, encircling me, waiting, watching, for I knew not what. And then, when I came to, I found myself walking down the street, dragging a locked trunk behind me, wondering if I had imagined all that I had seen and felt. All I knew with an immutable certainty was that the trunk and what it housed had now attached itself to me, and I to it through a covenant I did not comprehend. An empty trunk, with nothing in it but a creature of fire and smoke that had staked its claim over my body. And soul.

Teja

'We are our choices.'

–JEAN-PAUL SARTRE

SHE HAD BEEN SUCH A SPARROW WHEN HE'D spotted her at the railway station, huddled on a bench on the platform with her scruffy duffel bag with the fake logo of a brand that exhorted all those who used it to just do it, the 'it' something of much conjecture when he had been in college many, many years ago. A lifetime ago. It was a different Teja now, a different life. She'd robbed that bag off another passenger on the train, thrown away their belongings and stuffed it with her own, things she had tied together in a cloth bag and run away with. He would learn this later. She held it in a way that suggested she didn't own it, had never owned a proper duffel bag in her life. He could sense it, he'd been there, when he hadn't had anything but the shirt on his back. He'd travelled in a train that way, without a ticket, without luggage, using only his size, his muscles, wits and smooth talk to get him past belligerent ticket checkers and suspicious passengers who resented him occupying their seats when they clambered on. He had been young then, barely a couple of years older than she would perhaps be right now. She made him curious. And then, of course, there was the old lady who had told him to go to the platform, a young girl needed help, and he had gone, curious. Whenever the old lady told him to do something, he would have done it without questioning.

The goons were circling her like vultures spotting carrion, roadkill on a deserted highway, moving in to feast on her, fresh flesh for the taking. They fell away without much resistance when Teja had stepped up from the shadows and taken both her hands and her bag. She did not demur, perhaps she had been expecting him. He did not expect her to be so delicately pretty, a face carved out of the moon, with glowing alabaster skin, black eyes like round hard pebbles, a tiny rosebud of a mouth with no lip gloss or lip colour that could be made out, her nose tiny and pert, telling him she came from the hills. She was unlike the girls he saw in the city every day, in tight t-shirts and jeans, their faces painted into rictus masks, making them older than they were, their eyes older than they were, their gazes knowing and covetous when they saw him. He could see, even in the light of the halogen lamps that she would be glorious in daylight. Was it love then at first sight, as they said? It wasn't. It was just this fierce urge to protect this girl, waif thin and delicate, from those trying to pick her up and take her where they could have their way with her.

He was a lone wolf in a world of wolves; what he would do with her attached to his coat-tails he didn't know, he would figure that out later. These were garden variety goons who were intimidated by his size, or perhaps the rumours of the gun he was reputed to carry tucked into the waistband of his jeans. He had done nothing to dispel such rumours. He never carried a weapon except for a hit. His fists had always been enough, and his fists were always put into use when his tongue had failed to resolve the issue at hand.

Here, standing at this tea stall outside the bus depot, he waited for her to come after saying her goodbyes to this woman she had suddenly been so fascinated with. If it had been a man, Teja would have been jealous. It was a woman, an old woman, so he was amused, perhaps she saw in her the mother figure she had never had all her life. For a moment he thought perhaps he should just leave, free himself of her, it was not practical to keep moving with a young girl attached to him, it slowed him down, made him vulnerable. He would be free of her, an encumbrance to the kind of life he had become accustomed to leading, moving on without a second's thought, taking on jobs no one else would be ready to do, washing the blood off his hands without a moment's regret. Teja had done it, and more. That was how things went. It was survival. She was weighing him down. But she was what he had chosen to weigh him down. This girl, this woman, this rose that had bloomed slowly, petal by petal, while she had been with him, and he had opened her, layer by layer, until she was all his in a way no other human had ever been.

He put his hand in his pocket and felt the snub little jackknife nestled safely within. Its blade was tiny but sharp enough to take down an elephant. Much like Gulab, the girl who called herself Gulab now, he thought, a small smile crossing his face. Strange that she had forgotten her own name. She remembered everything else about her past in excruciating detail, except her name. She would find out her name once she went home, she said, there they would know her name, what to call her, the girl who had been left behind by her mother who had disappeared when the child was but a baby, and then had borne the trauma of a father who used her like a plaything, like a thing of flesh he had created for his own pleasure. The girl who now called herself Gulab had faded bruises mapped all over her body, cigarettes stubbed on her waist and buttocks, raised welts where a belt had split the skin on her back over and over again, thin stripes at the base of her neck where a knife had been held to her throat. Her body was a map of the pain she had borne. The bruises on her body had healed. Her mind had not, that Teja understood. There was much that she had forgotten or chose to forget, and with it was her name, and an entire phase of her life. She didn't remember or she didn't choose to remember who she was and what she had done. That was fine, sometimes one had to forget in order to go on. Remembering was debilitating. Forgetting was a salve when remembering was too painful.

Where was the girl who called herself Gulab? Why was she not here yet? He had not taken the Professorni's home number to call and check if she had left from there. It wasn't too far away, the *kothi* with its imposing wrought-iron gates. Perhaps he should just go there and check. But what if she came here and he had left, what then, would she panic, would someone see her panicking and take her with them promising to take her to Teja? She was so naïve, it flummoxed him that someone could be so worldly wise in some matters and so childlike in others. He would wait for an hour, Teja told himself, just an hour, then he would leave, he would take whatever bus caught his eye and go to wherever it ended. It was dangerous to go back, to look for her, he knew the dragnet was closing in on him, it had taken them a couple of weeks this time, but they had figured out where he was. The night was getting denser, the late autumn fog was rolling in, covering the early night with damp and grey, the buses would soon start leaving few and far between as the crowds thinned down. The night buses would rumble in, discharging their sleepy passengers, and the drivers would hunker down for a well-deserved nap before they moved on back to where they came from.

Teja looked at the crowds milling around, each rapt in their own personal world, the ones travelling alone, the ones in a group, engrossed in conversation with the others, invisible circles around them confining them to what was being said by the others. An occasional loud call for someone who had been spotted at a distance, a child crying, a woman haranguing an unfortunate spouse, a man's laughter, a fight breaking out. Normal sounds. The world was going on as it always had, Gulab would be here soon, he told himself, and they would be gone to where they could be safe. He lounged against the wall adjacent to where the ticket counters were, trying to be as unobtrusive as possible, which was next to impossible he knew given his height and his looks. He stood out no matter what he wore or how shabbily he dressed. Dressing shabbily only drew more attention to him, he'd realized. He'd learnt to dress as closely to how the men of his age in the town he was in dressed. It helped him blend in, as far as possible.

She caught his eye just then, a woman walking away briskly from the ticket counter having purchased her ticket. She was dressed in a drab brown salwar kameez, the dupatta draped over her head and covering her upper torso modestly. It was her gait as she moved away from his line of sight towards the counter that made him catch his breath. Even fully covered up, without a bit of her body showing, all the men there were undressing her with their eyes. The fragrance of roses hit him, straight to the limbic, burrowing deep into the recesses of his memories, taking him back to when he was eighteen and obsessed with this woman, this woman who trailed the fragrance of roses wherever she went. He'd moved away from her life over ten years ago, in a town not too far from this one. It couldn't be her, could it? And if it was her, could he bear to let her go again?

His feet began moving on their own and he found himself

walking behind her. It had to be her, he was convinced of it, no one else walked like that, a walk that was so sensual he could almost feel her hips undulating beneath him as he thrust into her over and over and over until he burst in an explosion, feeling her clamp down harder on him as she burst too. It was her. He knew it. He was close enough to feel the dimmed light coming off her, reaching towards him, where the light within him, long subdued by running and hiding, rose to meet it. She felt it and stopped still, mid-stride. He caught up with her in a few seconds, put his hand on her shoulder, the lights met, his feeble and second hand, what he had received from her all those years ago, hers a blaze of glory that suddenly flashed incandescent white, lighting up the dingy bus depot, freezing everyone around in a never-ending moment of nothingness. She turned around and looked at him, there was no surprise in her eyes. It was almost like she had expected him, seen him standing there, while she stood in the queue, her face draped, her eyes taking note of all that was around her, her light dimmed to let her move freely, at her will.

'Noor,' he said.

There was nothing more to be said. It was her. The same as she had been all those years ago.

The headlights from a bus coming into the depot swept across them both and lit up her face as they looked at each other for a long moment. Teja pushed the dupatta off her head and stared at her, taking in all of her. As he looked on, her face changed from the drably unremarkable it had been barely a few seconds ago and began glowing with an unearthly beauty that was too much to behold, a metamorphosis he wouldn't have believed had he not seen it happen in front of his own eyes. Her face was the same and yet not the same, her features were the same and not the same, the light now lit her up from within her skin, transforming her into a creature so glorious and radiant it hurt his eyes to continue looking at her without narrowing his gaze. Eyes green shards of stone and impenetrable, that firm bow of her full lip, her face full and round, her eyebrows thick and arched perfectly, her hair parted neatly in the centre, stray curls escaping from the side, her skin alabaster and ivory and rose. Her light pulsed strongly, its white cocoon embracing him too as he stepped into its circumference. She was what goddesses painted on calendars were like, beauty, terrifying beauty in all its glory. Beauty that could provide succour. Beauty that could destroy.

'Noor,' he said, after a long pause. '*Girgit*.'

'You finally found me, Teja,' she replied, her voice heavy and strange, weighed down by the struggle she was going through beneath her skin to calm herself.

'I've waited so many years.'

He gathered her in his arms, feeling the heat of her, feeling an ache he couldn't control, a need that consumed him uncaring of the situation they were in. No eyes were upon them. Everything and everyone had paused as they were, that was how she did it, she paused time when she shone. She pressed against Teja for the briefest of moments, feral and instinctive in her response to him, her body, her smell, the feel of her in his arms, was all familiar and hurting. She pulled away roughly, straightening herself, putting her dupatta back on her head from where it had been displaced and the world unfroze back into sound and movement. A bus honked, a child called out, the moment broke and dissipated into a million fragments that hurled outwards from the centrifuge that was the two of them, there, in the middle of that bus depot, surrounded by curious onlookers.

Men and women did not embrace in public at bus depots in this small town, they did not even touch, much less curve into each other so no part of their bodies stayed untouched by the other. Teja could feel his body trembling with the need for her. It was inexplicable that after all these years she still had the same effect on him, after all these years she was still exactly the same as she had been when he'd seen her last. Over a decade had passed, a decade of him never staying in the same place for more than a few months, of constantly being on the run until it became second nature, thinking of where he would run to next while he was still moving into a house in a new town, a new city.

This time he would not let her go, Teja thought to himself. And then it struck him as an afterthought, there was Gulab. He was already weighed down. He would go with Noor, he thought, Gulab could figure out her own life.

'Where are you going?'

She looked at Teja as if in a daze and then looked at the stub of the ticket in her hand like she couldn't quite remember where she was supposed to go. 'Wherever this ticket will take me. I don't know where it goes to. I asked them for the next bus that left the depot. It will leave any moment now.'

'Wait for me,' he said, grabbing the ticket from her hand and running to the ticket counter, pushing aside those who were in queue, not even looking at the destination on it. No one dared stop him or protest. Teja had that face now, the face of one you didn't mess with.

'Give me one ticket to this place, on this bus,' he said to the confused clerk at the counter, pushing the ticket under his nose to ensure that he didn't get the destination wrong. 'Make it quick,' he yelled. 'The bus is about to leave.'

He handed over the money, picked up the change and the two tickets and turned around, bounding without looking up towards where the bus was.

At the end of the long porch that made the ticket counter, looking at him with her pebble-like eyes that were now black shiny coals with anger, was Gulab. How long had she been sitting there, what had she seen, Teja didn't know. There was something different about her, something he couldn't quite put his finger on, something had changed about her. She was physically as she had always been but now she was terrifying. She was sitting on a small trunk, square and squat, locked with a solid lock that would need more than a crowbar to break open. Had she burgled the Professorni's home? He wouldn't put it past her to have done so. There was something about her, something that unsettled him, something that had absolutely no moral compass, beyond his kills.

'Where are you going, Teja, without waiting for me?' she asked, and as she looked into his eyes Teja had the uncomfortable feeling that something terrible was going to be unleashed upon him. It was Gulab and it was not Gulab speaking to him. Noor was somewhere in that bus honking musically to his left, a short sprint away, announcing its imminent departure.

'I'm sorry,' he mumbled, and pushed past her. 'I have to leave. I'm sorry, this is the end of our journey together. I'm really sorry.' He wasn't. He was just eager to leave, to go with Noor wherever it was that she was heading to. He had been given a second chance, Teja would be a fool to squander it.

She put out a hand and held on to his. Her grip was vice, a cuff of fire on his wrist that felt like it was burning his flesh to cinder. He screamed and pulled his hand away, there was nothing around his wrist, no burn, nothing. Had he been imagining it, no, he knew what he had felt and what he was seeing, flames in her eyes; eyes that had been black hard stones just a few seconds ago were now blazing orange and red. Then they were black again and filled with tears. Surely, he was losing his mind, imagining things that didn't exist. Teja stepped aside, dodging her as she stood in his path, dragging the trunk behind her.

'Please, Teja,' she whimpered. 'Don't leave me, where will I go, what will I do?'

He turned to her, apologetic yet incapable of doing anything but what he was to do. 'I'm sorry, I have to go.'

The bus honked again. She stepped back and looked at him again, a long hard look with eyes that were ancient stones from when the earth was forming and reforming, when the fire was in all the rock and the air was still sulphurous and acrid with the fumes of the deepest hells man would never know.

'Go then,' she said. 'Go with the knowledge that I am pregnant with your child.' This was not the scrawny, sparrow-like girl he had saved from a railway station. This was a woman in full control of herself, intimidating with the power of her self-awareness, of what lay within her, a woman who knew, no matter what his decision was, she would survive.

The huge green bus with its tinted dark windows gave a brief last burst of a honk before beginning to move. Teja looked at the tickets in his hand and then at the bus as it passed him, standing there, torn between where he should go, what he should do. Decisions were always difficult especially when there was no black and white rule book of prior circumstance and mandated responses. Seated at the window, looking impassively at him as it passed was Noor, her light drawn back into her, a regular woman in her late twenties, with nothing about her that would draw any attention from anyone, certainly no temptress that had him by the loins.

He ran a shaky hand over his brow, feeling like he was

just emerging from a deep, murky dream that had nothing he could remember in order to sift through the details and conclude whether it was an omen or a portent or just the stirrings of a disturbed subconscious. Gulab stood next to him, her hand on his arm, staking a claim on him. She was also holding on to that strange trunk like it contained her entire world now.

But the gap between Gulab and Teja widened after that night at the bus depot. Noor stood in the space between the two of them, a ghostly spectre. What Teja didn't know then was that late one summer evening she would land up at their doorstep, hammering at the door, barefoot and with deep gashes all over her body bleeding thick red blood all over the porch, gashes that only a wild cat could have made. And that, despite his misgivings, Teja would open the door, she would fall into his arms and into his life yet again.

Noor

'And he could go on in life, existing from day to day, without connection and without hope. For he did not know what to do with himself.'

– D.H. LAWRENCE, *Lady Chatterley's Lover*

I DIDN'T HAVE A TICKET, BUT IT DIDN'T BOTHER ME. I had lived centuries upon centuries without bus tickets, train tickets, identification documents, and I would live many, many more years without needing any. The bus conductor had felt sorry for me when I pleaded with him and paid him the money for the fare twice over; a kindly man who would die peacefully in his sleep eight years later, with no regrets and no misgivings. And if he had thrown me out of the bus, I would still be safe. I would find another ride even on the darkest highways. It was my strength, that I could draw to me what I needed at that moment, that she sent me what I needed to keep moving when my feet limited me. She. The mother. The one who watched over us all, scattered across the surface.

My ticket had been left behind with Teja. Strange that I had remembered him, of all the bodies I'd taken energy from. I'd given him some of my light, he still had the light in him, after all these years. It had reached out to me, seeking a joining with where it had come from like the rivers rush to the ocean, the droplets of water drawn inexplicably to the promise of home. I'd last met him when the early scratches of beard were still sprouting on his chin. Back then he had been but one amongst the many lovers I had taken. I needed human energy, and the quickest way to get it in doses enough to sustain me for months and years was through copulation. The easiest way for a short burst was a touch, touching someone in the first burst of their youth, a touch in which I unwittingly aroused sexual feelings in them. I didn't mind it. It was amusing, and the pleasure of the body I had grown accustomed to. Humans called it an addiction, I called it survival. Humans had no idea how much power they contained, for they could light up their planet if they were so inclined and run all the machines they had made to keep them living in convenience, if only they figured out how to harness their sexual energy. I felt kindly towards the ones whose energy I had fed on, as they were part of me now and part of me was in them, a bit of my shine. It hadn't dissipated me, this gifting of my shine, because it multiplied as it dissipated, scattered around wherever I had been. He had been an easy pick, a student at the local college. I'd noticed him because he was brimming over with raw uncontained sexual energy like a pot of liquid on the boil, simmering, overflowing, wasting all that I could have harnessed. I'd bumped into him at the gates of his college while passing. A touch from me was never accidental, I knew exactly the repercussions that would ensue should I touch someone I did not find attractive. People stuck to me like leeches once touched, and it was difficult to rid myself of them. I chose who I allowed myself to touch. I wrapped myself in the forcefield of my light so no one could get within touching distance of me without being stung by it.

I'd been watching him for a few days on the ground, his energy hovered over him like a flowing, live electrical field, sparking and fizzing bolts of electricity. I needed it. I needed him. Needing something makes you not heed the dictates of what humans consider appropriate behaviour. When I bumped into him, the brief moment of physical connection was enough to let my cocoon reach out to his energy and draw him into my forcefield. He was easy pickings after that. I smiled at him and he followed me, there was nothing he could do to stay away. It had been that easy. Twenty minutes later he had been thrusting inside me with an unpractised rhythm, the frantic movements of one who had never been inside a woman ever, standing against the wall of a disused godown, hidden from sight. That anyone passing on the street might come within the vacant compound to empty a bladder and catch us fornicating didn't bother me, I was worse than a street bitch in heat when I needed it. When he had spent his precious seed in me, I'd hardened him again with my fingers and thrust him inside over and over again until he was so weakened he could barely stand. Sticky with all of his spent fluid in me, I had walked off, leaving him leaning against the wall, telling him I'd meet him again the next day, the same time, the same place. He was there, waiting.

I couldn't really remember him too clearly, honestly, he had never meant more to me than just one more body, one more source to refuel myself. I should have moved on to the next town but he became a habit, an easy source of what I needed. He had a lot of it, the energy that fuelled me, the energy that fuelled my light. He quickly became obsessed with me though, spiralling deep into the antiquated notions of love and forevers and running off into the sunset – all quixotic ideas that I was quick to disabuse him of. One fine day he came to me at our pre-decided assignment spot, one that I had used earlier for other lovers before him, a dilapidated home owned by the old crone who didn't care what we did in the inner room, as long as I chatted and smoked a bidi with her occasionally. She gave me her key, there was nothing of value in her house, and she was at the marketplace all day. It was the perfect spot to take those I wanted to suck dry of their energy.

She knew me and I knew her, she watched over me, like she watched over so many of us, everywhere we were, all the forms of her. Here in this town, I was the woman with no past and no future, who lived nowhere, with the skin that was so pale it was almost translucent and you could see the veins running beneath it, blue and sometimes a flash of silver moonlight in them. She knew that I cast no shadow because the light shone through me, because I was light and light was me, she did not cast a shadow too, because she was of the dark, she absorbed the light and held it within her, captive. Her stall at the old market, near the steps leading down to the entrance, was what she did all day, selling strange trinkets infused with an energy to humans who needed them. They found her and she gave them what they needed to solve their woes. They didn't understand the how and why of how it worked, but I did. I could see the globules of energy each trinket sat within, hissing angrily, a plethora of colours that clashed and swirled around the matter.

I recognized her for what she was, someone bidding her time here, on the surface. In skin, temporarily. I was permanently in this skin, I had been so for aeons, unchanging, unageing, not decaying.

'How did you know about me?'

'I keep my eyes and ears open. You'll be surprised how freely people talk in front of you when you look like a very old person. You no longer matter, they don't even think of you as a person. You become furniture. You learn a lot of things. You'll know when you decide to let yourself look like an old human. It is very freeing.' She didn't feel old, she felt like she had been here on the planet before the gods had got to it, she had been here when the oceans were still throbbing with the earliest life forms building up the stromatolite reefs on the ocean floor billions of years ago.

'You need what you need in order to survive and walk this earth.' Her eyes, glinting hard in the afternoon light, were older than her face and younger than the fresh leaves glistening in the branches of the trees above us, fringing the path to the bazaar.

She lived in a broken-down house on the far end of the maidan, a short distance away from where I lived in a house where I had, for the moment, refuge. This was how I lived, finding refuge in homes that took me in when the hounds chased me, when I ran. I lived on the kindness of humans, it was getting more difficult over the decades to find such humans. Most humans were walled up behind mistrust, cynicism and suspicion. Some would take me in for lust, lust I refused to slake, their charred bodies were found the next morning, after I'd left and gone far, far away so I would never be tracked down.

'I live alone,' she once told me, her cough racking her sentences into intervals that then became words strung together with phlegmatic interruptions. 'Damn these bidis,' she said, looking at the one in her hand with scorn and then taking a deep puff from it. 'I'm not complaining, mind you. Only the weak complain. What I'm saying is there is my house if you need it, whenever you need it.' She coughed up phlegm and spat it inelegantly at the side of the porch down into the mud. It amused me, I who had been made where so much had been set store by appropriate behaviour, of delicacy, of manner, or grace, of etiquette. She followed nothing. And I followed her lead. It freed me. And so, I used the bed in her house, and brought to it an array of lovers, wiping their minds of me once I was done with extracting all the energy I could from them. Teja had run away before I could do so. He remembered me, he would never forget me now, he'd lived with the ghostly memory of me for far too long, it had imprinted itself into his mind.

I was indiscriminate: men, women, boys, girls. Humans. That was all that I needed to stay alive, to stay in this skin.

'Have your fun,' she exhorted me from lips that barely opened to let words pass, to ensure the bidi stayed in place. Occasionally, she sat guard outside, puffing at her bidi and warning me if she found anyone suspicious approaching. We sat together afterwards, sharing bidis and anecdotes, and I amused her with the recounting of what had just happened in the inner room of her ramshackle house.

'They call you a witch,' I said one evening, after the man had been hustled off once I'd got what I needed from him, and I had straightened myself back into respectability. Sometimes, I didn't even take my clothes off, nor theirs, just put what was needed where it was needed and felt the energy pour through into me, filling me up with life. She would hand me a bidi and sit quietly next to me on her porch staring out at the sun setting over the cemetery across the lane, and puff on hers.

'Then I probably am one.'

'You are not a witch!'

'What difference does it make what they call me. I know what I am. You know what I am. If they knew what

I am, they would be terrified.' She laughed, a laugh that resounded in the three worlds.

She was not a witch. She was immensely more powerful, she was the beginning of time and the ending of it. She was what ran the earth and the skies and the seas, and all that hung in the skies beyond our sight, behind the physical dimensions we could comprehend. She was the unending, she stayed in huts and hovels wherever she was needed, wherever humans had misery and she watched over them. And us. I found her wherever I ran. Or, to be more accurate, she found me.

She was never judgemental of what I did. After all what did the body matter to her, and the absurd rules about pleasuring the body that humans had put into place.

'A sole woman in a man's world needs power to survive,' she told me. 'Take what you want. You need to have the strength to run when they come.'

'I want to stop running. It is exhausting.'

'If you want to, you always can. If you don't want to, you never will. You have to gather courage.'

Then, one other day, she cocked a beady eye at me, after we had shared a cigarette, one from a pack I'd filched from a store while distracting the man who was sitting at the counter. Strong and thick tobacco that hit you in the gut and stained your teeth yellow. Back in the ancient days, tobacco and cigarettes came in packets with gruesome images of cancers. Now the manufacturers had done away with everything that would scare buyers away. And the tobacco was grown in the labs and not in fields. It claimed to not cause metastatic diseases anymore. We were immune to them, humans, we did not know yet, it was too early the generation after the switch to lab grown tobacco. Things had changed on the surface again, after the shift. 'Why are you giving it away for free when you can make enough money from it if you need. You need money to live amongst humans.'

'I don't want to be paid for sex because I want to choose who I fuck. I can't do it with anyone and everyone.'

She cackled. 'It seems like you can.'

It wasn't true though. I was picky. I needed attractive specimens, I needed to feel an attraction for them before I let my light touch them... To think I would bump into Teja now, after all those years in his time, a blink in mine. The boy who was so besotted that he wandered around in a daze through the day trying to find me, little knowing that I was of no fixed address, that I emerged when I chose to and went untraceable when I chose to, even if I had a home that I returned to when the sun fell into the horizon. I changed myself over and over, I was me and yet not me, I had passed him so often in the street and he never realized it was me. I became ordinary enough to melt into the crowd. I pulled my light deep within me, so deep that only darkness filled me. *Girgit*, he called me, he didn't realize how uncannily true the term was for me. How had I allowed myself to slip and let the shine out of me at the bus depot, it was a momentary lapse in concentration, or perhaps the light from him in me had reached out to me and spread out beyond the skin, as we passed, the lights embraced. I couldn't control another's light in me no matter how minuscule it was, only my own in my skins. There were thousands and thousands of borrowed lights within me, dimmed and nascent, waiting to be in the immediate vicinity of their owners in order to shine again.

I was glad he had not boarded the bus with me – he would hold me down, he wouldn't have enough light now to keep me going. There was no pleasure in this anymore, I wondered when I would be able to end this. I'd been around since the beginning of time, sucking out light from these creatures in order to survive in skin. Perhaps I need to give up skin, and return to what I was, a creature only of the light. Or turn to the darkness, the darkness would accept me. After all, I had shunned the light, I had chosen to fall into skin.

Teja and Gulab

'And it would not be a bad life. He knew that, too. Sometimes there is nothing you can do.'

– NEIL GAIMAN, *Neverwhere*

THE HOUSE WAS A MONSTROUS ONE. TO BE FAIR, it was a beautiful one, but an inconvenient one built without any forethought, with rooms piled on as the fancy possessed the owners. As a consequence, the ground floor opened up to a huge room which was supposed to be a living room, but which had multiple doors in every wall leading out to the various rooms that branched out from it. Not a single wall had enough space to rest a sofa or a divan against it, and a happy compromise was single chairs arranged around a sulky square coffee table plum in the centre. The exterior had once been painted a virulent blue but now had flaked into patches.

It had been unoccupied for a while thanks to the fact that the father's body was found in the ravines with a gunshot wound to the centre of his forehead, the daughter had disappeared and the grandmother found dead in her bed a few days after. No one wanted to live in it. It was haunted, they said. When Gulab returned after all these years, bearing a husband in tow and a child in her belly, no one disputed her claim to the house. Gauri they had called her once, but now she told them she was Gulab. That was the name her husband had given her. She would live in the house, she declared, and sought the key from the caretaker at the police station who had been in charge. No one had dared take it over, sell it, or live in it. It was haunted with the ill luck that plagued it, she was welcome to it. It was at a fair distance from people, far from modest neighbourhoods, and very far from governor's majestic residence, or the Mall Road, close to where the river gushed down the gorge at the very periphery of the town. They were curious, of course, about where she had been all these years; was there a connection between her disappearing and her father shooting himself in the head with his own service revolver? Did she not worry about what would become of her grandmother? Why had she come back now after all these years and who was this giant of a man she had come with, and claimed was now her husband, offering absolutely no proof to substantiate her claim? They kept their questions to themselves and welcomed her back with as much warmth as they could muster, veiling their curiosity thinly beneath discretely probing questions that she ignored. She was no longer Gauri, the child they knew, who had left town in the local bus and boarded a train at the main railway junction with just a bundle of clothes tied up haphazardly. This was a woman, a woman with a child in her belly, a woman who knew what she was here for and did not care to explain where she had been for the past few years.

She got an affidavit made with her new name, putting down the cause of change of name as marriage. Gulab Devi Singh. And she got the title of the house put in her name. The man, they told each other, was a smart one, who'd married a golden goose and he was making sure he got the paperwork in place so he could profit by this marriage. Where was the proof of marriage, they asked. He had flexed his biceps and no one dared ask again. No wonder she had run away, they told each other, she had been besotted by this chap who must have visited as a tourist and poor inspector *sahab* must have shot himself from the shame. Anyway, now that she was back, they would treat her with the love they reserved for their own, a wary love because she had left and returned. The man she called her husband would have to earn that love, they would weigh him and see if he came up wanting. Hill towns were strangely insular about those they accepted as their own.

It was hard to believe it was only three years since she had left. Three years were enough for nature to reclaim the house, slithering in with a determination that the primal force gives it, taking over the porch with creeping vines, letting the moss and the damp crawl over the once whitewashed walls. The pipes had burst within with the cold and needed to be replaced, the roof had been damaged by hail, and the rain had fallen into where the bedrooms were. The small garden was overgrown with tall grass and weeds that obscured what had once been a tiled path from the gate to the steps leading up to the porch. The timber pillars that held up the roof of the porch were sagging with the dampness and could give way anytime. Monkeys danced in abandon on the porch and the roof, the roof leaked, the walls were mouldy, the weather was incessantly foggy and damp. Nature crawled around in the form of snakes, scorpions, rats, stray dogs, ghosts, having taken shelter in the deserted house.

The disused house right on the outskirts of the town, where the ridge and the canyon intersected, where the deodars loomed, menacing and sentinel-like over the tiny path was worked on diligently by the man who hammered and sawed and replaced and repaired and painted until it became a place worthy of humans to live in again. They had a plan, they did, this couple; the sign went up a couple of months later, painted in a brazen blue, with a rose clumsily painted on the left corner. Rose Lodge. Into this lodge the occasional tourist or backpacker now stumbled and stayed the night when the lodges in town were full, assured by the locals that enough rooms were available here at a minimal rate, fascinated by the taciturn man who ran it and his petite wife, whose beauty flashed and burned the retina. But if asked to describe her later, one would be hard pressed to describe individual features that made up her face, except for black eyes, tiny nose, oval face, nothing in each by themselves to make anyone notice her. Yet together they came into a face that could have been described as pretty a few years ago, but was now simply glorious. The lodge was delightful and quaint, the food was nourishing, the rooms, two of them, were comfortable if a little basic. The guests slept the sleep of the dead in these rooms, dreaming dreams that took them through slimy warrens under the earth, dark tunnels with sulphurous acridity that burnt their skin and seeped into their lungs, fiery creatures that spat flames and ate humans. Most left within a day or two.

The bushes of wild roses that fringed the little patch of land around it with pretences to being a garden bloomed with an eerie violence, blood red roses guarded the perimeter of the premises, roses that were larger than any roses grown in the entire hill town, even the annual garden show prize-winning ones nurtured by gardening enthusiasts with love, scientifically vetted nourishment, temperature and moisture. The lodge grew a reputation slowly and steadily both for its wonderful views of the mountains unfolding from every window and for the wholesome meals provided. It was run on skeletal staff, the daily work was done by the proprietors and a man Friday, an old man who could be surly when asked to go beyond the call of duty, but did what he could without demur when asked to do so by the wife.

The man was called Tejinder Singh and his wife Gulab. The name suited her, she looked as delicate as a rose and as regal as a rose, the townsfolk soon forgot that she had been the inspector's daughter and she had another name, the name of a goddess, invoked with reverence especially during the nine days of Navratri twice a year, a name that was suffused with the power of feminine energy, a name she had given up for this triteness of being a rose. She smelt like a rose too, they realized, perhaps it was an *attar* she favoured, but when she passed by, the fragrance of roses suffused the air. Apt that she lived in a house surrounded by rose bushes and vines all over the property. In spring, the air around the lodge was redolent with the fragrance of a thousand roses blooming, and the buzz of the bees hovering around to suck the honey from them and the other flowers that made the flower beds on the green patch of land. It was a transformation indeed; they had taken over the old broken-down house and made it not just liveable, but somewhere travellers could stay.

'How could you do it so quickly,' they asked Teja when he went into the town to stock up on supplies. 'Have you enslaved a spirit to do the work for you?'

He laughed and said nothing. They were speaking in jest for he had the brawny arms to take on a superhuman effort of manual labour. And the other that had helped him, he didn't know so he couldn't tell. He didn't even realize that walls he began painting would get completed through the night, fences he began mending would mend themselves when he stopped for a break, the timbers were wrenched out and replaced in an instant before he could even turn around. He didn't notice this, or if he did, he did not question it. Perhaps he didn't even realize when human effort had stopped and what was not human stepped in, the others he could not even comprehend, leave alone explain if asked.

They made a strange couple, he tall and gangly, his shoulders broad and muscular, his gait silent and menacing, a hush descended on the crowd whenever he passed, they sensed it, the demeanour of a predator, stealthy and cunning, the danger his presence brought dissipating urgently into the air around him. She was different, his wife. Softer, gentler, with more grace and less urgency, she carried herself with an authority she did not possess but had conferred upon herself. He was deferential towards her in a manner that made the men in the village scoff at him. It was the respect of equals that the men in the town did not recognize or understand. Not man enough, they said dismissively, he lets his wife boss him around and tell him what to do, they swaggeringly added, deluded in their machismo that had them beat up their wives on a regular basis after a few drinks. The husband and wife visited the marketplace occasionally, early in the mornings mostly when the fresh produce from the neighbouring villages arrived. The folks were kind to her, she was after all one of their own and she was pregnant. She began showing a few months after they arrived in town. Her visits into town tapered off and their man Friday, Lachman Singh, a wheezing old gizzard who had fought in a war and lost a couple of fingers to it, came in each weekend to pick up provisions for the week. A couple of suppliers were fixed to supply them staples at the lodge twice a week.

The senior citizens sitting around the table at the local club, throwing down their cards and sipping from their highball glasses, made their guesses about why a young couple like them would choose to settle in their town and not have much to do with the rest of the citizens. Perhaps the womenfolk of the town should be more hospitable to the young woman who was to bear a child. Then the topic of conversation moved on to something else of immediate concern, the clearing of garbage, which had been long neglected by the local municipal authorities and the subject of much letter writing by the resident pillars of the local society to the local newspapers. Teja, Gulab and Rose Lodge were subject worthy of a single peg, but it wasn't worth wasting an entire evening's worth of drinks on them.

As for Gulab, she grew in stature and stomach from the time she first stepped off the bus at the small hill town bus stand, holding on to her little duffel bag, her eyes hard and bright with the high-altitude sun shining into them, her face that of a girl from the hills, a patina applied to her from her time away from town, the stays in other places had made her a stranger. This was the town she had grown up in, was familiar with, the language, the food, the culture, the people, she fitted in. When she went into town, they gathered her to their bosom, tut-tutting over this poor orphan girl, trying hard to unravel threads of the part of her life that they didn't know.

A strangeness lurked beneath the surface of Rose Lodge, a discordant note in the rhythm of the universe the small town lived in, something that one couldn't quite pinpoint but which definitely existed under the surface of all that went on in the course of everyday living. The lodge, as Teja worked on it, began regaining its earlier beauty, before the strangeness had invaded it. The heavy oak doors gleamed with fresh coats of polish, the rose vines blossomed against the stone walls, the patch of green around the lodge bloomed with care, fertilizer and regular pruning. The green sloping roof with the mysterious eaves was carefully patched up with the help of the local carpenter. Wood panelled rooms with fireplaces and high ceilings offered unfettered views of the mountains crawling in a jagged line at the distance across the drop of the ravine that the lodge was perched on the edge of, and the unheard screams of those who fell into the ravine, a slip of the foot, a gentle push, a loose stone under their foot, the reasons never quite clear for their falls. Those who slipped off the face of the earth, never missed, never searched for by their loved ones, those who disappeared forever into the echoes of the howling wind that corralled through the mountainside, those who became the mist and the fog that gently settled on the treetops and homes.

The mountains stayed impassive, unrelenting as the seasons changed. Gulab, who went to the doctor in town to check her baby growing within her, was told she would need a caesarean section as her pelvic canal was too narrow to risk a regular birth.

It all seemed okay, they would settle down to as close as what could be called a normal life, something she had yearned for ever since she was little, something he had hoped for ever since he'd first gone on the run. This was good, he convinced himself, this was comfortable, he had been on the run for far too long, it would do him good to settle down, live at ease. No one would find them here, in these backwaters of existence. What he had lost forever when that bus drove out of the depot he tucked away at the back of his mind, occasionally digging it out to pore over what could have been and then telling himself he did the right thing. Here at the edge of civilization, they could fall off the grid, forget what they had been running away from and be forgotten.

She waited, biding her time, wandering around the premises, helping the man with all that he was doing to make the place habitable. He didn't even realize how things repaired themselves when he turned his back or he chose not to. Accepting the strangeness of this was more difficult than questioning it. It was how it was once one was dead, one had nothing to keep oneself occupied with. She had infinity before her to wait or she could move to where the dead went, which terrified her. She was too young to have died! Now the woman had a baby in her, like the ghost had when she died. She would help her, the ghost told herself. The baby would be hers too. Humans had but a lifetime, and often they were too impatient to wait. But there was something else in this house, something watching this house, something that claimed all the residents of the house for its own. Something that was biding its time like the ghost was. Something that had staked its claim on Gulab and was waiting for the child to emerge in order to fully claim Gulab for its own.

Gulab

'He wasn't made of flesh and bone, or starlight. He was made of darkness.'

– VICTORIA SCHWAB, *This Savage Song*

IT EMERGED ONE EVENING, JUST BEFORE THE evening meal, when darkness had already descended over the mountains and the air was heavy with the crispness of burning leaves. Autumn had set in and the trees had turned orange and red, some had already begun shedding leaves. Walking down paths crunched fallen leaves underfoot, leaves gathered and burnt at the back of the house, where the small shed was. The fog rolled in earlier, staying longer until it submerged the day and spread over the nights.

The emerging of what it was began with a rapping on the roof, an insistent rapping that was definitely not the itinerant langurs running amok. Teja had just rushed outside to check what it could be when there was a roaring like the earth ripping apart and the roof breaking over their heads. The house was still, preternaturally still, with not a ripple of the shadows of the moving leaves from the trees outside on the windows shifting the light. The roaring was enough to shatter the eardrums of everyone in the vicinity. Lachman Singh had not yet returned from a trip into town to restock on provisions. There were no guests at the lodge at the moment, it wasn't tourist season. It was only Teja and Gulab. He ran back into the house to pull Gulab out, to bring her to safety from whatever it was that was ripping the house open.

The house was still, the noise swirled around the house like a tornado, a pulsating, living wall of sound that enclosed it within a sonic circumference that let nothing in and allowed nothing out. She was, he told her later, standing in the middle of the room having a conversation with someone or something he couldn't see. All the furniture in the room had been pushed to the other wall and the side she faced was emptied of every single thing, even the rugs had crumpled up accordion-like and were on the other extreme of the room. He clutched his ears, feeling his head rip apart with the pain and fell to the floor in a dead faint. What transpired after that he didn't know, and when he came to, Gulab was sprinkling water on his face, kneeling awkwardly on the floor, her belly hampering the ease of her movement, shaking his shoulders, slapping his face, her features contorted with worry.

'What happened to you?' she asked him. He'd looked around, disoriented, and shaken his head. The room was as it had been, there was no sound drowning out every thought in his head. Gulab was worried. Lachman Singh, who had probably returned in the interval between his passing out and coming to, was looking on with his regular expression of inscrutability. Nothing, he had replied, just a dizzy spell perhaps.

'What was it, that noise? Whom were you talking to?'

Her eyes were confused. 'What noise? How could I be talking to anyone, there was no one in the house except you. Are you losing your mind?'

She swatted him on the side of his head with the anger that came from worry. He gathered her to him and stroked her head. It was a tenderness he never showed, it surprised her, she pulled away, conscious that Lachman Singh had muttered something unintelligible and disapproving before walking off into the kitchen. He shook his head trying to clear it of the heaviness that had suddenly settled within – surely he hadn't been imagining what he had seen, what he had heard?

He touched her stomach reverentially, marvelling at what was growing within, life that he had created, a miracle that he had engendered. He would wait, for a movement, a sign, a kick to let him know the baby was fine.

'Is everything fine?' his voice trembled, his eyes were terrified.

She reassured him that she was fine, the baby was fine, she could feel its heart beating strong, kicking ferociously.

Silly fellow, she told him, who would have thought you

would become such a scaredy-cat when it came to your unborn child. What will you do when the baby is born, you won't let it out of your sight even when you go to the toilet. He laughed. And then was silent.

He couldn't explain what he had seen, heard. Perhaps he had imagined it. Perhaps he had gone into a fugue state. It did that to one, living so isolated here, in the middle of nowhere where the earth fell away under your feet and the sky refused to cradle you as you fell.

The next day he left for the city, a last job he had to do, an extermination, then hiding for a while, crossing borders, shaking the police off his track before returning here. It would take him a week or two, he told her, not more, but they would have enough and more money for the baby and all that they might need. The last one, she made him promise. He nodded, not committing to it being the last one with his words. Promises made by one's words were more *pakka*, more difficult to break.

Lachman, with his missing fingers and his limp, would keep her safe. He was fiercely protective of her, strangely enough, because there was no one else and nothing else he had to be protective about. He received a disability pension from the army that held his body and soul together. Working here at the lodge gave him a roof over his head since his sons and their wives had thrown him out as he'd become yet another mouth for them to feed.

The first day of Teja not being home felt like just another ordinary day, like any of the infinite others in which he had gone into town to get supplies and would be back when evening fell, a small bottle of whiskey in the pocket of his pant and melancholy weighing down his mind. When evening fell, the house became ominous and restless, rumbling with the discontent of what lay simmering, the one in the trunk, waiting until the child emerged from Gulab's body, allowing it to claim her for its own as it had been promised. The creature, of the smokeless fire and the wind who stayed confined for most of the time within his trunk, waiting and watching, sure that his time would come, and the woman would be his. It would be patient, it had all of eternity. It knew this was no ordinary child within her body, for her burgeoning belly glowed sometimes, a warmth that spread from it to her fingertips when she touched it. At times Gulab wondered if this was normal, that a woman's belly alight fiercely when it was carrying life within. She had never seen a pregnant woman uncovered so she would never know. But she remembered the whispers, the *daayan* who shone on the far edge of town, the woman Teja had been infatuated with. And sometimes when she looked at her forearms in the dark of the night, when Teja was snoring next to her, she knew that beneath her skin, her veins shone like they were ferrying pale blue light rather than blood. Her glow had intensified.

'What am I? Who am I? Surely I'm normal, the doctor checked me. I could be radioactive,' she thought to herself, she had learnt that in school. Materials that glowed and brought ruin on whatever living thing came into contact with them. Perhaps she was that. But she was not a substance, she was a person, and persons did not shine. Or so she had been told, by her father. Of course, she'd since killed him and no one else had mentioned her shine again to her face in unpleasant terms. She had not been required to kill again.

The shine that had always been within her was now coming forth even more ferociously, shining through her, and it was coming from what she was carrying within her womb. The foetus glowed, her abdomen under her kurta glowed. She covered it with sweaters and shawls, it didn't shine through so many layers. But it terrified her.

'Can living creatures shine?' she asked Reemaji, who lived around the corner down the path and taught biology at the big school in the middle of town, where all the middle school and lower school children went.

'Of course, some living creatures shine, it is called bioluminescence,' she told her. 'Like fireflies. And some sea creatures. Living creatures can shine too.'

Gulab twisted the end of her dupatta nervously in her hands. 'Can people shine too?'

Reemaji laughed; she didn't know why Gulab was asking these questions, but she needed to be reassured, she was pregnant. And she had the glow that all pregnant women did. Reemaji was stern and matter of fact when she taught class but warm and loving with her students when she wasn't teaching. She thought of Gulab as her student still, though she'd long dropped out of school and the rhythms of what a young girl's life should have been. 'Yes, they do, look at you, you are shining too, it's the pregnancy.'

It reassured her, these words. She thanked Reemaji and went back home, waiting for Teja to return. They had no guests now, it was a strange period of slack. Some days they would have both the guest rooms occupied, at others there would be nobody for long stretches of time.

She was consoled by this, perhaps this was what was happening to her too, she was becoming bioluminescent. Like the *daayan*. Like Noor.

And then there was the fact that she was losing time. Not just a second or two here and there when she went blank but entire chunks of time, minutes, hours, time that she fell into a blackness where she had no idea of what she did, and found herself suddenly elsewhere from where she had been when it went black around her, in her. And the day she came out of the blackness, a day when she was alone at home, a blackness she had fallen into when the morning was bright on the eastern horizon, only to emerge when the sun was high in the sky, standing on the roof, where a misstep could have her fall and break her neck, with no idea how she'd reached there.

Teja

'There will be killing till the score is paid.'

– HOMER, The Odyssey

THE CITY DEVOURED HIM LIKE IT ALWAYS DID, swallowing him in one huge gulp, sucking the fresh air from his lungs and filling it with the black acridity of smoke and exhaust and ten packs of cigarettes a day. Teja felt the soot take over his insides, the darkness reclaim his soul. It felt good to be back.

The weapon had been waiting for him at the hotel room, kept under the fake base of the mattress, the bullets carefully measured in a pouch next to it. This time it was a Glock 17, a black, metallic, snub-nosed beauty of a gun. He had used it before, he was familiar with it, he would hand it back to the ones who would get him out of the situation once the shots had been fired.

There was no room for any mistake. Teja wouldn't make one, he never had. His front as a roadside ruffian helped make him seem like someone who would perhaps indulge only in petty theft or be a pair of fists for hire. Only a handful knew that Teja was one of the most coveted sharpshooters in the business, and could pick out a target at fifty feet with the ease of a point-blank aim. Weapons loved him and he loved them, the cold hard heavy feel of an automatic in his palm was almost orgasmic to him. He worked with handguns, not with rifles, which were too cumbersome. He had been trained by the best in the business, he knew how to operate them all, the snub-nosed Glocks, the large calibre revolvers, the long bore rifles, the Uzis, the automatics, the semi-automatics, shotguns, but he preferred weapons he could tuck into the waistband of his trousers, and not have a problem concealing while he moved around, he just needed to ensure the safety catch was on. It was difficult to run with a rifle, it was difficult to get into position with a rifle, and the variability factor was immense.

Teja had never used a *katta*, the cheap country-made revolvers which were more hit and miss and could take your hand off with the backfire. He worked only with proper guns, Smith & Wesson, Colt, Glock 17, Beretta, Sauer. He had used them all. The one who trained him had taught him this: use the best equipment and pick and choose your kills. You can command your price. Teja had heeded his advice. Those who hired him knew he did not panic, he did not fail, and he would use only the best handguns to do the job. Teja never owned a gun himself. It would be too tempting to use it every time he lost his temper. It was simpler to not have the weapon with him once the hit was done, it allowed him to move quicker, without the fear of being stopped at check posts. When you towered over the crowd like he did, you didn't need something that would get you stuck at every search point.

Teja would spend a day or two getting used to the weapon, as every gun was different, one had to caress them differently to get them to obey you. Some with love and tenderness, some with a rough hand. Respond they would, his hand and his eye were accurate and steady. And his heart, well, he collected the souls, didn't he, he collected them once he had killed them, and kept them with him.

This faceless, nameless hotel room, with the uninviting bed and its sagging mattress stained by bodily fluids from being rented out by the hour was where Teja would live while he was here. He'd lived here before, they knew him and they knew that they didn't know him when they would be asked. Teja was a single-shot hire, that's why he got hired over and over again, and that's why he took in the souls he took out of their bodies, his punishment for terminating their lives before their time was up. No one knew of the trade-off that these one-shot executions wrought, that Teja was tied to these souls until the end of his life. They clung to him confused about where they should go, what they should do. Some were angry, others were terrified and yet others were resigned to having been ended before their time. Sometimes they quietened down once they realized Teja was neither frightened of them nor interested in their afterlife, others got belligerent and kept annoying him, clamouring for his attention. He already had fifteen of them in his duffel bag, he kept it zipped most times, except when he was putting in the next soul. The gaggle of souls kept the individual souls within the bag, none of them even contemplated escaping, humans were rather like crabs even when they were dead. It was a bag Teja carried with him everywhere and never let out of his sight. He kept the bag locked in a cupboard when he was not around and Gulab had learnt to not be too curious about it, and stay a safe distance from it. What she thought was within Teja didn't know, and didn't bother to explain either, she wouldn't understand. She had her own tin trunk in the attic that she didn't want him to touch. They kept their secrets to themselves, secrets they each thought the other wouldn't understand. Whenever Teja left town, he took the bag with him. They were his souls to bear after all, how could he abandon them?

This, he told himself, was his last hit. He would retire after this, live a simple life with Gulab, running the lodge with its two available rooms for hire with breakfast included, there in that quaint little town on the outskirts of civilization, where the mountains kissed the sky and houses tumbled down the steep sides of the road, and the roads curved sinuously through deciduous forests, with towering trees on either side of the road blocking out the sun. His last hit. Enough money to see them through the next few years.

He tossed and turned in the bed, cursing the lumpy mattress, the bedbugs and the flashing light of the neon billboard just opposite the road that made the room an unwitting discotheque. This hit was a simple one, a builder had to be exterminated. Teja had agreed to take this on because he had cheated innocent buyers. That was his determining factor when he decided to accept the hit, whether the person had wronged anyone. He followed the builder for five days, figuring out his schedule, when he would be vulnerable, and Teja would be able to make a quick clean shot and a quicker clean getaway. Both were of paramount importance. Teja had just one shot at him, from a distance. It would have to be precise. He would have to be able to get away without being intercepted. He would escape from the scene, pass on the gun to the person who would meet him at a pre-decided location, it would come handy for the next job, the one who assigned him these was generous in payments but pecuniary in the gathering of materials required to execute these tasks. Teja had spent the day tailing the target. His day, after a couple of days of observation, seemed to be uniform. He walked to the temple near his home in the mornings, returned home, had his breakfast, set out for his office, and from there to his various construction sites. His security men always accompanied him everywhere, except for when he entered the temple, where they waited outside. Teja had a chance of getting him here right at the entrance, there was always a crowded back lane to escape from, and an overshirt to be discarded, a cap to be removed, an appearance that could be changed right while fleeing through the crowd of a temple in a marketplace, and the duffel bag of souls in his hand he never worked without.

One more soul in the bag. A week in a safe home across the border, and then back to Gulab. That was the plan. The safe plan. If he did get caught, Teja would be out on bail within a day, he had been assured. He knew where to go. He was clean and methodical about his jobs, they were just those to him, jobs, hit jobs where he did what he was asked to, collected the soul he'd just separated from its body, and went off to lay low for a week or two until the trail went cold.

Today, Teja would complete this hit. He had already done the staking out he needed and conveyed the coordinates he would need a pickup at after the job was done, from the pickup point he would be moved from safe house to safe house, and then out of the city. It was all very methodical, Teja himself wouldn't know where he was being moved to. He'd done these before, many times before. Fifteen hits he'd done himself, dozens of others he'd overseen and planned. All that needed to be done now was the shot. Teja had no alcohol the previous night, nor any coffee or tea on the morning of the hit. He reached the site well in advance, finding his niche just behind a pillar.

He waited, the gun snug in the waistband of his jeans, the safety catch on, counting the minutes until the target would be in sight and within shooting range. When it happened, it happened all at once. The chap arrived, emerging from his car, surrounded by the men in dark suits from the security agency hired to protect him. Teja watched him, standing behind the pillar and the flower stall. They parted at the exact moment to keep his shoes in the shoe rack and he turned to the entrance of the temple, straight in his line of sight. He took aim and fired straight at the back of his neck, a split second and then him sagging like a sack of flour to the ground. Gosh, he'd forgotten the power of the kickback almost knocking his hand back out of the socket. He wouldn't survive that, no one would. It was a shot straight to the brain stem, Teja was good. It was a shot no one would survive, could survive. He'd put his years in biology to good use. Becoming a sharpshooter wasn't only skill, it was also knowledge of the human anatomy, and intense study of both anatomy, wounds and weaponry. The first murder was difficult. After that, it became routine.

He scooped the confused soul hovering around the dead body, with a lasso no one could see with human eyes, and put it into the duffel bag hanging from his shoulder. It was a rope, the old crone had given Teja. She had watched over him. She had turned up whenever Teja needed help. She'd given Teja this task of collecting lost souls. She'd turned up for Gulab when Gulab herself had no idea that she was of the light. She'd put the gun into Gulab's hand, she had pulled the trigger from Gulab's fingers. It had taken too long for her to find Gulab. The years of pain could have been saved had she found her earlier. Teja knew what Gulab was though, he knew the moment he saw her, that she had the light, the beginnings of it, and that was why the old crone had sent him to her. Gulab had no idea what Teja was, the harvester of souls. He would never tell her. Like she wouldn't tell Teja she had killed her father. That within the trunk in the attic she had brought back an entity from the Professorni's house, an entity that was just biding its time until she was once again a single soul in her body, and no longer shared it with the growing foetus. Teja's child.

We all had once come from the light into the womb, but most of us had lost the light. It lingered in others, in some like Noor it shone. She hadn't come through the womb, she retained it in its entirety, though not as bright as it was before she fell. Teja knew that now, after a smidgeon of her light had stayed in him. In others like Gulab it trickled in droplets within her veins, building up strength. Life would determine whether it swelled or diminished. The moon shone from her eyes. She would soon find out. It had already begun shining through her, brighter now, a pale blue phosphorescence that shimmered through her veins right now, it would soon spread, and then shine through from under her skin, a glow that would mark her out. Teja had no light, but he'd been touched by it when he'd touched Noor. Was that why he had recognized the light in Gulab, he wondered. Teja knew what would happen though as the light grew stronger within her. They would come soon enough. They collected those who shone and took them to a place where the light couldn't escape them, where they would harvest the light to feed themselves. And Teja knew she would have no idea how to protect herself from them.

That was why Bilkis Bi had him take care of her. Perhaps that was why she had him collecting souls all these years, perhaps he was preparing for a time when he would have to bargain and what better currency than lost souls to bargain with the hounds from hell.

When Teja reached home, he would keep the bag carefully, behind lock and key and wait, wait for the moment when he needed to release them all.

Noor

'She liked to keep only the bright side of herself turned towards him. She liked to shine.'

– MARGARET ATWOOD, *Oryx and Crake*

THE BUS CONDUCTOR DIDN'T PUT ME OUT OF THE bus. The seat was booked for, I told him, and my ticket had been in the hands of someone who got left behind. I offered to pay him double for the stub of ticket I did not have with me, but had purchased. It was an offer he could not reject, after all, who would find out, who would check? That is how it is with most humans, they would do anything that went against what was considered a moral compass if they thought they could get away with it. When I turned on my light and smiled at any human, man or woman, they could refuse me nothing. When the fragrance from my body entered their nostrils, they forgot all their anger and hurt, and resistance towards me, this unknown woman with no name, no home, no destination. I could flood them with light and fragrance and erase all their pain if I chose to. It was dangerous, what humans could not understand they did not trust, and what they did not trust they killed. I had escaped being killed a thousand times, but that was only because humans could not kill me. I could only be ended by those that chased me, and that too wasn't death, but an exile from this dimension into the other, the dark, sulphurous realm where hellfires burned and souls lived out eternities in torment. Death would be better. I envied humans their deaths.

I don't know what made me choose this town, or perhaps this town chose me. It was right at the end of where the roads took the bus, beyond this, there were no buses, only jeeps and private taxis, road enough for one vehicle to pass at a time. The roads led further on to where the mountains plateaued, touching the roof of the sky, and deep mountain passes gouged into the surface of the earth. They had seen men of yore painstakingly make their way through to reach the other side of the uncrossable heights, taking humans across to where man had created boundaries and lines of control, which needed passports, visas. Special permits were needed just to tread across the patches of land created all at the same time, formed from the same ever-expanding infinity into nothingness, spilling out from the nothingness into the dark with its light and energy and matter and antimatter.

We had spent hours winding through flat highways with only the darkness of the night draped over the horizon, sparkling with distant lights speckled through the black night, marking where humans lived in homes and demons did not prowl, searching for discarded souls released through accident, murder, suicide or painful illness. The ones who went peacefully were completely of no interest to them, the hellhounds. They sniffed out suffering and torment, and were drawn to it, to make it their own and to add to it.

The bus had stopped at regular intervals, to let some passengers off and let some on; the new ones clambered on, wrapped in mufflers and sweaters, clutching bags with zips held together by safety pins and cloth bags stitched from old bedsheets. It was not refined company. I hadn't expected better. I sat right up front, no one sat next to me. I felt a stray hand snake up to my breast on the side nearing the window as I dozed, and squeeze it. It was energy I didn't want, evil and malicious. I sent a shaft of what humans called current to the unwanted touch and heard rather than felt the crackle of burning flesh. The man screamed and yelled for the bus to stop, climbing down hastily in the middle of nowhere, spewing a string of curses at me, which deflected right off and landed back on him, intensifying his agony. That was the thing about unwarranted curses, they never touched the ones you directed it towards, but came back to you with redoubled vigour. The smoke continued to emerge from his charred hand as he stood there on the highway, screaming into the emptiness of the deserted night road.

The seat behind stayed empty for the rest of the journey. The other passengers didn't ask what had happened, nor did the bus conductor or driver. They were content to let the journey pass with no mention of the incident that happened barely an hour after we'd left the bus depot. When the flatlands ended and the climb to the mountains began, some on the bus called out for the bus to stop, their heads spinning and their stomachs heaving. The bus stopped to let them stand by the side of the road and throw up while yet others stuck their heads out of the windows to breathe in the crispness of the mountain air. I did so too.

The ramshackle bus depot was deserted when we got off, it was the strangest hour to reach a destination, not yet morning, not past night. Perhaps the term bus depot was too grand a word for what this was, a shed that was almost broken down with a tea shop attached to the only entrance and exit. And that too was shut at the moment, almost an adjunct to the ticket counter which was also closed. No one checked tickets at the end of the journey, here at the destination, it didn't matter if one had a ticket or not, one had reached where one was supposed to, and where one was not. The bus depot was off the main road, a turn away from what seemed to be the main area of the sleeping town which rose precariously from this road, houses stacked one on top of the other up the face of the mountainside. The circle of shops branched off into more shops down a road and up a road, into bazaars and temples and coaching classes, all closed right now. They promised to provide the residents of the town everything from clothes to luggage to groceries to home appliances, astrological consultations and de-addiction from alcohol.

This was a little bigger than a village, a little smaller than a one-horse town. The main road was a five-minute walk from end to end, and there was nowhere I had to go. Perhaps he would come for me, I told myself. He would take the next bus here after this one and follow me. He knew where the bus was headed to, he had my ticket in his hand and the one he had bought. I would wait. It was always good to have a companion in a strange place, even if in normal circumstances I preferred not to have anyone with me. I wondered why I was waiting for Teja. What was it about this boy? He was no longer a boy though, he was a man now. I also recognized my light in him, light that had moved from me into him, that I had forgotten to take back into me.

The tea shop right next to the bus stand wasn't yet open for business, but had a couple of welcoming benches placed right outside it, and a burlap draped over them for protection from the damp. I huddled myself under the burlap, which was also damp, and waited for the next bus to come in from where I'd just come. It would take hours, I knew. The buses between the two places were not frequent, not many people came here. Sleep would not come to me. What followed me there had not followed me here, that I knew. They had been distracted by the two souls drifting around aimlessly and got busy collecting them and taking them to where the souls were sorted into their various destinations. The thing with the hounds was they were easily distractible when one put souls in their path. I had put enough distance between them and me, perhaps I was safe here, for a while. For just a little while. Freedom was this interval between escaping what pursued me and waiting for them to begin pursuing me again.

The tendrils of mist curled around me as I waited. The next bus rolled in, I stared at all the disembarking passengers, trying to pick one out of the crowd, one with shoulders that could bear the earth, and the eyes of an eagle, one who stood tall in a crowd and surveyed it like he was the master of them all. It wasn't the bus from the town I'd come in. That bus didn't come in. It had been hours. The morning began whispering across the distant eastern horizon, a faint pink, the fog leavened and rolled past, the sky it left behind a light golden stain. The dog who had been curled at the foot of the bench stirred, got up to its feet and stretched languidly like one who has the luxury of all the time in the world. People who inhabited this world began drifting in, one by one, at first the tea stall owner himself, then the taxi drivers, wrapped up in mufflers and sweaters, ambling up to their individual vehicles, unlocking them, bringing out buckets, filling them with water from the tap by the side of the ticket office and washing their cars. There was a lot you could deduce from how a person washed his car. Some washed their cars gently and with care, the others did a quick job, focused on just getting a semblance of the vehicle being clean.

They didn't seem too surprised to see a lone woman sitting on the bench so early in the morning, although it couldn't have been a regular occurrence in these parts. The owner of the tea stall, a bulky squat man who had the demeanour of a retired wrestler was in a patched-up sweater and a woollen cap that covered most of his face. He switched on the radio and quickly lit a lamp and incense sticks at the little altar behind his counter. Morning *bhajans* floated out of the radio, an ethereal female voice took us to the divine or what human beings thought was the divine, then a prosaic male voice in a news bulletin brought us back to the mundane. All was well with the world. Nothing was well with my world, but then my world was not of this world and it was only fitting that I had timely reminders of the difference between the two and why I had chosen to straddle both, albeit clumsily.

The men respectfully stood at a distance from me, occupying the only other bench and leaning against the wall of the tea stall, fronds of smoke from the glasses of tea in their hands rising up to wreath their faces in smoke as they sipped. They sneaked curious glances at me, but did not speak to me. The owner came out and handed me a glass of tea, I took it with gratitude. The skin needed nourishment, at times even the light wasn't enough to keep me going.

'How long have you been here?' he asked.

His face was kindly and concerned. He couldn't have been much older than forty but deep creases already cut through the skin of his ruddy cheeks and cobwebs latticed the corners of his eyes. A few grey strands showed at his temples, under the grubby woollen cap he'd pulled on.

The single hand-knitted sweater he'd got on over a shirt had been inexpertly darned with different coloured wool in patches where it had given way. He could do with a bath, I thought, as the stench of accumulated sweat hit my nose. Most of them. It wasn't winter yet, perhaps they were accustomed to the idea of the once a week bath beginning at the end of summer itself.

'A few hours,' I replied, taking the glass of tea from his hands with gratitude, feeling its warmth course through my fingers, my light having withdrawn deep within where it couldn't be noticed, or cause trouble for me. That it was not yet winter had allowed me to sit on a bench outside a tea stall without shelter or warmth for all this while without freezing over. Hill towns were like that, a woman could wait at a desolate bus stand for hours without being in any danger of being attacked by marauding packs of men.

'What are you waiting for? Where do you need to go?' he asked. The men paused their conversations to listen in, turning their heads and their bodies, their interest was helpful, not lecherous, and for that I was grateful. I did not have the energy on this chilly morning to fight off unwanted attention. But then I was not sending out my light – I was mousy, ordinary and unremarkable, just a tired, scrawny young woman in patched and faded clothes, holding on to a small bag with all her might. They felt pity for me. I was brave, summoning the courage to leave was brave. They also did not want me to come near their womenfolk on the off chance that I transferred some of this courage to them.

Right now, they were content with pity. When my light didn't shine, I evoked this overwhelming sense of pity in whoever beheld me. This was my camouflage. *Girgit*. Chameleon. It kept me safe.

'I don't have anywhere to go,' I replied. 'I had to run away from home to save my life. I just got into the first bus at the bus depot. My husband...' Each filled up what I had left unsaid with their own imagination. I did not seek to correct their assumptions. There was no explanation I wanted to give that was false, and there was no explanation that would come close to the truth. They would not understand the truth anyway.

He looked around at the gathered assembly for some solution to this issue of a young woman with no place to go to and no money either. The collective brows were furrowed in what could only be deep contemplation. They looked at each other, hoping the other would have some solution to the crisis.

'Perhaps she could go to the boarding school, they would take her in if she worked there for a bit.'

That seemed to be the only sensible solution, as none of the weather-beaten faces there would dare take the onus of taking an unknown lone woman to their home. For one, it would never pass societal muster, for another, it would mean anarchy in the home. One of the men offered to drive me to the school, he knew the staff there, his daughter taught in the senior school and would put in a word. He made a quick call home and spoke hurriedly to his daughter,

I did not listen in. I gathered my bag and got into his taxi with a polite temple to three gods right on the dashboard, fragrant with freshly lit incense stick and a small garland of flowers placed reverently around them. A red and gold strip of silk was tied around the neck of the rear-view mirror, to give a clearer view one supposed and to protect the vehicle from the error of a misjudgement, which on these curving, narrow roads, could be fatal. There were no second chances here, what crashed, fell. What fell, died.

The bus stand receded behind us in the rearview mirror, a bus roared in and turned in, it would drop off its passengers like little afterthoughts from the journey when it shuddered to a stop. They would pick up their bags and suitcases, and emerge, moving jerkily like marionettes, their bones and muscles stiff with the journey and elated with the arrival at their destination. The boarding school he deposited me at was an imposing and sprawling stone and mortar structure, with walls and walls that went on forever on a long winding road, which ended in imposing gates. After a brief conversation with a grouchy warden who looked me up and down, and then took pity on me, taking me in, I heard the clang of the tall gates shutting behind me, shutting the world out, the hellhounds would bound over it in a moment, but the gates needed to be opened to them, they could not enter unless the doors were opened. This was the law that governed them. This school was off the main road, a fair distance away, high up where only a determined climb for an hour on sturdy legs or a vehicle could take you.

The hounds would find me here, I knew. But till they were sated, I was safe. I had to find a place where I would be welcomed with love. The love would keep me safer.

'She can stay here and help in the kitchen and the housekeeping for a month. We'll see how good she is before we decide whether we will keep her on,' the lady told him, a trifle too sternly for my liking, looking me up and down before smiling at me, a smile that was as graciously warm as the sun. She was a formidable woman, built like a tank. Her unruly hair was tied back into a no-nonsense bun, her body enveloped in layers of a salwar kameez with dupatta and a sweater that gave her the appearance of a tree trunk shorn of its branches. The taxi driver nodded and indicated to me that I should follow her now. I thanked him for his kindness and he patted me on the shoulder paternally. No one felt any lust for me when I shrank my light.

'If you don't like it here, you know where to find us. Come to the bus stand, we'll find you another place to stay.' It brought unexpected tears to my eyes and a sudden sinking sensation in my stomach. I wasn't afraid of being alone, I'd been alone in this world for centuries, moving from place to place, trying to shake off that which had been chasing me wherever I went, my punishment, facing the eternal consequences for my arrogance in believing that no harm could come to me. Now all I did was run every few years, few months, whenever I sensed they had sniffed me down and would come for me, no matter how many kilometres and boundaries I moved, across cities, countries.

The stone walls of the convent were not yet warmed by the morning sun, a crisp autumnal wind cut across the quadrangle as I followed her to wherever it was she was leading me. The chatter of children in the adjoining wing which housed the school livened up the bereft morning, the bell had still to ring, class still had to begin. I was here early. She led me through a maze of corridors ending up two levels below the main level. Here tiny cubicles branched off the main corridor, this was where the staff lived, I realized. She opened one door of the many and directed me to step in. The room was cold, I shivered involuntarily as I stepped in. There was no window, not one that I could open, except a half window at a height I could not reach that would let in the morning sunlight. In the afternoon, the sun would have changed direction and the room would be cold until the next morning.

'This is your room, keep your bag, go to the bathroom at the end of the corridor to freshen up and meet me in the kitchen as soon as you finish. I'm in charge of all the kitchen and cleaning duties, I will introduce you to the rest of the staff and give you your duties for today.'

I nodded.

'What did you say your name was?'

I didn't. I hadn't told her my name. Nor the men at the tea stall. No one had asked me my name.

'Noor,' I replied. 'Noor.'

I didn't call myself anything additional, not my honorific,

nor the dignity provided by my family name nor my husband's family name. I had none.

'I'll need your identification,' she said.

'I don't have anything.'

She sighed, looking up at the ceiling. 'How am I to keep you here then, child?' I wondered how old she thought I was, then decided not to correct her misconceptions about my age. It was possible that she had taken me in just because she thought I was a young girl down and out on my luck, or running away from something unmentionable in polite society.

I kept silent.

'Okay, so listen. You are my niece if anyone asks you. My cousin's daughter from the village. You haven't made your identification papers yet and I will vouch for you.' I nodded. She gave me a raking look from head to heel. 'Don't let me down. I'm taking a risk on you. I don't know why I feel sympathetic towards you when I don't even know your story. We have a few rules here. Jobs have to be completed without excuses. No men in your room. You are young and beautiful, you will get attention, don't get sucked into it. It is not worth it. None of them are, men are a waste of time, before they marry you and even after they marry you.'

She was softer than she looked. That's what humans were, completely unlike what one assumed they would be like on the outside.

I could feel the light ripple within me, I held it tight, I couldn't let it spill, not here, not now. I couldn't raise any suspicions, I had to camouflage myself to be as human as I could be. This was a stopgap arrangement, a roof over my head until I found Teja. He would be here, somewhere close by, I was sure of that, I could feel it in my bones. I could sense it now that our lights had touched again, my light reaching out to the light I had put into him. A man who did not care where I came from or who I was or what I had now become was the one who'd keep the hellhounds at bay. As for the girl I had seen standing next to him at the bus depot as I passed, she would not have any objection to me living there with them. I would make her fall in love with me too, I had seen the light in her too. She shone and she didn't know it.

Gulab

> *'The place where you made your stand never mattered. Only that you were there... and still on your feet.'*
>
> – STEPHEN KING, *The Stand*

AND JUST LIKE THAT, ONE DARK EARLY WINTER afternoon, when the fog had begun rolling in from the distant mountains, bringing with it the damp, unsettling sensation of being underwater, there was a frantic knock on the front door. A woman's voice called out to Teja, begging him to open the door, to let her in. I recognized the voice, it came from the woman who had come to meet me a couple of days ago, asking for a room to live here, a request I had thought absurd but had strangely found myself acquiescing to despite all my initial misgivings. I could be a sucker like that. Teja had returned after two weeks away just this very morning, the beard thick on his face, his eyes heavy with the lack of sleep from being on the move for the past fourteen days. Part of the job, I told myself. If he wanted a settled life he should have become a bank clerk.

'I went to ten different places before I could come back to you,' he told me. I smiled. If he expected gratitude he wouldn't get it. He hadn't left me as I constantly worried he would. And anyway now, the woman he would have left me for had come here, following us. Or had we followed her here? I would never know. It would be interesting to see how he reacted when he saw her. I hoped I wouldn't need to kill him too.

Outside the windows, the fog began glowing a strange flickering orange and red, the condensation trickling down it, like someone was breathing heavily on the windowpanes, on the house, on the path, on the entire town.

A low growling rumbled the floorboards, making them quiver, a growling that seemed to come from deep within the bowels of the earth and higher than the clouds, a feral snarling. I felt my heart freeze with an unnamed dread of what unholy thing had reached our doorstep, a dread I could not comprehend, given I had lived with strange things in this house for the past many months. There was the creature that had tethered itself to me from the Professorni's basement, now in its bottle, up in the tin trunk in the attic, vaguely discontented and angry, emerging occasionally to reassure me that once I gave birth, I would be permanently bound to it, to him. Then there was that other thing that had once been here, crawling up the face of the cliff that it had fallen from, the gunshot wound in the middle of its forehead now with the scalp falling off, the rotten flesh and bones showing through where flesh had fallen off or eaten by creatures of the wild, hiding in the basement, crawling back down the face of the cliff, crawling up again when it felt like, revealing itself to me when I was alone, and helpless, and begging my forgiveness for what it had done to me when still alive, asking to be set free, to be released into the afterlife. The ghoul, once the man who called himself my father, had no power over me anymore now.

Also, with us in the house, what lived with us when she wasn't living on the banyan tree in the lane outside, uncoiled herself from around the chimney where she normally perched and came into the parlour, a cold moist presence that only I could feel, or see when she chose to be seen. She was frightened, I could sense the fear emanating from her in waves, this *bhootni* who was protective of me, of the child in me. I was terrified. If she was frightened, I didn't want to think about what it could be that was outside the door, it wasn't something I had ever encountered in all my years of sensing things that other people could not.

Teja was upstairs when the first knock sounded on the door. When the voice called his name, he rushed down towards the door. I put a hand out, stopping him, the dread of what was outside sliced ice through my spine, chilling the blood in my veins.

'Don't open the door.'

He looked at me with anger, and pushed my hand aside. 'How can I not? It's Noor.'

As he threw the door open, a sulphurous fetid stench rolled in and almost made me gag. It overpowered even the fragrance of roses. Noor stood there at the doorway, leaning heavily against the door jamb, looking at him for a long still moment. Around her the light rippled, broken and in pain, a cocoon of moving pulsating energy, now dimming, ripped and slashed by claws we could not see. The sky outside was dark with the fog, a strange reddish-orange light lit it up, an eerie otherworldly son et lumière that pulsed with a life of its own, framing her in a way that seemed to swallow her up, her light and her body. There was blood flowing from the gashes in her arms, her clothes ripped by the force of whatever it was she was fleeing from. She was no longer the siren I feared, but a tired, traumatized woman I felt pity towards. I surprised myself. Pity was not an emotion that came easy to me these days.

'Please let me come in…'

I could not turn her away in such a state, so I nodded. She stumbled as Teja took her towards a chair. She sat heavily, her breath coming in low rattling rasps, like death was invading her chest. The glowing neon orange-red light that had lit up the fog disappeared, leaving an overwhelming greyness behind. There was a huge ripping sound like the sky was being torn apart and then a silence, a silence so deep it hummed across the entire sky like strings of a guitar being plucked over and over again by an uncertain fingernail. The putrid stench that had come in when Teja had opened the door to her, cleared up instantly. Whatever it was, it had gone away. The fog rolled over, the clouds parted, the evening outside was soft, pale and fading into night, the stars still keeping their light to themselves across the vastness of space and time.

'Thank you,' she muttered, clutching my hand and Teja's with both of hers. 'Thank you.' Her hands were soft, hands that had never done any manual labour, the hands of a queen. Or an angel.

Teja was bent over her, checking her wounds, murmuring to himself. I ran in to get water to clean her wounds, cloth to bandage them, feeling the terrified kicks of the baby against my diaphragm as it struggled with the accelerated adrenalin rushing through my bloodstream. Noor had slumped now into a dead faint. Teja lifted her and took her to the divan in the parlour. I sprinkled water on her face, but she was unresponsive. Beautiful and unresponsive. Damn her. She had no business being so beautiful when I was bloated and grotesque with child. I couldn't hate her though. There was something that tied me to her, the light.

'Is she dead?' he asked me, his expression terrified beyond measure. Her light had withdrawn deep into her. Unthinkingly, I reached out to her with my light, pouring what little strength I could from me into her. Teja looked up at me, shocked. He had never seen my light when it emerged beyond my skin, I had never allowed him to. It was something I'd learnt only recently, that I could control the light, that it was growing within me, with the child, and that it had power I could not explain. He stood still for a long moment, then put out a trembling hand, touching the light from me as it reached out to Noor and embraced her, warming her up, feeling for her light, drawing it out from the deepest recesses within her consciousness it had withdrawn into.

'You…' He didn't complete his sentence, he didn't need to. I knew what he wanted to ask, and I smiled. He seriously hadn't realized that he probably needed to be protected by me, rather than the other way around. I'd allowed him his silly misconceptions.

'Me.' Yes, me. And her. I touched my burgeoning belly, feeling the light from within it, nascent, trembling, reaching out to touch my fingers. And us. The baby shone brighter than I ever could, even through layers of skin and muscle and the uterine wall.

Things, as he knew it, would never be the same again.

Noor

'He was glad she had come; she was for him, as he for her, "another place".'

–IRIS MURDOCH, *The Message to the Planet*

I KNEW WITH A CERTAINTY I COULD NOT EXPLAIN that he was in this very town, a certainty that grew a couple of days after I'd settled into my small, coffin-like room in the school. I saw him only a few months after I had arrived, driving through the main market road in a battered pickup vehicle. The town had just one main road that took ten minutes to walk through, lined with stores on either side and two restaurants bookending it, one Chinese and one for Indian food. There was also a momo stall and a tea stall. That was all the town offered to sate the appetite. A bakery that provided breads and cakes was amongst the more popular shops for the children on their weekly trip to town, it had expanded its repertoire over the years to include burgers and fried chicken.

My duties included going into town with the school

van and collecting the weekly provisions. When the matron realized that I was literate and could manage lists, duties and calculations of money, she put me on this weekly duty. I had a list, a list dictated telephonically to the storekeeper who would have everything packed and ready when I reached and all I needed to do was to corroborate my list with what was packed and take responsibility that it reached the kitchen pantry on time. We were not allowed to run out of provisions no matter what. The school van was driven by Kuki Daju, an elderly local.

Our paths didn't cross, the first time I saw Teja. He didn't see me, he couldn't have, which in retrospect was a good thing to happen, it allowed me to collect my thoughts and to figure out what I needed to do if I bumped into him unexpectedly. Even if I had presciently shrunk my light, as I did on a regular basis these days, the light in me and the light in him would reach out to each other. The light had its own reasons, reasons I did not know and could not control when it came in the proximity of another with light. My light surged and reached to the door of the store, exhorting me to move out. Startled, I pulled it back into me before anyone else in the store noticed it. Luckily, the store owner had his back towards me and no one else was in the store.

A horn sounded impatiently on the road outside. I kept a tight hold on my light, and turned around curiously to look at what could have caused it to leap out of my body unbidden, and what could have caused this honking on a road that would barely have two or three vehicles at any given point in time. A ramshackle jeep was outside the shop, blocked by an errant cow with no interest in crossing the small road. Teja was at the wheel, his hair cropped tight to his scalp now, but still unmissable. He was wearing a plain checked cotton shirt, first three buttons open, over a vest at a time where the rest of the population was already tucked into their first layer of thermal wear under their sweaters. By the time I'd rushed out to check if it was really him or if my eyes been playing tricks on me, he had roared past leaving behind only a cloud of exhaust, dust and my certainty that it was indeed him.

'He followed me,' I thought to myself, the relief flooding me like a sigh that found no escape from my lips. 'He did indeed follow me here.' I was being silly, there was no reason for him to follow me here. It probably was just fate and happenstance that made me book a ticket here, climb into this bus with this destination, and have him land here too. Happenstance was this strange thing that moved in predatory patterns of its own choosing, humans had nothing to do with it. It was the fates that decided what was to be, who would come into your life, who would exit it, what would happen on a particular day, what wouldn't happen. It was strange that mankind had not created a god of happenstance and worshipped it, it was the only god that made sense in this world where most gods were capricious and happenstance ruled.

In the past few months, I was no longer a stranger here, in this strange town where the people were kind, the language was like pebbles being cast into a pot, where the mountains fringing the horizon were forbidding and remote and what had chased me, slavering in anticipation of taking me with it, had disappeared back into the depths of the earth. For now. It would return some day that I knew with a certainty I could not erase. Nothing would deter it, not even the fact that there was a small chapel on the premises of the school. The holy was holy to only those who believed in it, who invested in its holiness with the power of their own belief. The unholy did not fear the holy, they did not believe in its power, they only bowed to what held more power than they did. And sometimes, the unholy were the most powerful around, at a particular moment.

The store owner looked at me curiously when I re-entered the store to pick up my parcels which were ready, packed in brown paper, tied in string. There was no harm in asking him if he knew the man who had just driven past, honking loudly.

'He's moved recently to town with his wife, she's a girl who grew up here, a local girl. The father and grandmother died a few years ago, the mother had died when the child was young. She left town when her father died and no one knew where she was all these years. Now they're living in her house, the house of her father. This is the abandoned house right on the top of the ridge. Curiously enough, no one ever wanted to take that house, or live in or even buy it, even though it was empty for so many years. Not even vagrants stayed inside. She's pregnant now. She's very young, I wonder where she met him and married him, and why. He makes me uncomfortable, he's polite enough but there's something unsettling about him I can't quite put my finger on.' It was quite a long speech for the store owner to make. Bishtji as we all called him, was a man of few words.

'He scares me to be honest. His eyes are dead, it is like looking into blankness when one looks into his eyes. There is no expression, if you understand what I'm saying.' He shuddered involuntarily and continued.

'It's like looking into the eyes of a corpse.'

This was not the Teja I had known, alive, vibrant, bursting with light and pure energy. What had I done to him when I had taken the light from him all those years ago, had I drained him of all that he had contained, had I only left darkness behind? No, there was within him some light from me, that I knew, it reached out to mine every time we came in close proximity. Had I removed all his light and replaced it with a tiny bit of mine, making him only a receptacle of darkness when he was not in my immediate vicinity?

It was of no consequence to me, I told myself. He was dispensable. All humans were dispensable, them with their grandiose notions of being important and valued, they were less than ants in the grand scheme of things. But they were of use to me, and that made them important to me. He had a fraction of my light in him, light I hadn't taken back, a thin skein that bound him to me, no matter where he was. It would reach out to the light in me if I let it. I would be safe in their home, I knew, he would protect me. I needed to move there, but first I had to get her permission and approval to do so, the woman who was carrying his child in her stomach.

It had been six months now at the convent, six months of sleeping without being coiled to spring up in an instant and flee, six months of luxuriating in the calm that pervaded before the storm. Six months of peace and shelter I was grateful for. I had cut and scrubbed and cooked and cleaned and done the grocery runs and slept in a tiny room as cold as a box, emerging to light only when I stepped out of it. I had learnt in these six months that the Christian god was benevolent and all-forgiving even if he had been nailed to a cross by human arrogance, and even a sinner like me could hope and pray for redemption should I begin believing in him. But belief was a strange thing, and I knew that the world was not what humans saw with their eyes and heard with their ears, and between the visible and the invisible was all that they still couldn't comprehend, couldn't dare comprehend. And perhaps, all that the gods gave humans was the temporary solace and hope that this was not all just some cosmic dice.

This was just a hiatus until I regained my bearings and could set off to find my space in this world. I would need to recharge myself soon, it had been a while. I would prowl the touristy parts of the town when I needed to and find someone who I could use. Someone young, vibrant, bursting with the power and glory that the transition after adolescence and before adulthood brings. Then, I would go to Teja to be safe, when I had filled myself with enough light to survive for a couple of years.

It was hope, barefaced, shameless hope that filled me. Hope that I would be safe, hope that someday I would no longer have to flee from that which kept chasing me, which had been chasing me over and over again through centuries. Perhaps it did not really want to drag me down to the depths of what humans called hell, perhaps to it, the chasing and giving up was part of a set routine, something to assuage its masters that it had tried. It didn't try hard enough, I realized that. Perhaps it was tired of the game too, chasing and not catching, allowing me to escape, allowing itself to get fobbed off by distractions. Perhaps it was more human than it would like to think, it with its ten heads and snarling fangs dripping acid, eyes that blazed red and sulphurous, breath that charred whatever it landed upon to crisp. Perhaps it didn't really want me, perhaps it was being kind to me, perhaps it would tire of this cat and mouse game eventually. I could hope. But what was hope but the shiny tinsel draped carefully around relentless despair, its party hat askew, blowing into its whistle, hoping to distract you from what was to come.

When it came for me, it would come without warning, screeching its vileness at the windows, making human ears bleed with the intensity of the sound it made, something that no human ears were created to endure, rasping my name, the one humans could never pronounce because they did not have the language nor the vocal abilities to do so, calling out to me as they emerged, tearing through the layers that separated us from the worlds we could not see, rending the skies red and orange with pain. It would sniff around, slavering acid on to the houses below, on to the roads, the people. No human would be able to see it unless it chose to be seen, to be smelt, to be felt. All they would feel would be an inexplicable chill up their spine and look over their shoulder. Those who followed the Christian god would cross themselves and say themselves a *Hail Mary* or an *Our Father*, those who followed Hindu gods would recite the Hanuman Chalisa, and hurry to wherever it was they were headed to. Those who were safe within their homes would call their children in, draw their curtains, close the door and huddle in a corner, unable to explain the strange change in the air that made them uneasy. It would advance, it that no human could see, but only sense, singeing its funereal dirges on the wind with a voice so silvery that the air would cleave in front of it, riding the hounds it rode, the hounds with the heads that looked in every direction, sniffing me out, chasing me. When it found me, its arms would reach out to me, arms that were smoke and fire, talons and claws, arms that had slithered through the dimensions, rising from the hells, demanding what had been promised to it hundreds of years ago. A fallen angel. Me.

It would stand helpless at a doorway of wherever it was that I had taken shelter in, the horrific thing from the seven darknesses. The one who rode the hounds, now clad in the garb of a lost young child sobbing piteously for his parents, a feeble old woman shivering from the cold, a young girl bruised and bleeding, a dog, a cat, someone in need of help, or even me, staring at myself when the door was opened to it. It would stand there helpless and trembling until it was invited in, and then devour everything and everyone within. It could not cross the portal of a home I had been invited in with love. The only thing that protects another in this dimension is love, unfortunately humans don't realize the strength of love. It is in fact, the only power they have against the darkness.

Only I would be able to see it in all its horrifying monstrousness, the flames and the fire surrounding it when it came. I would run out of whatever exit I could find, a backdoor, jumping off a balcony, chanting the words that had been taught to me by the one who had tempted me to fall, the one who kept me safe and provided for, who watched over me from wherever she was. She was everywhere and nowhere. It was a chain of words I had memorized from repeated chanting, in a language that mortals had never heard, words that had been in existence back from the beginning of time and existence, when the old gods had risen from the air, the earth, the sun and the seas, and claimed dominion over each of them. Anyone hearing me would think I was muttering unintelligible and nonsensical syllables strung together in an inchoate order as I ran, it couldn't touch me as long as I chanted, and the words I chanted wrapped themselves around me in a cocoon of light and protection so strong that nothing could pierce it, not even the darkness of the netherworlds. It would exhaust me in my running from it, until I would ward it off as long as I had the strength in me to chant without pausing. Or I needed to reach a home that had not yet opened the doors to it, a home that welcomed me within without reserve.

When the time came to run again, I would run to him I told myself. I would not be safe at the school, no one there had let me in with any love. I would run to him, Teja and his wife, that girl-woman now rotund with the child in her belly, her face wiser than her years, her eyes black appraising stones in their sockets that were hardened with what life had thrown at her, things that I could sense, pain and shame so horrific that she had folded it all up into a tight little packet of emotions and tucked it deep inside herself, locked behind a door she did not open. It contained her name too, a name she could not remember, even though everyone in the small town knew her by that name. To her, it was the name of the other girl, the girl who had been raped every night by her father until she killed him, shot him dead with his own service revolver and kicked him off the narrow path into the ravine below. I knew that. I had looked into her and opened the secrets she'd hidden within, reading them out of her thoughts. I had watched them over and over, in their freshly painted bright blue house with the tin roof painted white, the slight patch of a garden where she had planted enough vegetables to ensure that she wouldn't need to go to the market every other day, the cobbled pathway leading up to the porch from the hand-hewn gate. I saw the *bhootni* who swung indolently most days and nights from the branches of the banyan tree on the small path leading up to the house, the one who lived in the trunk in the attic, the one who crawled up from the valley in the dead of the night, his broken body rotting and miasmal, begging for forgiveness from a daughter who would not forgive and was not afraid of what he had become, a ghoul with no redemption in either purgatory or any of the seven hells. I knew them all.

Teja would, I knew, always open the doors of his house to me, take me in and shelter me. I would lie low and wait until it was time, I never knew when that would be. Sometimes it took years for it to come back for me. At others a few months. I couldn't understand why it did so.

It was fraught, living on the edge, waiting for the whispers to begin in my head, it calling my name, telling me it was coming for me, talking to me in the voices I'd loved in times gone by, times when I was not of this earth, not of the surface. I would be tempted to throw the door open and confront whatever it was that stood on the other side, the thing on the hounds, their gaping maws of fire that would grow till it blotted the sky as they reached out to take me with them, through the crack in the skies, in the ground or whatever it was they had emerged from. If I was outside the shelter of the house when they arrived, I would begin chanting my prayers, chanting for my life, without stopping to breathe, running barefoot if I had to, until I found a home filled with love that would take me in without any reservations. That was difficult, most homes had no love, only a thinly veiled tolerance for each other, and most times not even that, just anger that skittered around in corners and leapt up, unfettered with a careless word or a gesture.

Sometimes I had ample warning to leave, at others I didn't. I ran with only the clothes I had on my back, sometimes barefoot, without having had the chance to put on a pair of slippers. Sometimes, if I had the chance, setting fire to what and whom I was leaving behind, it was distracted by fire on the surface, it would stay back to play with it, the marvel that it was. At others, I would just run in the hope it couldn't follow me into a house that would not let it in. How long would I run, how long before it finally caught up with me, how long before I would not be able to protect myself with talismans and amulets that I tied around my neck, my ankle, with the words I chanted, with the feet that did not flee as fast as I could wish them to.

I kept track of Teja and the woman he now lived with. I went to the end of their lane whenever I got some time and stood there hidden by the shrubbery just watching their daily routine. A stalker, if you would call me that. That's how I knew about her, and what she had done, what she had been through, about all that were in the house and around it, staking their claim to it and to her. She was what drew them all together, she had the light too, faint as it was. It was her own, possibly this was why Teja had been drawn to her, the light in him had reached out to the light in her.

'They came to town around the same time as you did,

maybe a day or two later,' Kishan Singh, of the bus stand tea shop, told me when I went across to meet him a couple of days later. 'He and his wife, came from the plains. She's a hill girl though, from this town itself, you can see it in her face and the way she speaks. The house was vacant all these years, she ran away with God knows who, probably this fellow, and her father killed himself from the shame. She moved right back into the house and they made it habitable again. What luck for the girl, she is the only claimant to that house now. No one else seems to want it too, strange things kept happening to those who lived in it. He does odd jobs in town, bookkeeping for those who need it, tuitions for those appearing for competitive exams, but that doesn't fetch them much money, I think. They also give out rooms to boarders, two rooms they have, bed and breakfast, very cheap but very few people want to go all that way out there, so they get few boarders. She rarely comes down now that she's pregnant. Wonder what their story is, how they met, why they got married, why they insist on living in that house with all those strange things happening in it.'

'What strange things?'

'Nobody has lived there since the previous owner killed himself and then, the local broker gave it to a family who had nowhere to live after their house collapsed in a landslide. They found their bodies…' He shuddered. 'They put it down to a wild animal entering through a broken window, but…'

No one who had lived in that house had stayed more than

a couple of months since. It was an ugly squat house, just a single floor with what seemed like two rooms, a parlour and a kitchen. In the manner of most of the traditional *kath-khuni* homes built in the region, it was made of interlocked black slate stone and deodar wood, with a roof that was part slate and part tin, possibly replaced with the tin when the slate broke over the years. The wood, the locals maintained, would last for thousand years even if soaked in water, and ten times that in air. No one would have checked the veracity of that outrageous claim in terms of documentation but there were temples and houses in this town probably older than what the locals could count back to.

The houses were interesting here, in this part of the world, they clung precariously to the edge of the roads, built into the slippage of the mountainside, searching for precarious bedrock to tether their foundations to, vulnerable to falling rock, to erosion, to a storm. They hung on tenuously, like life itself had in these inhospitable parts, a hardiness that one saw in the people too, with their determination to survive in places where only mountain goats could reach when the rains washed away the roads.

For the moment I was safe at the school, with its peaceful chapel, students who skittered in and out through the day, the resounding chimes of the huge bell in the belfry tolling at the canonical hours, and the other shrill electrical bell which was more buzzer than bell, to mark the start of the school day and the division of the hours of study. The nuns firmly stayed out of the way of the housekeeping staff communicating through the supervisors. As long as one did one's tasks relatively efficiently no one hassled you; in fact, they took pity on me, I didn't know what exact story had got around about how I'd come here. No one had asked. There was in the place of natural curiosity a strange patina of deference and empathy which I had done nothing to deserve. I realized that it was a month or so down the line, when one of the kitchen girls asked me how many rooms there were in the palace I was born in. I had smiled enigmatically and said nothing. I had not been born into a palace, I had fallen from the skies. The skies had been my palace. I had fallen from my palace centuries ago. The rooms there were beyond human count. I didn't tell her that.

'One can make out, you know,' she said, chewing her lip as she looked me over from head to toe, assessing me. 'The way you look, your features are too fine, your mannerisms are too gentrified for you to be one of us. Even though you wear these hand-me-down uniforms and don't even line your eyes with kohl, you look like a movie star.' I laughed. If she had seen me in my full glory she would have been blinded by the radiance of my light.

Bala, for that was what her name, was barely eighteen, and had the colour of youth still high on her sun-chapped cheeks, and the fierceness of a gaze that had yet to be wrestled down to the ground by life and circumstance.

'So tell me, were you a queen?' she asked. 'Did you live in a palace with a thousand rooms?'

I laughed. What could I tell her that would make her believe the story I would tell her? 'All I can tell you is that I ran away,' I said. 'I would have been killed had I stayed.' It was the truth. But it was enough. I had run away, hadn't I? At first, I had run away from the light. And then for millennia after I turned away from the light, I had kept running away from what wanted to cast me into the pits of darkness.

Her gaze melted, she could identify with it, all women ran to survive in different ways. I became a project to her, a fledgling to be cared for, taking me under her wings so to speak. It was amusing how protective she became of me.

It was she who came with me into town the first time round to procure the weekly rations when required and showed me around the main street and the various lanes and pathways and stairways that made the small town. I then wandered through them alone when I had the day to myself on alternate Sundays. Being alone had its pleasures, one was not beholden to make polite conversation or to follow the whims of the other when it came to where one might go. It also allowed me to go to the house and watch the occupants. This was my escape plan, it wasn't too far from the convent, around twenty minutes if I ran really fast; I could hold my breath for twenty minutes, I could chant with faith and I could invoke the one who would sluice the air with her curved hook and send it back into the netherworld. I mapped out the route in my mind, figured out the negotiations I would have to make with the corners of the pathways, timed myself in the cover of darkness and waited. And waited. What would come would come soon enough. Days passed, then months. I waited. Waiting is all one can do when one is doomed beyond what any human can comprehend.

I sometimes wondered in what misplaced moment of aesthetic decision-making had they decided to paint the house such a virulent blue that ricocheted off the retina. Maybe, over the years the rain and sleet would tone it down and make it tolerable to the gaze. There must have been a reason for the blue, the townsfolk thought, blue was the colour of Neelkanth, the god of the mountains, him of the animal skin around his waist, the snake around his throat, the skin blue with the poison he drank to save the earth, the moon imprisoned in his hair, the Ganges flowing from his matted locks, the ascetic, the destroyer of the triumvirate. The reason was more prosaic; someone had ordered the wrong shade of blue from the paint store and refused to take it now that it had arrived in stock from the paint company that refused to take back the order. Teja had managed to get it at a throwaway price. That was what life was, simple answers for what seemed like complex questions.

The blue made the house stand out from the end of the lane through the curtain of the shrubs and the foliage as one looked up, a lighthouse of potential refuge to me, a shrine to safety.

And then there was the radiant beauty that youth conferred on Gulab. It pierced me, her youth and her beauty, a youth I would never have, not in skin, I was a million years old out of the skin, this skin was already centuries old, well preserved as they might say. But within her was a hard core that I sensed, I sussed out her memories, going through them carefully, skein by skein, taking care not to alarm her, she barely sensed it, a whispering through her mind, as I blew away what she had constructed to block the memories that troubled her. As I watched them over the next few months, her belly swelled up, her steps became heavier, her face, as delicately chiselled as it was, became broader, swollen with the additional weight and water.

There was one day a week that I got to myself, when I went to the market, to the bus stand, when I walked down the main street, that stretch which ended before it even began, fringed with stores on one side and the drop of the mountain on the other. Or I sat for a while on one of the benches around the main chowk, the one with the statue of a national leader standing with one arm raised, as if hailing a taxi, or walked down what they called the mall, which had at the very most forty to fifty shops crammed cheek by jowl, selling everything from shawls and caps to wooden artefacts and soft toys, all targeted at the passing tourist. I would buy nothing. I needed nothing, except some warm clothes, I had carried none when I fled, except the couple of sweaters I had pulled on. The occasional tourist taxi would roar past, bearing a family taking in the crisp mountain air, a honeymooning couple, mehndi still dark and fresh on the hands of the woman, the hope of a blissful life ahead still to fade from her eyes. At other times, I would walk up the hundreds of steps up to the small temple that housed the god of these hills, a tiny stone construction that was as old as the hills itself, a rough-hewn sanctum sanctorum. You had to bend in order to enter, the gods insisting you pay obeisance with both your posture and your mind. I didn't feel any safer in the temple than I did in the convent. Both were homes of gods. God would not protect me, only humans could, by offering me shelter. Sometimes, I needed light and would find myself a stranger and take them in whatever deserted spot I could find. Behind a wall, against a tree, in a field. I would wipe out their memories of me once I drained them of their light. Some would last me a few days, some were good enough to go for a month or two, very few lasted for years. Teja had been one of those, bursting with enough energy to keep me alive for a year or so. Why had I not bothered to erase myself from Teja, I wondered, it hadn't been an omission, a momentary forgetfulness. I had been fascinated by this human and his raw energy, perhaps I had wanted to stay connected.

I met Bilkis Bi the fourth time I went to the marketplace, her stall was right there at the entrance, like she had always been there, forever and no one dared oust her from that prime position.

'I knew you would come here,' I said to her.

'I knew you knew I would come here,' she replied, and continued arranging her wares in the haphazard order that only she knew, but I had over the years begun to figure out. The useless trinkets sprinkled all over and interspersed, at nodal points the ones which really had the power to change lives, to help lost souls, to contain demons taking over innocent bodies, and she would know who needed what when they approached. Sometimes she refused to sell something that had caught someone's eye when it wasn't what they needed, at others she gave them what they didn't want without charging them a rupee, because that was what they needed. She would be there too, at the market back there.

'How did it take you so long to get here, I've already been here months.'

She smiled, a smile that was both a pondering and remembering.

'I was trapped. I was stuck within the body shell. What I had been trying to trap, trapped me instead.' She laughed, a laugh that shook the earth and the sky, no one else heard it like I could.

'I'm here to trap it and confine it, and you will help me.'

I couldn't understand what she was saying but I listened nonetheless. We spoke in a language no one else could understand, it was a language that had fallen out of use for thousands of years, a language that had sprung up, word for word, syllable for syllable, letter for letter, when humankind had just about begun settling themselves into walled cities where they learnt to harvest, to hoard grain, to create gods and worship them, to build temples to the gods they had created, huge ziggurats that went up to the skies, where writing was on clay tablets, an alphabet that researchers now called cuneiform, and had spent decades trying to decode. We had made our way here, as I shifted bit by bit both my location and my form, moving where I hoped the hounds wouldn't find me, further away from the gates of hell little realising that the hounds would tear through the crust of the earth and create new gates each time.

On the fourth Sunday, I spent part of my day in the thicket outside the blue house, now Rose Lodge as the board ambitiously proclaimed it to be, I felt someone behind me, not right behind me, mind you, but at a little distance. I turned around instinctively. A young woman, perhaps just out of her teens, sat on a huge stone that fringed the path, swinging her legs. She shimmered in the daylight, or was it the light that shimmered through her? Her face was pretty in the way young women are pretty, without much effort, with youth bestowing a magnetism that makes it impossible to look away. There was nothing else that was remarkable about her; she was wearing a salwar kameez of some indeterminate hue, faded with too much wash and wear, and a fraying hand-knitted pink sweater over it. Her feet, without socks, were in slippers. It was not the weather that allowed you to roam around without your feet covered. It was almost weather for mufflers, overcoats, thermal wear, shawls and multiple layers that protected you like a carapace from the biting winds that rolled in from the north, sweeping over everything like the promise of death and resurrection.

'What are you looking at?' she asked.

'How long have you been watching me, and how did I not hear you coming up the path?'

'I didn't come up the path, I was right here,' she replied. 'I've always been right here.'

Perhaps she had been in the thicket, relieving herself. Even then, I would have heard a rustling, a cracking of a twig underfoot, a subtle shifting of the air parting around her as she moved. How had I not sensed her behind me? Years of being constantly on the run had made me acutely sensitive to what was around me. My very survival depending upon it, it was an acuity I had honed over many, many years of listening to shifts in the air, sniffing for sudden whiffs of sulphurous odours permeating what seemed to be a regular evening breeze.

'Now tell me why are you watching this house?'

She could be helpful, this young girl, staring at me with a saucy insolence that told me she knew more than she let on.

'I'm curious about these people, they're new to this place, aren't they?'

'As are you,' she replied, her tone matter of fact. Her voice had a curious ring to it, sharper than any voice I'd heard, echoing within my brain like it went directly into my head without the intercession of the eardrum.

'I've never seen you around earlier, and now you're here most days hiding in the bushes just watching the house.'

I started. Had anyone else seen me too? Did Teja know

I had been watching the house, assessing them both, trying to figure out whether I could rush here if I needed to seek a safe house again.

'Why are you spying on me?' I asked her in response. Attack has always been the best kind of defence.

'I live here,' she replied. 'What is your business here? You are the one spying, not me.'

'You live here? With them?'

She nodded, her eyes cold as stone, an anomaly in her face that was still flushed and plump with youth.

'I lived here long before they came here,' she said, her voice suddenly years older than she seemed, a voice that rang through the ages, that had lived lives I could not even ken, 'I will live here after they go away, after they die. I live here with them. I let them live here because I like them. I didn't let the others live here because I didn't like them, they were disrespectful of me. Now,' she smiled, a smile that pierced icicles into the deepest recesses of my brain, still sitting on the rock swinging her legs like a child, 'do I like you or do I not like you? Do I let you live or do I not let you live? Are you respectful of me or are you not? And if I do let you live, should I let you live in the house with them, as you want to, or should I give you up to the one from the eternal darkness who wants to claim you?'

A chill crawled up my spine as I looked on at her, and she looked back, smiling a slow smile that was at once both conciliatory and a warning. How did she know about me, how did she know about my intention to live here in this house, and most importantly, how on earth did she know that I was fleeing something that no human being could see in its true form, in its horrible entirety?

She pointed at the house with a slow deliberate gesture that made me turn my entire body to look at the house. Standing on the porch, looking straight at where I stood, was Gulab. It was a gaze that was as direct as it could get. I froze, the blood ran cold in my veins and then hot lava seared my insides. Teja came out and stood next to her, looking in the same direction, directly where I was, the thicket between me and them, a distance of ten yards perhaps and some odd shrubbery acting as further veils. She couldn't have seen me, he wouldn't have seen me. I was well hidden, I told myself, I'd been careful. I stayed as still as I could, terrified to move, to breathe. I had plans. With all my plans, I knew, nothing would matter when it blew in on the wind and chased me down, demanding my body and my soul. They turned around and went into the house, I sagged with the tension leaving my body in a sharp gush.

'That was close, do you think they saw us?'

There was no reply. I turned around to the girl. The pale, watery, late afternoon sunlight glinted off the sloping rock she had been perched on a couple of seconds ago, her feet dangling merrily like a child's. There was no one there, except for the echoes of the chill wind whistling eerily through the deserted pathway, rustling the fallen leaves, making some take flight, and the dappling shadows of the feeble sun struggling through the towering deodars fringing the narrow path making their own bioscope production of a ghostly procession of figures on the damp earth of the ground. Carrying on the wind, the rustle of leaves and from a distance high above, a high-pitched laughter that could have been a bird, a girl, a child and when I looked up, I saw nothing but the thickness of the tree cover and the mist rolling in, coiling around the tops of the trees, blotting out the rays of the sun and the blue pockets of sky. A blue that was trembling in wait of the virulent orange fire of the worlds beyond it that would tear it open.

Rani

'Well, get out of hell then! The gate's open and I'm holding it!'
'I can't. I'm hell, myself.'

–IRIS MURDOCH, *The Sea, The Sea*

GULAB HAD BEEN A DISRUPTION IN OUR ROUTINE. She'd slipped in, my curiosity about her had made me let my instinctive guard down and she had been what I had been told to look for, the rose. I'd been fascinated by her, the hard edges on her delicately pretty self, her voice a bright and chirpy patina over a core that was disconcertingly self-preserving. And now she was gone. With the trunk. She had no idea what she had carted away voluntarily, the immense favour she had done me. If there were any misgivings in me about the burden I had selfishly shifted from myself to her, I chose to bludgeon them down. The release was exhilarating, even liberating.

I was no longer terrified to do as I wished, there would be no reprisals now, no sharp pains piercing my insides, no red-hot skewers through my brain, no sensation of being completely dipped in boiling water. No longer would I wake in the middle of the night, paralysed, being penetrated and sexually used by something I could not even see, but could only feel and smell, a weight on my body that was no heavier than air and a smell that was burnt incense, dry and evocative, a coupling that was not a communion of body or soul, a coupling that was possession by something that was far more powerful than I was, intercourse that seared my insides, but showed no scars. I dreaded being alone at home, it was the time when it chose to emerge, toying with me like a cat would with a mouse it had cornered. It was a creature of many moods, much like a human. Sometimes, it was like a lover, gentle and seductive, caressing me with breaths of hot air over my entire body, a slow warmth that built me up to an uncontrollable orgasm. At others, it threw me to the ground and the walls like a rag doll and pierced me every which way it could. Vicious and jealous, a possessive lover that had staked its claim to me without my consent. But then, when had a woman's consent been of relevance to the taking of her body?

When I thought back to the morning my life began derailing, I rued picking up that argument with the crone outside the market, Bilkis Bi. It had led to me being taken away into a limbo, returned unharmed, sent into exile by my family, then latched on to by something I had not wanted, an entity that had followed me home, and taken charge of me. I should have held my tongue and my peace. Surely, now, I realized that a bracelet was not worth having had my life upended into existing in the intervals between being tormented by that which had possessed me.

I should have tied up my hair tight in a bun, pinned it safe instead of that loose knot which I knew kept unravelling, I should have not daubed the attar of jasmine on my wrists, my cleavage, the nape of my neck, behind my ears, I should have realized, I should have known. Unknowingly, unwittingly, I had done the forbidden. By visiting there, with my hair falling loose to my waist, by perfuming myself, by just being a young woman revelling in the glory of my youth and beauty I had given it permission to claim me for itself. Was this the payment it extracted from me for bestowing the favour I'd innocently asked, writing it down on paper and pinning it to the walls of the *dargah*? Was this the entity who bestowed favours at the *dargah* or was it something else, another virulent one, one that had nothing to do with the benevolence of those who harkened the pleas of all those who came to its doors with supplications?

I had tried to rid myself of it, over and over, in the intervals when it withdrew from me and wandered elsewhere, I knew not where. At others, it rested in the trunk, instructing me to keep it locked and hidden, so that no one would unwittingly open it and disturb its repose. A lock, though, couldn't stop it from emerging if it wished, it travelled through tin and stone, space and time in the blink of an eye. When it was gone I knew, I was me again. And when I was me, I visited holy places, I beseeched exorcists, healers, babas, I went wherever I heard a whisper of success with ridding those afflicted with unwanted entities taking over their bodies, begging them to rid me of this, this creature in the trunk back in the basement of my home, this creature of air and fire and smoke that had claimed me for its own. The one who had first confined it in a bottle was no longer in the marketplace. He had disappeared they said, a pile of ashes had been found where he'd been sitting seconds after a client exited and another entered.

I went back to the town, to the market where Bilkis Bi had her stall, in the vain hope that I would find her and convince her to take back the curse she had bestowed on me. My parents were long dead now, and my sisters were married across the country. The family home, when I visited, had been razed to the ground and a swanky new multi-storeyed apartment complex had come up in its place. I stood across the road and stared at what had become of the humble single-storeyed home I had grown up in, with its low-brick compound wall, the gate inset into the wall, the courtyard where Ma began her cooking early in the morning during summers, the rooms leading in from the porch, the charpais on the ground where my father took his post when he returned from the office and where my grandmother sat through the day supervising the comings and goings of all us girls. Five girls, she would moan, how will my son marry them all off, and she would berate my mother in a continuous harangue. Nothing about this building or the redeveloped constructions around it were remnant of what still existed in my memory. The proceeds of the sale of the home, if any, had never reached me, my sisters having conveniently discarded me from their lives. As had I them. Surely they knew where I was, it wasn't difficult to find out where I'd been, where I had gone, for someone determined to track down someone they had grown up with and loved. But perhaps that was the differentiator, perhaps they did not love me anymore.

'Why do you want to go back after all these years?' he'd asked me, the Professor sahab, when I told him I wanted to make a quick trip home. 'It's not like there's anyone there waiting for you or missing you.'

I couldn't explain to him why I wanted to go back, all I wanted was to see if there was a possibility that I could undo what had got me here, in this situation, attached to this entity that wouldn't leave me, and wouldn't let me be. So, I lied.

'I want to go back to meet my sisters,' I said. 'I'll go alone, you don't need to accompany me, it might be uncomfortable, I don't know how they will respond to meeting me after all these years. I'll be there for just a couple of days. I'll stay in a hotel.'

He booked the room for me at a comfortable three-star hotel not too far from where I used to live as a young girl, and contacted an old college classmate to make sure I would be taken care of while I was there.

'It will be walking distance for you from the hotel, your home, your college, your entire neighbourhood.' He looked uncertain. 'Are you sure you don't want me to accompany you?' I reassured him I did not want him to accompany me. I was quite comfortable on my own.

He was only too pleased not to have his routine disturbed. My woman Friday, Lachmi, would run the house in my absence. I had trained her well, she was used to the usual rhythms of the house, it was the unusual ones that she didn't know, nor did anyone else except me. I had managed to, thus far, keep it secret, that which had attached itself to me. It was one of those phases when it was resting, or travelling, or somewhere that wasn't with me. I had a few weeks of being myself, alone with myself. It could be in multiple places at the same time, I knew that. Sometimes it got me things which could only come from hundreds and thousands of kilometres away, just to please me or terrify me, depending on what mood took it. A lotus flower from a lake, a box of sweets from a sweetmeat shop in Delhi that I had been fond of, a frayed prayer flag plucked out from where it had been living a peaceful existence streaming in the icy Tibetan winds, jewellery from some store in Mumbai that I had been admiring the ad of in some magazine, a finger from the hand of a child whenever I felt the pangs of missing out on motherhood. Little tokens of its appreciation that it wooed me with, almost like a lover, an abusive one.

'Show yourself to me,' I'd asked it, in the early days of it latching on to me. 'What do you look like?'

'I look like nothing. I can look like whatever or whoever you want me to look like,' it had replied. The next moment, a handsome young man was sitting in front of me on the ground, wearing a cotton shirt and trousers hanging loose on his body like it was stitched for someone with a much broader torso than his. His feet were bare, he had nothing else on his body, except for shirt and trousers. No watch, no ring, no shoes. Clothes he had deemed important for what he assumed was modesty. The rest he had no need of. He was beautiful, so beautiful that my heart ached to see him. His features planed and sharp, as though carved from the finest block of marble by the most skilful sculptor that creation could find, his shoulders broad and muscled under the loose shirt, his eyes shut and his expression expectant. He was silent, not even in my head now that he had taken on solidity. I reached out my hand, involuntarily, to touch him, to feel the reality of his presence. He felt solid, real, tangible. Flesh to my flesh. At my touch, he opened his eyes. Where eye sockets should have been, there was darkness, just a deep blackness with smoke emanating out of them, I fell unconscious. He never appeared before me again, but the image of him, what he showed of himself to me as, persisted, terrifying me.

'That's why I didn't want to show myself to you, it would scare you.'

He'd never appeared to me again in complete solidity.

'What is your name?' I'd asked him once.

'Call me whatever you like.'

I began thinking of him as Majnu. Majnu he was. A terrifying, predatory, jealous, constrictive Majnu, who was stuck to me no matter where I went, how far I ran. I didn't see myself as a Laila though, there was no love I bore for the creature that had claimed me for its own. I just did not have the wherewithal of how I could escape from its clutches. Majnu. Possessed. It seemed appropriate. I was possessed, a strange possession that was almost human in its stalker-like intensity. I managed to wrest out a strange truce with it, that allowed me to live as normal and regular an existence as I had pleaded for. It would let me live the normality of a life as the wife of a respectable man in society as long I allowed it complete dominion of my body and self in the time and space when I was alone.

When I reached the old market, Bilkis Bi was not where I'd expected her stall to be. Instead, there was another stall of brick and cement with a proper shutter and shelves, one that displayed pieces of jewellery that had lived many lives before they had reached here, in this shop at the entrance of the marketplace in a mofussil town right at the edge of a country where the border was just a walk away. Set in silver, stones with power. Topaz, agate, jet, obsidian, jade. I wondered how these pieces of jewellery had come to this humble stall, they were too powerful and too intricate to be found at a roadside stall. My eye was untrained, but I could recognize things of value, it came naturally to me, perhaps a remnant of a former life when I lived in close contact with beautiful and precious things, given I had no truck with them in this life.

A young woman was perched on the stool behind the

counter, puffing at a bidi. Her skin was the clear skin of those from the land beyond the mountains to the North West, the blush of youth tingeing her cheeks and lips, her eyes sharp and dark, two vertical lines furrowing her brow as I hovered over the stall. She wore what looked like a long tunic over a full skirt and a scarf tied around her head, from which a few tendrils of curls escaped, almost guilty in their indiscipline, her eyes and her hair were the deepest black, obsidian. She narrowed her eyes and looked at me carefully, I looked back at her. She looked away, almost guiltily, and took another puff of her bidi. The way she held her bidi was strangely familiar, I wondered where I had seen it before. I stopped in front of her stall and made a show of going through the trinkets on display, but she did not exhort me to try any or appeal to my vanity as most shop owners do in order to flatter one into buying something. The stock on display was what was available at any Tibetan stall in the hill towns and tourist spots, that I knew. I had seen them at the Dilli Haat when I lived in the city, exquisite carved stones, precious crystals, silver jewellery, prayer flags.

'How much is this?' I asked, picking up a silver ring with a green stone.

She smiled. 'How much would you pay for it?'

I put it down again. If she wanted to haggle, I would. I didn't like it too much too, it made me feel uneasy, like I was holding something warm, alive and squirming in my palm.

'That one is not for you,' she said, putting it back in its place. 'It will make things worse for you.' She wasn't making sense.

'How much is this?' I asked, holding up a ring that looked like an oval topaz set in silver.

She looked at it scathingly. 'You'll need something a lot stronger than that to rid yourself permanently of it,' she said, her voice now suddenly raspy and reedy, the vocal chords much older than what she appeared to be. A familiar voice.

Chills trickled down my back. She picked up a pendant with ancient carvings on it, a square green marbled stone set within. Jade. Ancient jade. As I touched it, I felt the power of the stone course through me, making me shiver, the grip of what held me loosened a bit, a mere fraction.

'I knew you would come back,' she said, taking another puff of the bidi. 'What took you so long?'

It was then that it hit me.

'Where is Bilkis Bi?' I asked. 'Are you her daughter?'

She smiled at me, a slow deliberate smile that sent icicles down every nerve in my spine, raising the fine hair on my arms, on the back of my neck. She couldn't have been more than eighteen.

'Rani,' she said. 'You haven't recognized me, but I recognized you the moment you walked in. You haven't changed much. After all these years, how many has it been? Thirty? Forty?'

'How can it be?' I asked, grabbing one of the poles that held the awning up to steady myself.

She smiled, looking into my eyes, her eyes the same as they had been all those years ago, all knowing and ancient, with the ability to look inside your head and shift things around.

'When you haven't changed even after three decades, why can I not go back to what I was over a hundred years ago?'

'You still remember me?'

It was a superfluous question, I knew it as I asked it, but was somehow compelled to ask it, to clear the misgivings in my head.

'Of course, I remember you.' She smiled and there could be no doubt it was her, it was the same smile, a smile that was a promise and a threat, a smile she had smiled after she'd condemned me to suffer over and over. 'I cursed you. You have suffered that curse all these years, you've come to get me to take it back.'

'Please. I need your help. We need to have a talk,' I replied. 'But not here.'

The crowds were milling around throwing curious glances at us. It made for an unlikely sight, the two of us, engaged in conversation far deeper than what should have been the cursory of a buyer-seller engagement.

As I watched, she closed her eyes and opened them to reveal complete blackness. I took a step back, the entire marketplace turned black, the sun turned black. She picked up a small sharp needle and, as I watched, scratched something out on the back of the pendant and then held it between both her palms, muttering something unintelligible. When she opened her eyes again, they were rheumy and regular.

'You must wear this at all times,' she said, pulling out a black cord from a box on the counter and threaded the loop of the pendant into it. 'I've carved his name on it, it will keep him from entering you again or tormenting you.' She handed it across to me, I put it around my neck, examining it closely. It was an unusual one, it had an oriental design, something that had probably been carved thousands of years ago, and then made a tumultuous existence through dynasties that had created the Great Wall, and gunpowder and firecrackers and silk, and found its way here, through circuitous routes, into India, to this small town, into the hands of this woman, who looked like she'd barely stepped out of her teens with ancient eyes that had seen waves breaking on the shores of land as it rose from the primordial oceans. I could not see what she might have written on it, it was invisible to my eyes. She threw her bidi to the ground, stubbed it out with her *jutti*, put the cord strung with the pendant to my throat, knotting it swiftly at the nape of my neck, muttering something unintelligible as she did so.

'It has no power over you now. I have written its name on this. He cannot defy the one who commands him by his name. Keep this on you always, never remove it, until you feel the weight of him completely lifted from you.'

I felt the heat of the pendant as it found its way deep and low where no one could see it, nestled in the valley between my breasts, covered with layers on layers of fabric.

'Whatever troubles you, find out its true name. Only the knowledge of the true name can render it powerless against you.'

'How did you find out its true name?'

'I asked one of his kind. No one can refuse to answer me.'

A weight lifted off me and disappeared, a gust of breeze that had so far been within me was now outside of me. She looked into the distance and smiled, a smile that had not a trace of regret in it, rather was smug with satisfaction.

'I'm sorry for what I said unthinkingly all those years ago. You should have known better than to annoy me. Now. Come on.'

She swiftly pushed everything displayed on the board into a box and clamped it shut, pulling down the poles and the awning with efficient precision, and tying them up back tight. The shutters she pulled down, and slung the bag over her shoulder.

'Aren't you going to lock it?'

'For what?' she laughed. There was a loaded pause while she looked back at the stall and those who were standing around in the lane, watching us. 'And no one would dare steal anything from me if they want to stay alive.' I believed her.

I followed her as she walked down the narrow lane, a swing to her hips and a lilt in the tune she was whistling, an old Hindi film song from the black-and-white era, with romance and longing and yearning, that suddenly transcended the reedy bars of her whistling and suffused me with desire for I knew not what. I walked behind her unresistingly as she wove her way through lanes and by-lanes, noting how people fell back as she passed, a sense of ferocity preceding her that made those around keep their distance. The pair of anklets on her feet tinkled as she moved, as did the many silver bangles on her wrist. A dog picked up her trail as we exited the crowded market area and fell in step at the main road. She didn't shoo the dog away, it followed like it had walked this way with her a thousand times. It walked along complacently, leading the way at times, falling back at others to investigate interesting odours and possible sources of food, barking at other strays on the way, pissing on specific lamp posts and trees.

The sun was bright and high even though it was late afternoon – it was still summer after all, the end of June. The main road was framed with rows of Amaltas trees on either side, Cassia Fistula a term I had learnt from being with the Professor all these years, which had blossomed into a yellow canopy, spreading a yellow carpet of their fallen petals to be trampled underfoot as we walked, and at other stretches ashoka trees stood guard over those who passed. She then turned off into another, less crowded lane, which further branched off into another lane. The trees changed here, no longer were they the planned glory of civic beautification, tended to with care, but the random springing of hardy trees where the seeds fell, a neem tree, a babool tree, shrubbery that grew unfettered, thorny, dry and untended over the decades, reaching for the skies while the earth held them secure. We reached a deserted unpaved pathway which I knew led to the cemetery. It had been built back when the British still ruled this small cantonment town, and some of the graves told stories of lives cut short young far away from the home country. The tombstones were broken and mossy, some sunken into the ground, crushing the bones within, the wall surrounding the graveyard had given way in parts, allowing vagrants to find within a safe refuge to chase drugs.

'Where are we going,' I asked, hesitant, and feeling the oppressive miasmal presences from the burial grounds floating around, watching us, wary of approaching us. She could sense them too, I knew, and she had a healthy disdain for them, that I knew too. They did not dare intrude, but hovered, attentive, like staff at a formal dinner, waiting to be beckoned if required.

'Why, I'm taking you home. Like I should a guest.'

'What is this you've tied around my neck?'

'Call it a *taaveez*, an imported *taaveez* if you like,' she laughed a brittle laugh. 'It is an old and an effective one, it will protect you from whatever it is you seek riddance from. When it has served its purpose, please return it to me.'

'How will it protect me?'

She smiled beatifically and did not reply. I knew better than to try and force an answer from her. I did not wish to annoy her again, after all these decades.

We had turned off the path adjoining the burial grounds and had reached what seemed to be a dead end. As she walked right through it, there was a momentary flash of light, like a curtain that had been pierced and the opacity of the dead end peeled away.

I could see her within, but she seemed to be at a fair distance away, not just a few steps away as she should have been. She turned around and beckoned me to follow her. I hesitated, but she gestured again, this time more insistent. She was saying something I couldn't hear. The curtain of light seemed to be narrowing, I stepped through without thinking. Here the air was crisper, lit by a light that was not the sun I was accustomed to. It was gentle on the skin, even a caress of light if that were possible. As far as the eye could see, fields stretched out in every direction green and lush, the sky was the kind of blue that one saw only in paintings, and in the midst of it all, at a distance was a little hut. She beckoned me to follow her, and turned to walk towards the hut. A path formed under her feet as she walked and a huge spreading banyan shaded the hut from the gentle light of the sun, so soft it could have been the moon. Its aerial roots hung down over the path like a curtain, its branches and canopy blocking out the sun, a preternatural shade that made standing under it just that bit cooler than it had been on the rest of the path.

The hut, as one saw it from the porch, if it could be called that, was a ramshackle construction which was sleeper wood, brick and mortar all jammed together luck by chance to create a standing structure with a roof. Two windows on either side of a door winked as the late afternoon sun caught the glass. There was no lock on the door. She stepped in, gesturing at me to walk in. I did so with great trepidation, the unfamiliar feel of the pendant nestled between my breasts strangely warm and comforting when I needed it. Where were we, what was this place?

I followed her into the house, bending a bit to enter the low door and then standing up again to take in my surroundings. The house was huge. The space within was nothing like what it seemed from the outside. This was a palace. My head spun. The dog who had slipped in after me went to a corner and settled himself comfortably there for what seemed like a long nap in a familiar spot on a rug.

'Not quite what you expected, is it?' she asked, her voice and her diction now completely changed. She was changed too, when I turned around and looked at her. She was the same to look at, but she was somehow more imposing, more terrifying. I saw rather than felt myself trembling with fear.

'Don't be afraid, I'm not going to harm you.'

'Who are you?'

'Not of your kind, as you must have guessed.'

She gestured at a chair, her gestures now elegantly imperial.

I sat down gingerly expecting it to give way under me, looking around me with the same wonder that a tribal from a remote forest might have on their first visit to a metropolis and being confronted with chrome and steel edifices to modernity, and the push and throb of the crowds that streamed through the roads and the public transport.

The room was lavish, velvet and leather upholstered chairs and sofas, hand-woven silk rugs and carpets with designs so intricate many weavers must have given up their eyes in the process of making them, crystal chandeliers that hung from high ceilings, ornately designed with gold and mosaic, a span so huge that my eyes didn't take in the room at a single glance. And there were rooms shooting off from the main room we had entered into.

'What is this place and what are you?'

She laughed, and sat down opposite me, her ghagra and long kurti which had been faded and threadbare until she'd stepped in, now seemed the stuff of rich coloured silks and gold-embroidered velvets. And then for the flash of a second, she was an ancient crone, stark naked, with grey hair streaming behind her to her ankles, her skin wrinkled and sagging, her breasts parched and pendulous, a grey thatch of hair covering her pubis, her eyes bright and piercing. I gasped and she was back as she was, a young woman dressed in clothes fit for a queen.

'This,' she gestured at what seemed to be the inside of the mansion we were sitting in, 'is my home. It can be anything you choose it to be, and you made it a palace. I am happy to keep it a hut, I need nothing more. I am the keeper of secrets, the watcher of the worlds, I am the vacuum of space and time, I am the fullness of the universe. You knew me as Bilkis Bi, the old lady with the stall at the market. I will save you from what has claimed you.'

Fear racked my body, tremors I could not stop. I tried

to spring up and rush to the door. My body stayed locked where it was, a kind of paralysis I had never experienced before. The room around me began swaying gently whether from my terror or actually moving back and forth I did not know. I looked outside the window and there were no trees, no grounds, only soft cottony clouds streaming past gently. We were now in the sky, the house was in the sky and I was trapped here, in this house, with this woman who was nothing I could ever understand or hope to understand. Anything was possible, either that or that I was fast asleep in my hotel room and dreaming, those vivid dreams that gripped you by the throat and didn't let go even if you screamed and shouted. She came to me and sat next to me, taking me by the hand. Her hand was soft and comforting, her breath warm and fragrant, washing over me, soothing my panic. She became my mother, she became my grandmother, and she turned back into the old woman with nothing covering her nakedness but her hair and laughed. She stood up holding out her hand into the air and what seemed like a sickle manifested into it. Sparks flew into the room from the clouds outside which had become dark and menacing, lightning lit up the room with sudden sharp cracks of luminescence, the thunder roiling behind not too far after.

'What am I? They call me and my kind by many names. *Chudail*, *daayan*, *dakini*. Some call me a goddess. We were here since the beginning of time and will be there at the end of it all. You don't need to understand how they define us or what they say about us. You don't need to fear me, I will not harm you. I will save you, my child. And you, in turn, will save me.'

Gulab

> *'Do not neglect to show hospitality to strangers, for by doing that some have entertained angels without knowing it.'*
>
> – ANONYMOUS, The Holy Bible: King James Version

I NEVER SPOKE TO TEJA OF WHAT HAD HAPPENED between the time I'd reached that evening at the Professorni's house and the time I'd left the bungalow. He had never asked. To be honest, I couldn't quite remember what had happened in that interim. If you had asked me, I would be hard-pressed to give you a coherent answer. And he would laugh at me. The trunk I had dragged along was heavy as I dragged it and light as a feather when we opened it. There was nothing inside it, except a glass bottle which had nothing within.

'This is what you dragged along all the way? An empty trunk? With an empty bottle?' he laughed. I laughed too, uneasily. Some secrets were better never told. I couldn't tell him I was biding my time until the baby was born, and that once the baby was born, something, something I couldn't explain, would become my lover and my possessor. Something I couldn't fight. Something that had been let out, something that should have stayed confined within, something dangerous, a sudden scent of jasmine, a string of flowers tucked carelessly into the hair, redolently sweet through my memories, probing my thoughts and emotions through the passages of my consciousness. Then, an overwhelming rush of hot air that came upon me like a blanket, covering me like an embrace, the sense of a breath hovering at the nape of my neck, a breath that was almost a caress, a forbidden one that made me feel aroused in an inexplicable way. I was wanted, desired. I knew that with a certainty, but by whom or what I did not know. I was imagining things, I told myself, I was imagining it all. And then it withdrew, like a man in lust would when he realized that time of the month was on you.

I had started losing time from the moment I'd opened that trunk. Seconds, minutes, hours. I had lost time from the moment I stepped down to the basement and only came to myself when I reached the bus depot. I had come to myself only to see Teja and that woman embracing, an embrace that should have been a public nuisance and a bookable offence even though they had all their clothes on. I was not going to give him up so easily! I didn't want him, but damned if I gave him up so easily to another woman. If I ever let him go, there would be claw marks on him.

I realized it had all started with the trunk, all the instances when I was there and not quite there. I didn't dare voice my fears to Teja, I preferred for him to think of me as stupid and forgetful rather than not all there. He had his own worries, the hit jobs he took on and went away to complete, only to return, too exhausted a week or two later, content to only lie in the bedroom, his eyes closed, his soul unsettled, his duffel bag by his side, a duffel bag I was not permitted to open ever. One he had attached a small lock to, the key to which he kept in his wallet, and one that occasionally rattled and had voices coming from within that deterred me from investigating the contents. I had no desire to investigate it, opening empty bottles in locked trunks had been mistake enough.

The ones who had been chasing him had now backed off, or so he thought mistakenly. He was still easy to track down, but after all these years he assumed they had just about given up on finishing him. And there was no one paying to have him done away with, and those who hired him to finish the ones they took contracts out on were invested in his safety and well-being. Between the two warring factions, he'd eked out a tenuous peace and stability.

'They won't look for me now,' he said. 'They're just happy I'm out of sight. It was an honour thing.' Though what honour his death would bring to those who ran cartels of all that was illegal from smuggling contraband and drugs across countries and continents, I did not understand.

He couldn't believe I had lugged an empty trunk. It hadn't been empty when I took it, I told him. He hadn't taken it to the bus, he had been too shell-shocked by what he had let go to carry it. I had dragged it to the bus where the conductor had loaded it in the hold. I had dragged it out, he had watched on bemused, yet unthinking to open the trunk and check what exactly it contained. For an empty trunk it was very heavy, like it contained the weight of the universes within it.

'You just picked up the trunk and dragged it behind you?' he had asked later, incredulous.

'Yes,' I had replied, that was exactly what I remembered.

'But why?'

'I don't know,' I replied. Perhaps it is an antique, I told him. See the work on it, we could sell it for a lot of money. He scoffed.

I remembered nothing and sometimes I could remember the Professorni lying supine on the floor in a dead faint, and me dragging the trunk up the stairs from the basement, and shutting the door behind me. At yet others, I couldn't remember how I'd made it to the bus stand dragging such a heavy trunk. It was almost as big as I was. Perhaps I'd hailed down an autorickshaw. I couldn't remember. I'd waited and waited until we reached the town the bus took us to and found ourselves in the house before we opened it. The trunk had been heavy. When I wasn't paying attention, it would become light. The trunk had been what I had wished it to be, I realized that now.

It was an unnecessary precaution not opening it in public. There was nothing in it. Absolutely nothing, except that empty bottle and the hot air that emerged when I unscrewed it in confusion. Again. At that moment, I had forgotten what had happened in the basement. I would now keep oscillating between the forgetting and the remembering. We had stared at it disbelievingly for a long moment and then collapsed into laughter.

'All that effort of lugging it across state borders for this!'

It came in handy though, it gave us an aura of respectability. Anyone lugging around a trunk couldn't be vagrants, they had to be a down on their luck couple, looking to start afresh. Folks were sympathetic. The taxi drivers at the bus stand recognized me even after these years, and one agreed to drive us to the house for no fare. After all, I was a daughter of the town, albeit one who had forsaken it and then never looked back to check what had happened to her father and her grandmother. My grandmother had passed away a few days after my father, in shock, he said. My father probably paid her a visit in his current state and gave her that shock, I imagined.

He filled me in on how the house I had grown up in now came to be deserted and haunted, the rumours of the *bhootni* guarding the approach road, sitting on the peepal tree that spread its branches over the house and the small patch of land that surrounded it. I would like to meet her, she would make for good company, *bhootni*s always did.

'I don't believe in *bhootni*s and *chudail*s and *aatma*s,' Teja had stated to him flatly when he'd warned us about the house. 'The living are scarier than the dead.' I agreed, but didn't voice it. It wouldn't do to unnerve him.

Nonetheless, we appreciated the man warning us in advance, it was done in our best interests. He'd shrugged and helped us put our trunk in the carrier on the top, tying it safely with ropes. Sometimes a memory flashed deep in the back of my mind before I could grab it and examine it, that of a thing, something I could not explain, a thing, a person, a being, a creature, that had crawled out of the trunk, something that was fire and air, a person and not a person, something that had entered my nose, my ears, my mouth and rushed through my body trying to find something I didn't know what. And then there was the blackness, a velvety blackness that had no beginning and no end, only a susurration of sounds as something whooshed through me and I whooshed through something.

The first of the blackouts. I had been having blackouts ever since, for short periods of time. Sometimes I would be gone for a few minutes, at others it would be hours. I didn't tell Teja about them, he would worry. I would worry too, I wondered what it was that I did when I lost time. I'd blacked out about how I'd managed to get to the bus stand, and only come to myself when I saw Teja holding on to that woman like she was life and death and everything beyond it, in a way he had never held me. She glowed, that woman, she glowed like she was dipped in moonlight, like her veins under the skin were a riverine map of mercury, pulsing, flowing.

As I looked at them, she opened her eyes and caught my gaze. She knew. I did not know how she knew and how

I knew that she knew, but she instantly stepped away and walked away to the bus without a backward glance, releasing him from any obligation to go with her. It was a gesture I appreciated, relinquishing her claim on him. The decision, I realized, she'd left in his hands, whether to follow her or to go with me, and I felt unequal to the challenge. And of course, then I rose to it.

Would he have left me without a second's thought, a backward glance, had I not told him I was pregnant? Had he felt anything for me, any sense of love or affection or even obligation to me? Had he stayed back merely from a sense of duty? There was no answer to these questions, and I didn't dare ask them. It was too terrifying to think of what I would do if the answers weren't to my liking.

We shifted with our trunk and duffel bags into the house and set about making it habitable. The impolite name for the house was now '*Bhootni ka ghar*.' We heard of it, of course; it slipped out unbidden, when folks spoke with us, at first curious and then intrusive in their curiosity. There were bets, we learnt later, as to how long we would last in that house. No one would come to work at the house or to help with the repairs – it was cursed, they said. Teja began doing the work himself, untrained as he was, buying bits of wood, sawing, taking measurements, setting up his work bench in the yard, hanging around at the supplies store, befriending the handymen who came there to buy their stock and figuring out how things needed to be done. Over the days he made friends with some of the handymen, and they came to help. That's how the townspeople were, they came forward to help eventually, overcoming their initial reluctance, these folk with the open smiles and hearts.

Teja asked around in town for odd jobs and figured out clerical tasks he could perform for the shopkeepers and restaurant owners in the main street, helping them with keeping their accounts and managing their stock. He did this to keep himself busy. Occasionally he went into to different cities for jobs he was assigned. It kept us more than fed, what he did. I didn't ask him what it was that he did that paid him so much that he kept it all in wads of cash in the trunk, now locked with a huge old-fashioned lock and secreted under piles of old rugs and blankets in the loft. He divided his days, and kept busy. I was alone in the house for most of the day, he came home in the evenings, and we lived, like a married couple was supposed to, in the intervals between the passing of the day into night and the next morning. When he was not around, I kept losing time. Seconds sometimes, hours at others. I would be pouring out something and then come back to realize I had poured everything on the counter. I would be folding clothes, to find I had been sitting holding a shirt unfolded in my hand and the sun had moved from early morning to late afternoon. What happened to me in the time that I lost I didn't know. Sometimes I emerged with an inexplicable bruise, at another time my finger was cut, dripping blood. Once I found myself on the roof, standing surveying all that was visible before I came to and froze in terror at where

I found myself. Another step and I would have tumbled down from the roof, over the fence, down the drop at the back of the house, rolled straight down the steep slope that went past the roads and the pathways. We both would have died, me and the child within me. I didn't tell Teja about these time lapses, they were infrequent and no real harm had come from them. It would worry him, and nothing had happened. Nothing to worry about, I told myself, it was probably the pregnancy.

I should have known better. Like mould, what was growing over us, the miasmal presence, was biding its time, making inroads occasionally, testing how much it could take over me. How could I fight something I could not see? Even if I had a gun, I could not shoot it in the head and be done with it. And I didn't know any other way of ridding myself of it.

Teja took me to the lady doctor in town to check if all was well with the baby and with me. Not once, by word or behaviour did he ever suggest that we get rid of the child. Honestly, I had hoped he would ask me to do so. I felt inadequate to bring up a child. I dared not bring it up, after all, it was the only thing I had to ensure he stayed with me, and now that she was gone it was the only thing keeping him from going out in search of her.

'Perhaps we could keep a lodger or two. We have two extra rooms,' he suggested one morning over a breakfast of parathas and aloo sabji, before he set out for his day's work. 'I just need to get the pipes working again and the roof repaired. These goras pay a lot of money for what they think is the real experience of living with local families.' We were a family in his head, a family of two and a half. Or probably a quarter, what number did one put to a child in utero? He paused, looking at me to check my expression. 'I want to stop doing what I do.'

I didn't ask him what it was that he did that he wanted to stop. But if he wanted to stop and we had to find an alternative. A lodge, if we could manage it, seemed a good option. The house was cosy, it had two extra rooms we could let out, the room my grandmother had died in and the room where I had faced torture at the hands of my father. We had taken the biggest room for ourselves when we had moved in, that was the room my father had lived in, the room he still crawled up to on the nights that he crept up the steep ravine, rotting off the bone, the maggots in his flesh, the hole in his face where life had left him and death had not taken him. That he would end up the undead was something I hadn't bargained for when I'd killed him. That he would return over and over again to beg my forgiveness was something that would have terrified me if I'd known of it back then, but now he didn't bother me. He was powerless to hurt me anymore. He needed my forgiveness to release him from his body. I couldn't find it in me to forgive him. Not yet at least. Keep rotting, I told him. Soon you'll be only bones and nothing to hold the bones together too.

'Are you up to it? The baby will be here soon.'

I didn't know if I was up to it, but I could try, and if I had some help around the house we could manage, that I knew. It was a good suggestion. Money would come in. He had over the past couple of months made the house habitable with determined functional repairs. I had strung up curtains rustled from cheap fabric I'd sourced from the market when we'd gone down; we had found furniture being discarded from a restaurant that was renovating its premises and convinced the owners to give us a few chairs and a table, a bench. The beds in the rooms were still sturdy, the cotton in the mattresses we got fixed again, and the covers changed. Someone passing through, looking for a cheap room to live in, could live here pretty comfortably. There were enough *angeethis* for cold nights, and Teja had arms sturdy enough to get the wood.

'I can make basic meals if they want,' I mused. 'I don't know anything fancy.' Our food was simple, I could educate myself on more elaborate dishes if needed, the phones had everything now, cooking videos, cleaning videos, childbirth videos. Teja had a phone with data, I had no phone, never had one.

He thought about it. 'That should be enough. If they want fancy food, they wouldn't stay here, would they?' He had a fair point. He got a board made, which he nailed outside the door. 'Bed & Board Available', it said, painted in a painstaking hand which didn't quite read the English language comfortably, but could copy what was written with precision. What would we call it, he asked, and then decreed it would be Rose Lodge. After me, Gulab.

For days, we had no takers. We waited. The baby grew within me. I lost some more time. Some minutes one day. An hour another day. I flooded the kitchen, leaving the tap running. I sat in the afternoon sun, curling up with the cat on the bench outside, soaking up its warmth and woke up to realize I hadn't slept but it was evening and a chilly wind had begun blowing in from the north, locking all my bones into position. Perhaps it was this way when women had children growing in their stomachs, sometimes the children took over their time, I told myself, perhaps it was normal to just keep blanking out. At others, I worried that I had a worm in my brain that kept eating up bits of it, and I lost time whenever it did so.

One afternoon, after I'd eaten a light lunch of roti and aloo *sabji*, tidied up the house a bit, and was just about to go lie down for a bit, the baby within already sending fumes of fire into my windpipe, the scent of roses wafted over the wind and through the windows filling the room with a fragrance so sweet that it brought tears to my eyes. The door knocker sounded. I opened it, to find her standing there, that woman, carrying a cloth bag and wearing a rough sweater over a badly fitted salwar kameez in a regulation brown fabric of an institution. It had not been stitched to her measurements, it had been meant for someone bulkier than she was. Despite the clothes, despite the complete lack of adornment, she was glorious. Her face a perfect oval, her skin pale and translucent, her hair a black that was meant to drown in, her eyes, under two sharply defined brows, doe-like and clear, shining like the stars hid themselves behind the eyelids. A luminosity ran beneath her skin and leaked into the air around her, surrounding her with an unearthly nimbus as she stood at the door looking at me with an expression that could only be construed as hopeful. I stood still for a long moment as I took her in.

She was beautiful, not in a way that strikes you immediately as beautiful but a strange, compelling allure that made you want to look again at her over and over again, and with each glance notice each individual feature, the composite of them all and how they all came together to make her exquisitely and compellingly beautiful. She was unearthly, I could now understand what Teja saw in her. The late afternoon sun was behind her, beyond where the trees obscured it, and the filtered rays came through her, light that sparkled and danced. Teja was not at home.

'I was told you take in boarders.'

I stood there, one hand on the jamb of the door, the other on my belly. It had become a reflex action I realized, touching my belly constantly, to reassure myself of the child growing within. The baby within kicked. A kick of recognition?

'Can I come in?' she said, her voice refined and elegant, her diction polished with the rigour of tutors and being born to wealth. It was a voice that was soft because the world would hush itself to hear what she had to say. It was rude to make her stand at the doorstep, so I bade her to come in. The room seemed to get brighter with her entering it, and the energy shifted just that bit, a slight flare of iridescence, setting light to all the molecules of air within the sitting room. She entered on noiseless footsteps and looked around with the unabashed curiosity that I had hitherto seen only with young children when they entered a new place. I looked around as she did, following her gaze: it was a humble room, with furniture salvaged from the discards down in town, but it was a cosy room. It was a room Teja and I had worked on with love and parsimony. It was my first permanent house, the others had all been resting houses, so to say, this was a home that would see us become a family in a few months. As far as a hitman and a killer could be family.

I gestured towards the parlour, she stepped past me. Something crackled, sparks leapt off the floor and the wall, and I felt like I was seeing the residual images of firecrackers at the back of my eyes. Then it faded and all was normal again. I sat down on the sofa indicating she sit on the divan opposite.

'Why are you here?' It was the only question to be asked, the most direct one, and the only one I needed an answer to.

'I need a home,' she said, her voice soft and pleading, quite unlike what I had imagined her to be. This was no seductive siren luring young men to their death and devastation, she was a woman, a gentlewoman, who was obviously down on her luck and trying to survive in a hostile world.

We sat opposite each other, looking at each other, not as

adversaries now, strangely enough, but as women in difficult circumstances.

How did you come to this town, how did you find us? I held the question in my mind and didn't speak it out aloud. What is this light that is shining through your skin that also faintly shines through mine, why did you come here when there are so many boarding houses in town, where were you all these days? These were questions at the tip of my tongue that didn't get asked. There would be time to ask these, now was not that time. She seemed, I realized with a sudden shock, ageless. I could not place how old she would be. She smiled, a smile that told me she knew what I was thinking. A smile that told me she was older than anything or anyone I could imagine, even my dead grandmother. Maybe she was older than the hills or the oceans. A frisson ran over my spine. She had some great skincare regime, I thought to myself.

We recognized each other and our place in Teja's life, this was not acknowledged by anything either of us said. There was a certain wariness, and an acceptance of what we were to each other, antagonists of sorts for a man's affection. Strangely though, now that I saw her close up, I felt no antagonism towards her. She was a woman, a lovely one, albeit one who had the affections of the man whose child I was carrying. She made you feel good just by her presence. The light pulsated around her, like an energy field, but far from scaring you, it made you want to reach out and touch it, enter it, be in it. It spread outwards from her and reached me, enveloping my belly with a suffusion of love and warmth, holding what was precious within me with a tenderness that made me feel, for the first time ever in my life, truly cherished. I wanted, at that moment, to always keep her by my side, to have that warmth and joy fill me like a benediction, to suffuse me until I felt no worry, no fear and no cold ever again.

'How much longer?' she asked, gesturing at my belly.

'Any time now,' I replied.

'It will snow,' she said.

For some reason, her words terrified me with what they implied. It was snowing the night I killed my father.

'Do you have a child?' I asked. It was a superfluous question as she didn't have the look of a mother in her eyes, an expression I'd noticed only mothers had, because now they no longer thought of themselves first. I would have that expression in my eyes soon enough, others would look at me and know I was a mother. I would soon be a mother, life as I knew it would change irrevocably and I didn't know right now just how it would – it just loomed ahead of me, a threat, a promise, a benediction.

'I can never feel enough love for a child.' It was not the answer to my question, but it was as good an answer as I could ever get. She paused briefly and then looked into my eyes. 'May I touch your stomach?'

I nodded, I realized then it would be impossible to refuse her anything she asked of me when she asked it with such love. She reached out a hand and laid it gently over my belly.

The light crawled out of her and spread over the floor from where she was sitting, spread gently along the walls, a silvery light that danced with an emotion I couldn't quite understand, then wrapped itself around me before suddenly withdrawing. I looked at its spread, flummoxed, I'd never seen anything like it. She smiled and the light disappeared, withdrawing back into her like it had never expanded beyond her body and spread through the room, lighting it up with an unearthly radiance.

'Your baby is blessed,' she smiled. 'So, do you have a room you could let me rent?' It would be churlish to refuse after she'd blessed my baby.

'We do,' I replied, conflicted about whether I wanted to have her in the house, in such close proximity to Teja. I could still see him holding onto her like his entire universe was balled up within her body. I straightened my back, I had within me his child. He had chosen to come with me, I couldn't lose the first long-term boarder we had because of my insecurities. A fixed income was always preferable to folks who came and went. And if she was a good cook, I didn't mind lowering the rate for the room. When the baby came, I knew kitchen duties would be tough to handle.

'How long do you plan to stay here?'

'For as long as I can.'

I told her what we charged for the room, and that we offered a basic breakfast and meals. She nodded. It wasn't a huge amount, but it was enough. Would she have the money, I wondered, but that was not my concern. If she was taking up this room on the assumption that Teja would not charge her any money, she was mistaken, and I would ensure that she paid up as promised. Could she cook, and help with the household chores, I asked. I would lower the rate. She nodded. Behind her a tablecloth that was askew, straightened itself obediently. I winced. Not one more, I was exhausted of having creatures here who did the work when they thought no one noticed.

'When can I move in?' she asked, a slow smile lighting up her face like moonlight had just dappled through the afternoon breeze and settled on her face. 'Can I move in immediately?'

'I'll have to discuss it with my husband,' I said, feeling the word 'husband' roll off my tongue with an unpractised ease.

She smiled, she knew we were not married, but she did not correct me or indicate in any way she knew I was trying to make ours a legitimate relationship. For that I was grateful. I rose heavily to bring her a glass of water, it was only right to be hospitable.

'Would you like some tea?'

'No,' she waved a hand to dissuade me.

'Don't trouble yourself. Can I move in today?' she asked. 'I just have a few clothes of mine, nothing else. I can go get them if you say I can have a room.'

'I'll have to check with my husband,' I replied.

'I won't be any trouble,' she said, her voice pleading. 'I just need a place I can be safe in.'

'Why do you think you'll be safe here?'

She looked down at the floor for a long moment, as though she was deliberating about what she could safely tell me and what she couldn't.

'This is a safe house.' She smiled. 'I will be safe here, that I know for sure. It cannot follow me here. I will be protected here.'

'Protected from what?' I couldn't understand what she was getting at, the light that surrounded her rippled and flinched as though terrified of what she was going to tell me. She looked straight at me, and there was pain and terror in her eyes.

'Protected from that which has made my life a living hell, a punishment I have brought upon myself. Hell on earth.' She straightened her back and stood up, suddenly taller and imposing in a way she had never seemed before. The light glowed again, strong and liquid washing over the entire floor, the walls, unfurling itself from her like an oil spill of iridescent luminescence, that spanned both sides of her, wings that extended far beyond what the tiny room could contain. I put a hand up to shield my eyes from the brightness, perhaps I needed dark glasses if I was to look at her full in the face, like looking at an eclipse or risk blinding myself. Her voice echoed, the ground trembled as she spoke.

'I am, little girl, what you might call a fallen angel. I have fallen to earth. It was a choice I made for succumbing to mortal desire. What I didn't realize was that fallen angels aren't allowed to live on earth, we must go to hell. And what I need to be protected from are the ones who keep trying to drag me into hell. And what you have in your womb is the one that will protect me if I stay close to it, it has your light and his seed which has my light. And the purity of the unborn.'

When she withdrew the light, I quoted a week's advance and she paid it without question. And that was that.

Rani

'By the will art thou lost, by the will art thou found,
by the will art thou free, captive, and bound.'

– ANGELUS SILESIUS

I RETURNED HOME WITH THE JADE PENDANT UNDER my kurta on the cord it was tied with, invisible to a casual glance, wreathed by my dupatta. The stray ginger cat who had adopted us mewed in greeting as I walked in through the gate, her saucer of milk was not put out. There was no one at home, I opened the door with my key.

'Channi,' I bent down to stroke her. 'Are you hungry? Did they all forget about you?'

She came up to me and curled around my legs, sinuous and warm, fur that stroked my bare feet as I slipped out of my shoes and put my home slippers on. Her eyes, as she looked up at me, were like the eyes of the woman who had put the jade pendant around my neck. Was it her? I had lost my mind, the past couple of days had made me lose my mind, there was no other explanation for the thoughts I was thinking.

Lachmi had forgotten to put the saucer out for her, so the first thing I did as soon I entered the kitchen was to pour out some milk from the fridge into the saucer and set it out. She lapped it up with a quick efficiency in a few seconds and then looked up at me with her yellow inexpressive eyes, demanding more. I poured her some more. She was the closest I would come to having a child, I realized. A ginger cat, one who had given kittens in a niche behind the kitchen some months ago and stayed back when all her kittens had grown and wandered off. I sat on the porch watching her with a strange relief that returning to what one considered one's normal brought about.

The Professor arrived an hour later, after I'd freshened up and set the house in as much order as I could after few days of neglect which left nothing askew except that which was visible to my own eyes. A hair grip that was not mine, wedged between the pillows and the mattress. I picked it up, it was a cheap one with fake diamantés on it, the kind one who seeks to draw attention would use. Had it been left there deliberately, I wondered, looking at it, noticing how the bedspread had been tucked in a trifle carelessly, hurriedly, a swift departure in the morning before the house help arrived perhaps. An indicator for me, I would think, to know that the bed had been used in my absence. I felt no jealousy, if anything I was relieved. The Professor had spent enough years reining in his desires because I wouldn't, I couldn't, let him consummate our marriage. I had been keeping him safe. Now I no longer cared either way after all these years.

If the Professor was perturbed that I'd come home a day earlier he didn't say a word, but just smiled with placid joy as I handed him his evening cup of tea when he returned from college that evening. I hadn't called. We were not the couple that called each other when apart. We were back to routine. His hadn't been unsettled. I'd smashed my life to smithereens and returned to collect and reassemble the shards.

'Did you manage to locate your sisters?' he asked, sipping his tea, reading the project submissions from his students, a messy pile on the dining table. I would take them to his study later just as they were.

'No,' I replied. 'I realized I didn't want to meet them when I reached. I didn't bother asking around for them. I just wandered around the old neighbourhood and then came home when I'd seen all I'd wanted to see.'

'Your old home is no longer there? Are the neighbours still there?'

'No. Everything has changed. Most people have moved out. Almost all the families in the lane have gone to Canada.'

He nodded, not taking his eyes off the paper he was going through. What had hovered around me all these years was no longer there in the same room as us; I could sense its absence, he couldn't. He had never even noticed it ever. Often one chooses not to see what one doesn't wish to see, it makes for peace of mind. I could see the absence when I looked at myself; no shadow followed me even in pitch darkness anymore, no shadow that had claimed me for its own, and used me like its plaything, no wind whipping around me, smoke and ash, even when the air was still.

The Professor, I realized, no longer looked at me like he used to, no longer the same man who had taken me in with no hesitancy, merely happy to have me with him. There was affection in how he treated me, but there was no longer love. Something intrinsic had shifted and I hadn't realized when this had happened, or how it had come to be. Had it been the years of familiarity which had eroded the longing for me that had consumed him when he didn't have me next to him, had having me with him and not being able to love me like a man should love his woman done this to us. He had also made out his will, something he had kept from me, which I had learnt on an off-chance when I had opened the door to his friend, a lawyer who practised in the sessions court and helped us with our documentation when needed, one morning a couple of months ago. He handed me a thick, important looking envelope.

'Please give this to Professor sahab,' he had said, politely declining my offer of a glass of water or tea. His gaze was cryptic, even sympathetic. Of course, I had steamed the envelope open. His will, signed and notarized, had left all he owned to his sister's children. I was not mentioned. I had never let him touch me or given him the children he'd hoped for. This was his way of paying me back for all those years of lying next to me in bed, backs turned towards each other. He didn't know that I never allowed him to touch me in order to keep him alive. Had he tried to consummate our marriage, he would have died. It would have killed him in a second, a death so excruciating that his soul would never wish to be born ever again. How do you tell your mortal husband that weeks before he had taken you for his mortal wife, something else had claimed you for its own, something that had never been born, would never die, something that was born of the fire of creation and would end when all the worlds ended.

I didn't speak to him of the will I had read, a will he hadn't spoken to me about, or about Bilkis Bi, and why I had sought her out, nor what I had experienced back there, in my hometown or even shown him the jade pendant that she had given me, the power it emanated in gentle waves, touching my skin at all times, a protection that I felt, a living pulsating egg of energy that now enveloped me. It was protection given to me by a being so powerful I couldn't even assimilate what she was and where she came from.

Bilkis Bi was back at her spot at the marketplace when I had visited her the next day after I'd returned to my hotel room, shaken and tremulous.

She pulled out a small stool from under the counter and made me sit next to her.

'Do you remember what happened yesterday?'

I didn't. I could only remember the swirling sky outside the windows, the lightning snaking into the room and rippling into the sickle she wielded, her body in a flash, naked, an old grey-haired crone, at the next instant a beauteous imperial woman of middle age, and the next a young pubescent girl, her breasts still buds, her pubic hair yet to grow. I could see the sickle in her hand unspooling something out of my body, a something that seemed like luminescent steam that pulsed and danced with a life of its own, and pushed into a glass jar. It felt like my head would burst and my body too. The next thing I felt was an all-enveloping darkness that gathered me to itself and flung me down through what seemed like a long draughty tunnel where I could only feel the whooshing of cold air as I fell through it.

And when I came to, with the feeling of something cold and wet pressing against me, I was back on the ground, lying on the floor of the shanty, which was no longer the majestic house I had entered, but just a humble, decrepit old house, crumbling to pieces, with the plaster falling from the walls, no furniture except a mattress on the floor, and a few small trunks stacked one on top of the other in a corner of the room. The dog that had followed us on the road and entered the house with us now hovered around my face, pushing his snout into licking my face solicitously. That was the wet and cold thing that had woken me up. I opened my eyes to his eyes looking into mine. If there is unquestioning love for a complete stranger, it has to be the one only dogs can give a human, a human they have met for the first time ever, and don't know if they will ever meet again in their life.

Sitting across me on the ground was Bilkis Bi, now in

the body of the old woman I'd first seen her as, dressed in the clothes that a street vendor would wear, faded, ragged, patched together with mismatched bits of fabric.

'Sit up gently,' she said. 'You might feel a bit strange.'

I did. I felt lighter, it was as if a burden had been taken off me, a weight I hadn't even realized that had been pressing me down had disappeared.

'It's here,' she gestured, at a bottle next to me. 'You know what this is, you had this before, you were careless with it. Take it with you. Put it in that trunk, the lock and key are right next to it. Don't ever open it, not even out of curiosity. Pass it on to another soon, don't let her open it in your presence.'

I nodded.

'You know where to find me. And when you do pass it on, bring me the pendant back.'

What she had managed to confine into a bottle and I'd then doubly secured within the trunk didn't fit into anything that we understood as space. The lock was iron. The lock could not be broken or opened without its consent.

Why this trunk, I asked her, this ordinary trunk of tin – who carries trunks around anyway? She laughed, a laugh that echoed in the emptiness of what we were traversing. This is an ordinary trunk, something that is so commonplace no one would think of stealing it from you. The pendant would protect me if it ever managed to wander out, but she had confined it to the trunk for now, and hopefully would stay within. The trunk was something I could not understand. I did not know what it was made of. Smelted into its alloy was sky iron that bound what it contained within its confines. All I knew was that I had not encountered it before, and at times it felt immensely light and at others it was too heavy even to be moved a millimetre.

It would pass on to whoever it chose, it would choose who could drag the trunk away. But even if what was within the trunk could no longer touch me, it was still with me in my house, and the clock was ticking.

'She will come to you,' Bilkis Bi had told me. 'I will send her to you and you will recognize her immediately. She will wear red and she will be a rose.' How would she be a rose, I wondered but had not the courage to ask. What Bilkis Bi had cleaved from me with her sickle up in the skies, she had rolled into a ball and put into a jar.

When Gulab approached me in the store I knew before I asked her name that this was the woman who had been sent to me by the fates. If she was the right one, the trunk would allow itself to be taken. If she wasn't, I would need to keep looking. There was nothing I needed to do but wait and watch, and let things unfold. They unfolded sooner than I had bargained for. All I had to do was hope.

That evening when she came home, I knew in my heart that this was the day it would unfold. When she left, dragging the trunk behind her in a daze, I did not stop her. Her memory of what she had seen, what she had experienced had been erased, all she would remember was that she had entered the house and taken the trunk from the basement. She would start forgetting herself, bit by bit, as I had, until I had finally remembered. Where she went with the trunk I did not know. I didn't ask, I didn't choose to try and find out. Time and distances meant nothing to what was in the trunk, it could return if it chose to, it would do that while it had attached itself to me, go back to where it had originally come to me from. Gulab was gone and with her the trunk, just a couple of days before six months were up from the time the trunk had first entered my home. She was a beautiful thing, Gulab, a rose who was still to bloom, bearing a fragrance of roses that emanated from her without her realising it. Sharp, fragrant, definite, not the artifice of attar or a rose-based cheap scent bought at a street store. It came from her, she wafted of roses, she fascinated me in a way that no man had ever fascinated me, reminding me of a woman who had touched me all those years ago, kissed me against a crumbling wall in my lane, and asked me to run away with her. A woman I didn't know, a woman who told me she would reverse the curse the crone had set on me, a curse I didn't know would begin taking effect immediately after I'd backed away in fear of what it meant, and what I felt for that woman who was nothing like any other woman I'd known then, and know now.

I needed to travel back to return the pendant to Bilkis Bi. I made up a story about having been contacted by someone who knew where my sisters now lived, and boarded the morning bus to my hometown. I would reach in a couple of hours, just in time for the market to open. I'd go straight to Bilkis Bi and catch the earliest bus back. I'd told the Professor I would return the next day. He hadn't baulked too much about my going away again, in fact he seemed almost glad to see me go. Perhaps it had been too much to expect fidelity when I offered nothing except my presence in his life.

At the old market, Bilkis Bi had not yet arrived when I reached. I found myself a spot in the shade under a spreading peepal tree that stood majestically fringing the pathway. The rays of the sun darted through the gaps between the leaves, slivers of light that swayed and darted around as the wind playfully brushed against them. It was a pleasant autumn day, a precursor to the colder days that would come.

The old man at the stall selling bangles opposite Bilkis Bi's had been watching me curiously. Finally, he decided to amble up to me. 'No point in waiting for her,' he said, revealing stumps of teeth sacrificed to a *gutka* habit. 'She won't be coming. Hasn't come here in over a month.'

I stood up. 'Has no one checked up on her?'

He shook his head to indicate a negative.

'Must have died in her sleep. When the body stinks, someone will complain to the garbage collectors if they pass by her hut.'

No one had bothered to check on her. She didn't need checking on, but that was something I knew, that she could more than take care of herself and anyone else she chose to take care of. I thanked him and picked up my bag. I would go to her house, or whatever it was that was her house.

Would I be able to find my way to her house, I wondered. Perhaps I just needed to go to the cemetery, I would know my way from there, the broken-down walls, the banyan tree that grew there, spreading its branches over much of the pathway, its roots hanging down to the ground like so many otherworldly tentacles in search of hapless souls to coil around and pull up. As I walked down the main road, a dog fell in step next to me, the same dog that had accompanied us the day Bilkis Bi had taken me to her home. After a while, it began leading the way, looking back to see if I was following it. So, I did. When I reached the cemetery, the morning light had already changed to the directness of the pre-noon. There was nothing ghostly or unearthly about this place now, not even the crumbling tombstones over the graves and the charnel house at the far end of the grounds for those hapless enough not to have their own individual resting space. I turned into the little pathway fringing the cemetery that led to Bilkis Bi's house. There was no membrane, no portal I had to step through this time. I could see the little hut at the end of the lane. The dog stopped and looked back at me, and then with a movement of its head that could be interpreted as a beckoning egged me to go up the pathway towards the house. It shrank back, refusing to go further.

'What is it?' I said, bending down to stroke it. 'Why won't you come in with me?'

It whimpered and took a few steps back.

'Okay,' I told him 'I'll go on ahead,' noting now, that

this was a male dog, hardy and street-wise, with a torn ear from what seemed to have been a savage street fight, and a pelt that was patchy and in need of a good hose down. He was a respectable street dog, one who owned his territory judging by the number of tree stumps he had marked along the way as we had made our way down here, and one whom the other street dogs gave a wide berth to as we passed. But here he was, whimpering in fear, refusing to go into Bilkis Bi's house. I squared my shoulders and walked to the door. I knocked. No one answered. I sat on the porch and waited. The pendant hanging down my neck suddenly felt hot against my skin, like a live coal. I pulled it out and placed it outside my kurta so it didn't singe my skin.. I had the sense of someone else sitting next to me, a shimmering vapid presence, I turned to look but there was no one there, just the sense of being drenched in moonlight and starshine. The hours passed, the shadows lengthened, I stood up and walked around to ease the cramps in my legs. My shoes, sensible slip-ons, were chafing against the back of my ankle despite the socks, my feet had swollen from all the walking and the sitting. How long should I wait, I wondered, when there seemed to be no clear indication of when Bilkis Bi would be back? I would have to come back the next day, there was no alternative. Perhaps she had gone off somewhere, a trip, something. There weren't any neighbours one could ask too, except of course, the residents of the cemetery whom I definitely wasn't going to ask, though I was sure they had something to tell me. I wouldn't know how to ask them anything. The dog skulked by the broken-down gate, running up and down the lane, in a frenzy and finally settled down, licking his paws, ready for a long nap. I stood up, what shimmered next to me raised itself as well. It was like a shadow presence, strands of light and dust motes.

I turned to look at it, and felt it turn towards me, echoing my movements, a mirror reflection of myself in what I could only describe as a shimmering shadow, a reflection of me that was nothingness except light. Nothing surprised me about what I would experience anymore at Bilkis Bi's home, not after all I had experienced.

'What are you?' I asked, surprising myself with courage I never thought I would have had. There was no answer, just the sense of a smile washing over me, a soft gentleness that was comforting. I was not afraid, this was a protective force.

The dog at the gate noticed me standing and stood up too, looking at me expectantly, perhaps sensing I was ready to leave. Something though told me to wait, I needed to wait. I sat back again on the porch. Hunger was gnawing at my stomach; I drank some more water, not too much, there was no toilet around and I didn't fancy relieving myself in the shrubbery, one could never tell if a snake would suddenly emerge and sink its fangs into my flesh. As the sun sank into the ground, shadows began uncoiling themselves from the tombstones and floated across to the dilapidated wall that demarcated the boundary of the cemetery, beyond the kachcha path. They hung around there, curious. Perhaps they had something to tell me, I thought, perhaps I should go to them. I rose again. Nothing seemed to frighten me anymore I realized. I had seen strange things and experienced even stranger things in the past so many years, things that regular people would be far-fetched to even comprehend or explain and I had survived it all. I walked up to the wall, seeing the wisps of light hover above, waiting for me.

'She's inside,' a voice inside my head told me. 'She's being held down by it.'

'By what?'

'It.'

They crowded around, glowing balls of light, some misty, some fierce, none like any human shape I could imagine.

'Go in,' said another voice in my head, more authoritative, more definite. 'Go in and save her.'

'What do I do? How do I save her? And what is *it*?'

'Don't look at it in the eye if it appears. And you must put water into her mouth. That's all.'

The dog skipped around my legs, impatient for me to get on with it. I rushed to the house, the door which I had assumed was locked, swung open at my touch. Within, the room was dark and a foul stench of the graves hit my nostrils as I entered, gagging me, almost making me retch. I could barely see anything right in front of my eyes. I pulled out my phone from my handbag and switched on the torch. The hovel was as it was the last time I had been there, humble and worn, the stack of tin trunks against one wall, the mattress on the floor against another. Lying on that mattress was Bilkis Bi, in what seemed to be a deep sleep, her hair grey, her skin wrinkled, her clothes arranged carefully around her.

Water, they told me to pour water into her mouth, I looked around desperately for some water by the light of the torch. In the corner of the room, on the floor, I could see a pot covered with a steel plate, a steel glass kept inverted over it. I reached out and picked up the glass, taking away the plate and put my hand in with the glass to fill it with water. Something within grabbed my hand and pulled it. I pulled back with all my strength and found myself lying on the floor from the rebound when what had grabbed my hand suddenly let go of me. I sprang up to my feet, decrying the fact that I was a little less agile these days, it felt like all the years that had not passed me had suddenly caught up with me all at once. Quickly putting the lid over the pot, I looked around for some water. There was the bottle in my bag, outside on the porch I remembered. I stepped out, grabbed it and ran back in. The door slammed shut behind me with a force. Whatever was in the *matka* had begun slithering out, a faint hissing sound that filled the silent room. I rushed to Bilkis Bi and opened her dry lips, they were rigid, locked into position. Something called to me from behind me, a susurration of sound that was both seductive and threatening at the same time, a sudden increase in the stench that was already pervasive in the room. I quickly poured a few drops into Bilkis Bi's lips, holding them open, praying to whatever God still watched over me to bring her back from whatever place she was locked in. The whispering from behind me grew louder, as did the stench. A voice called me, 'Rani!' a long forgotten, familiar voice, that of my mother. My head jerked back, involuntarily, when a hand rose up and turned it back to face the front, away from what called me.

Bilkis Bi sat up, looking to all purposes like she had just woken up from a refreshing afternoon nap.

'Whatever happens, don't come back. Get out of this room and wait outside.'

I stood up to go out, and the voice called me again. It was my mother, my poor mother who had never been able to defy my father all her life, and watched sobbing as I was sent off to another city in disgrace. She was dead, that I knew, and I fled out of the room, catching my breath only when I reached the gate. The lights hovering solicitously at the cemetery wall were comforting.

'You did well,' they whispered to me.

'Of all the people she has helped, you're the only human who came hunting for her.'

'She will be forever indebted to you.'

'She has been held down for months now.'

The shanty was eerily quiet and then it began to quiver and roar until it was shuddering uncontrollably like a person in the midst of an epileptic fit. And then there was a stillness, an eerie stillness that not even the occasional squawk of a bird returning to its nest could disturb. I walked gingerly to the porch and stood there, waiting, listening. The silence was loud. I could hear the thumping of my heart in my ears, the rush of the blood in my veins. I knocked at the door gingerly, there was no response. I waited, wondering.

Nothing moved, not even the leaves. I pushed the door open and went in. The room was rippling with a strange light, and sitting cross-legged on the floor in the middle of the room was Bilkis Bi but not Bilkis Bi. This was the one who had taken me to the skies and cleaved what had attached itself to me, this was the goddess or the demoness, whatever one chose to see her as. Her eyes were closed, her body radiated waves of light that were causing the shimmering in the room.

'Shut the door,' a voice inside my head commanded. I did so without questioning where the command came from. Her lips had not moved, her eyes had not opened.

'Sit,' the voice commanded. I sat, not knowing where to sit, across her, where she was with her eyes closed, hands in her lap, her body still and motionless, emanating waves of what seemed to be some energy I could not understand nor explain.

'Put your right palm out,' the instructions came from within my head, clear as a bell.

As I did, something hot and dry was put into my hand. I looked down at my open palm, I could see nothing, there was nothing in my hand.

I closed my hand around it, it felt like a hot coal and was singeing my skin but I could see nothing, nothing that I could even throw away. Bilkis Bi opened her eyes and looked at me, her eyes were dancing flames.

'Swallow it,' she said, and there was no refusing to what she commanded. I lifted what I could not see to my lips and put it into my mouth, feeling it burn my tongue, my palate and my throat as it slithered down my food pipe, into my stomach, settling itself there a hot coal I could not see but only feel, filling up my insides so I could no longer feel anything apart from the heat that was radiating from my stomach.

'Rani,' she said, her voice thunder and lightning and mountains smashing against the sky. 'You came at the right time. What had confined you had held me down for months. You now have part of me in you. That is the only way I can protect you. I need to find out its name, its full name. What I had been told was only part of its name, I could confine only part of it. I know that now. To find its full name, I need to go into the place it came from. Once I find its full name, I will have dominion over it and send it away. What I had cut away from you and confined in the trunk is only part of it. It cannot claim the body you passed it on to, that body bears a child in its womb and it cannot enter a body of such purity. The other half of it is roaming free. You need to be protected again.'

I looked at her, disbelieving, feeling my eyes burn. She put her hand on my forehead, tapping lightly until a fire rose within me and churned me into a pillar of flame.

'Go find it. The bottle. Destroy it, bury it deep within the earth, where no human will dig it up and find it, bury it with the trunk it is in. You cannot break it, you cannot burn it or fling it in the ocean. Just bury it in the earth. Pray that it is never found, never opened, that she hasn't flung it away yet. That is your only hope if you don't want to be taken over by it again.'

Noor

'How did I escape? With difficulty. How did I plan this moment? With pleasure.'
– ALEXANDRE DUMAS, *The Count of Monte Cristo*

IT WAS TIME. THEY WOULD ARRIVE ANY MOMENT, I knew it, I could smell it in the air, on the breeze, taste the sulphur with my tongue. The susurrations would soon begin in my ears, behind my eyeballs, in the folds of my brain. They would find me here, here would not protect me, there was no love here. Only an enforced togetherness through happenstance and duty.

I had been to the house some afternoons ago to speak with her, the girl they called Gulab. I needed her to let me into the house, willingly.

She was a tiny creature, would have barely reached a little below Teja's shoulders, but then he was massive, a tree trunk in flesh and muscle wrapped over bone. Anyone would be tiny in comparison. But though she was tiny, she was the stronger one of the two, that I knew. In her eyes was immense suffering, strength congealing into a paradoxical hardness and softness that existed simultaneously, a state of being that only another who has walked a similar path through hell could recognize because they had been that way too, and learnt to keep it hidden from the world. I recognized it even at a distance. I had walked through another hell, and emerged scorched to a cinder, my wings bruised and bloody.

We, the fallen, didn't choose to be human. We first came to earth as emissaries of the divine, guiding humans to be better, to make better choices, to deny the evil that tempted them, they were not meant to be tempted by evil. We stayed and then were tempted to find out why humans experienced the vacillation of emotions that meant nothing to us, what was it that roused such fierce passions within them, why would they do things that made absolutely no sense to their well-being, why did they need the body of another human so very much, what was it about flesh on flesh, touch on touch, why did humans copulate. I had been curious, I had succumbed thousands of years ago, touched a human male I had found exquisite, his touch made me flesh and his seed made me as human as someone like me could be. Once he had poured his seed in me, I had doomed myself to an eternity in flesh. He had been a scribe, his job had been to maintain the administrative records for the temples, he had been devoted to his God, the god of the scribes, I was the angel deputed to watch over him, to keep him awake as he wrote with his stylus on the clay tablets before they would be fired in the kiln, to take the stylus from his tired fingers and lay it aside, and blow a soft, fragrant wind on his face to lull him to sleep. I began by stealing into his dreams, and then getting bolder and bolder. One night I manifested to him in the flesh, and there on began my journey in skin. I became his woman, I sang to him in the day as he worked, hymns that I strummed on my lyre, hymns to gods and goddesses as capricious as humans were. And when he lived out his mortal life in skin and died, I went away for years to other towns and came back to a new generation of priests. It was only natural that a beautiful young woman with no family to claim her became the handmaiden to the moon god. I stayed in the divine bedchamber in the Great Temple. I was fed the best of foods prepared for the god, in the kitchen of the temple, to the northwest of the great temple complex, just off the main stairway. The priests who had chosen me for the divine sometimes thought they could use me for their pleasure. They were scorched when they touched me, and never reached out to touch me again.

Some sacrosanct nights, the moon god descended upon me. His wife hated me, I was amongst the most favoured of all his human consorts. But she was strong and powerful herself. The people sang hymns to her, hymns that are still sung to this current day. She knew, as he did, that I was not all of the flesh, that I bore within me the light. I bore him children. They were taken from me when they were born and given to childless couples to raise as blessings from the divine. I didn't know where they were, how far they had been scattered. He filled me with enough light to fuel me through generations and generations, until the invaders came and we all fled. I bore no child from human seed. The gods did not descend upon the earth anymore. Only we, the fallen, walked the surface for as long as we could, before we were dragged off to the hells of our choosing.

I walked down the road from the school through the main market and across the path that rose beyond the main road and twisted into the one that would lead to Rose Lodge that sunny afternoon. I could not stay on at the school I knew, already whispers about me had begun circulating amongst the staff and most of them had begun looking at me askance. Sometimes when I slept, my light spilled out beyond the closed door of my room and rippled around the corridor like the moonlight shimmering on the surface of a placid lake, luminous and disturbing, before I could draw it back within me. At other times, I got tasks got done in minimal time, raising eyebrows about how it was humanly possible for a person to mop an entire floor of classrooms in a couple of minutes. They did not know that time bent differently for me, things moved to my command, inanimate things, animate things. The whispers had begun and I could feel the growing unease. It would boil up soon enough, and the humans who felt threatened by me would hunt me down before the hellhounds came for me.

I asked Kishan Singh if he thought I could move to Rose Lodge since they were taking in boarders and lodgers. It would be safer to live with a family than to take a house of my own. I did not want to live at the convent anymore. He agreed.

'I wondered how it took you so long to decide to move out. You aren't of our kind,' he said.

I started in surprise. 'What do you mean?'

He laughed, shaking his head. 'You aren't accustomed to hard labour, that is obvious from merely looking at you. I was only wondering how long it would take you to give up the room at the convent. How will you pay for the room if you want to take up the lodging quarters?'

'I have some money saved up,' I replied. 'I have some jewellery I can sell.'

I saw the glint of lasciviousness come into his eyes for a moment when I mentioned jewellery. He fought it down. Humans were like that, they were all tempted, some resisted it, some let temptation take over.

What I needed was a room with windows that looked out to the sun, the moon and the stars, I needed my light to be fed by the light from the universe that touched the surface of the earth. I bent towards the light, the light fuelled me, even more than food did. The light could keep me alive in this, this fragility of human flesh, prone to degeneration and decay. I basked in as much sunlight as I could grab in the little snatches of time that I spent out of the convent, or when I was free to roam the grounds, feeding myself with all the light I could absorb. Humans did not realize just how much they were blessed with the light of the creator, all they needed was light. Food was what degenerated them, even if all they did was bathe themselves in sunlight, they would survive. I had always been pale, pale enough to be white of skin, with my hair black and long till my waist. Shut up in this windowless room I had become pearlescent, my glow had dimmed, I would fade away. The only company I had were the langurs that ran riot on the roof above, creating a ruckus that was only matched by hailstorms when they occurred.

'I'll drive you down there,' he offered kindly, I declined the offer. I could walk down there myself at a time when I was sure Teja was not in the house and I could speak with the girl alone. I didn't want his reactions to influence her decision. It had to be her free will that allowed me into the house. After all, wasn't that what humankind was about and why I had fallen from grace, the pursuit of free will, to do as I pleased, to sin as I pleased and to suffer as was mandated after I had done so.

The girl who had chatted with me the last time I'd watched from the thicket was not around when I went this time. Perhaps I had imagined her, but I knew with a certainty that I had not. Our paths would cross again if I lived in this house. We had already established tenuous boundaries of understanding, we would negotiate it further.

I carried nothing on my person right now, I would go back and get my bag if she agreed. If she didn't, I would take the next bus out of town and go elsewhere. This being confined to a physical body was limiting, to be encumbered by its corporality, by how fast one's feet could move, or by how fast whatever mode of transport one took could transport one.

When I knocked at the door, I knew she would lumber towards the door, her steps heavy and weighed down by the child growing in her belly. I knew that she would stop for a moment and catch her breath, holding on to the door jamb before she threw the door open. I did not know what to expect after that. I could feel my light growing as it absorbed the feeble rays of sun filtering through the clouds that rolled in and out, the walk up to the house would recharge me enough for me to last a couple of days or more. I needed light to fuel me like humans needed food and water.

The girl came out of nowhere and fell into step with me as I turned off the main road to go up the narrow path that led to the house. It sat at the end of the path, perched high above the town, at the very top of a steep climb and surveyed the range of mountains unfolding accordion-like in front like a watchtower to the heavens.

'Here you are again,' she said, after we'd walked a few steps together.

'Here I am again,' I replied.

'Don't I scare you?'

'There's only one thing that scares me,' I said. 'And that's why I'm here.'

'They are coming for you, but you know that.'

I did. I needed to shift my presence from there immediately, be taken into a house willingly and with love. Love would save me when nothing else would.

'I do. And I need to escape them.'

'Why did you choose this?' she asked.

It was a question I'd asked myself a million times over down the centuries. Why did I choose to be flesh, why had the passions of the flesh, being human, enticed me so much that I had chosen to give up all that I had been made for. And now, having tasted the pains and the passions of the body, did I yearn for them anymore at all? I did! The body was an exquisite machine, those of us condemned to live without its pleasures had no conception of the bliss something so base could bring. Copulation was the only gateway for every single human to glimpse a fleeting fragment of divine bliss. But human energy was powerful, immeasurable, they did not realize just how powerful. Some had, of course, down the ages, and they had tried to explain to humans just how that power could be harnessed. Humans misunderstood and made them divine, when they were just the messengers of the divine. The energy they had been gifted with, that lay coiled, waiting, unstirred at the base of their spines, waiting, at times for an entire lifetime, to be awakened. Most lifetimes passed in a human without them ever doing so. I helped some of them discover that energy, and then I took it from them, I fed on it, their energy, draining them, fuelling myself with it. Sometimes I thought I was an abomination, at others I told myself I was doing them a favour, giving them a glimpse of something they might have never experienced had they lived an entire life until the ripeness of senility and death. Perhaps that is why

I chose this, to live tremblingly on the brink of existence and danger forever and ever. To find nourishment, to be chased by danger.

She continued her questioning. 'You could have been invincible, unassailable. They would have never dared to look you in the eye. Now they hunt you down like the dogs they are.'

'I have no intention of letting them win. They haven't till now.'

She laughed, a laugh that tinkled merrily. 'Don't worry, we won't let it drag you off to hell.'

'I need to be accepted into the house by those who live there.'

'They will,' she replied. 'They have no option but to. There's already too many of us living there. You'll be just one more.'

What did she mean *too many of us*? I turned to look at her, but she had disappeared into the shimmering sunlight that struck the path and I was already at the gate. I pushed it open, noting the fresh coat of paint and the signboard fixed at the gate post, inexpertly painted and yet sincerely tacked onto the frame.

'Rose Lodge. Boarding and Lodging.'

The gate creaked a bit for lack of oiling and the invasion of rust, the creak carrying on the gentle breeze that blew in, announcing my arrival to the house, where Gulab was in the kitchen. She peered over the sink through the window at the gate. When I stepped on to the path leading up to the porch, I sensed the girl was now watching me from the branches of the oak that spread all over the fringes of the path, shading the house and the gate. I looked up and smiled at her, she smiled back. The *bhootni* of this lane. Why did the townspeople fear her so, I wondered, she was just a young girl, one who had died here, at this spot. I knew these things, it was something that being human had not taken away from me. I could sense the stories behind the people, even if they were disembodied from their skins. The *bhootni* was a confused soul; once I was settled here, I would help her go on her way, stuck as she was from the confusion of finding herself suddenly dead and anger over her child dying as well. She was waiting for her child, to take her child with her. Little did she know that her child had been pulled back to the between world, the world between lives. She was kind and benevolent to Gulab because Gulab was with child, it was the one thing that had saved Gulab and Teja from her wrath at what she now considered as her territory being intruded upon. Ghosts, like wild cats, were territorial. They did not like intrusions, by either humans or creatures that were not of this dimension. Gulab knew that too. And there was something else within the house, something restless, angry and biding its time. I could sense its presence and knew it had terrifying power of its own, but had been contained against its will. When it emerged, it would be roiling with rage.

It was trying to claim Gulab for its own, but couldn't. The child within her protected her, and the few times it did succeed in entering Gulab's head she lost herself, she was taken over. I could only call it a spirit spouse, the closest term I could give it, an entity that staked its claim over a human. It would attach itself to Gulab and suck her soul out of her, bit by bit, until she was just a shell of a body, a shell it could use to its pleasure and command.

Gulab opened the door as I knocked. When she gestured me to enter, I saw that the house was swarming with presences that humans would not sense unless they were consciously made aware. The *bhootni* was but one, the man who had owned the house and had been found dead in the ravine below was another presence, silent and foreboding, filled with regret and guilt, unable to leave this plane unless he found the redemption he sought. The third thing would be of no help to me, that I understood, it came and went as it pleased, angry at being cheated of something Gulab had no control over, yet unable to inflict any harm on her.

'We'll keep you safe,' the *bhootni* whispered into my ears, floating down from the ceiling and passing through me, a shock of ice through my body. 'You keep her and the child safe.'

It was a bargain I accepted; I had no choice.

I could sense them around as I sat in front of Gulab and felt her child within her react to my presence. All the unborn did, pure as they were of spirit, untainted with what growing up outside the womb would do to them. I reached out to it with my light, enveloping it in the embrace of the little I had left of the divine within me. It was joyous and accepting, the fledgling consciousness within her.

'Can I live here?' I asked her, my desperation dispensing with the pleasantries of initial conversation. 'I need a safe place to live in.'

She needed to welcome me with all her love, she had to. How could I make her love me with all the love she could give when she knew that I was the one the man she loved had been ready, at a moment's notice, to desert her for? How could I get her to accept me, except by enveloping her in my light and drowning her in the embrace of the little of the good and divine within me that still remained? And so I did.

'Yes,' she replied. 'I will tell my husband. You can stay with us. But…'

'I promise you I will not seduce your man, I walked away from him when I saw you and I knew,' I replied, voicing her fear. 'I will not allow him to touch me. He will no longer want to touch me in that way that bodies have when they want release.'

'I trust you.' She was fidgeting with the edge of her dupatta, her forehead was breaking out into a perspiration which was strange for this time of the year when the air was chilly enough to have folks begin to bring down their heavy woollens and their thick layers of *razai*s down from storage. 'You won't do this to me, not when I'm in this situation.' She told me how much it would cost me to rent a room for a month, and she would give me breakfast and, if I chose, a meal as well. Or I could cook my own with my own provisions. There was a week's advance to be paid. I did so.

It was a humble amount; there was no way a home would run on what they made from taking in boarders. Strange that they chose to do so when there was so much effort involved. There were no other boarders at the moment in the house, this was not a town that was geared to many tourists, and those that came did not choose to come so far out of the way to a small boarding house.

She placed her hand gently on the swell of her abdomen. I could sense the life within unfurling at her touch, reaching out to reassure itself that it would be loved, that it was wanted.

'I will come back,' I told her, 'I will bring my things and return later in a day or two.'

I went back to my room and told the matron that I wished to leave, and she wished me well and told me I would have to wait till the end of the month to receive my pay for the days I had worked, and was I okay with returning later to collect it. She was sorry to see me go but paradoxically also glad, there was a strangeness about me that made it difficult to keep the whispers about me down. I was sorry to go. She had been kind to me, a stranger who had been foisted on her doorstep by an acquaintance. Humans were like that, they could be immensely kind to strangers and unbearably cruel to their own.

The next day, I packed my single bag after my duties, and set off for the lodge, swinging my bag in my hand. The day was glorious, a pale autumnal sun shone over the hills, over the asphalt of the newly paved road, over the uniform sameness of the pines that arranged themselves politely in what seemed like velvety rows of green in the distance. The town had fallen away a long way back, and as I walked, the stray houses that clung to the sides of the road began thinning out as well, I could feel the air changing around me. The brightness of the day began dulling down into an ominous grey pall, suddenly heavy, weighed down with what felt like the crackling crispness of the static electricity before the clouds discharged it with a crack of lightning. A faintly sulphurous odour wafted in over the wind. I could taste it, smell it. I knew now without a moment's doubt that the doorway to the seven hells had opened again and the hounds had been unleashed, commanded to fetch me, for others like me.

They would be here any moment now, slashing through the layers of the dimensions and emerging onto the surface, sniffing me down, chasing me, their fangs dribbling acid, their maws craving flesh and blood and soul. They were here to make me them, to make me one of those who devoured those she seduced, to be the harvester of souls, it was a pact I would not make. I began chanting, calling out for help to the one who would come for me, who would save me, who would slash the earth and the skies with her blade and bring the starlight down to the earth to protect me.

There was nothing to be done but to run again, panting up the road, chanting continuously, sensing that which was loping across thousands of miles having emerged from the cracks they created on the surface of the earth, in pursuit of me, hoping I made it into the house that would shelter me, cocoon me with love and acceptance, and hope that I would escape again, find the time and space to breathe and live in the intervals of being almost human. Not an angel, not a demon, not human. What made me less of an abomination than those which had been chasing me down over the millennia? I was also, I knew, a monster.

Gulab

> *'But this was what happened when you didn't want to visit and confront the past: the past starts visiting and confronting you.'*
>
> – BRET EASTON ELLIS, *Lunar Park*

SHE WAS EXQUISITELY BEAUTIFUL, I REALIZED AS I looked at her up close, in a way that grew on you, feature by feature, and then you didn't see each feature for the beauty of the whole. You first noticed the skin, untouched by the sun or by the years, the firm arch of her thick brows, the liquid green-gold of her eyes, the chiselled imperiousness of her nose, the plump pink of her lips, and then all at once you couldn't take your eyes off her face. Now that I had sat opposite her, spoken with her and heard her out, I felt no envy, no resentment, no jealousy, no hatred. You couldn't hate her. You could only love her, in a strange way. There was no other way to describe her, she was love. That she was different was apparent when I first felt the light emerge from her – she wasn't like any other human I had ever known.

I knew the light, it was familiar, I had it too, though mine was nowhere as strong as hers was. It did not scare me, this difference, a difference that strangely enough made me want to protect her in a way I could not comprehend. She was vulnerable, she was sinking. Her light was getting feeble and she was being chased by creatures; she had not enough light to defend herself from. And yet, when she had drawn herself up to her fullest and unfurled all her light, my retina had protested. For a moment, after she'd shrunk it back to within her, I had seen only black.

The days were going to be short and dark soon, the nights would be long, wet and cold. I had a child growing within my belly which would emerge any time now, and I was losing time in a way I could not understand, time snatched from me in minutes and hours, bits and pieces of thievery that could not be explained, could not be replaced. I needed someone to watch over me. She could do it, I knew she would do it.

And did she say she was a fallen angel? Angels didn't exist, and fallen angels didn't walk the earth, they lived in the holy books and in the words of the storytellers who told us about them. We told ourselves stories about them to keep believing in them. Witches or goddesses who drank blood, ferocity incarnate of the divine feminine. I had heard of these, I had been to temples where these goddesses were worshipped. But I had never yet heard about fallen angels, and that they walked the earth amongst us humans. If she had the light in her, and I did too, did that make me one of them? Why did I have the light in me? Where had my mother found me, who had birthed me, was it one like her? Did that explain why I was able to see the things that others could not even sense around us, on this corporeal plane of existence? Was I a fallen angel too like she was, where had I fallen from, why did the light glimmer within my veins at times in the dark, in the night, when the lights were out? There were too many questions in my head.

The baby kicked in my stomach weakly, and then delivered a flurry of punches to the side of my abdomen, stretching the taut skin in fierce bumps that came and went, the contours of a land being made and unmade. Teja returned home in the evening, tired from a day filled with what I did not know. I realized, this man I had put myself in the hands of, had changed from the man I had met and taken up with. The rakishness that had characterized him when I had first met him had all but disappeared, in its place was a cautious weariness that now weighed his every step, his every word. He had become, I realized, a householder. As perhaps I had too. We had changed, and what had changed us completely was perhaps this child growing within me. We no longer lived till the next move, we had put down roots and were growing around it. We stocked enough groceries and provisions to last us for a month or two. What could be more indicative of us not planning to pick ourselves up and run at a moment's notice? My pride and joy were no longer what I'd managed to nick from a store with an unguarded storekeeper, but what I managed to stock in my pantry that would see us through being snowed in for a week. I was becoming one of those dreaded creatures, a house-proud woman. It was a depressing thought.

'What is for dinner?' he asked, a standard question he always asked me five minutes into the house. There had never been sweet nothings between us even in the early conversations we had had when we had just begun reaching out for each other's bodies, and now those too had disappeared, what remained was the grey sludge of the perfunctory, functional and precise. Of domesticity.

'What is for dinner?'

'We're out of rice and flour.'

'Pick up some vegetables on your way back tomorrow.'

'The tap in the backyard is leaking.'

'Iron my blue shirt in the morning.'

The love between us, if it had been love, was now the comfort of the quotidian. Passion had cooled down, he was terrified to have sex with a pregnant me in case something went wrong. The more I insisted, the more he withdrew from me. The one time I forced myself on him he couldn't get aroused no matter how much I tried with my lips and hands. I couldn't blame him, I was like a rotund ball needing to be careful around sharp objects in the event a poke would deflate me.

'Your body doesn't excite me anymore,' he had said, a hint of apology in his voice. I had swallowed my hurt. It would be okay once the baby was born and I went back to what I had been like, I told myself. And now, she was coming to live with us, she of the body so luscious that he still cupped the memory of her buttocks in his hands when he was drunk.

She had promised me she would not allow him to touch her while she lived here. She would keep her promise, and strangely enough I trusted her to keep her word, a woman I did not know at all and had spoken with for the very first time today. Would he be able to keep away from her, that I did not know? He would, if he knew what was good for him. He knew better than to anger me when I was already irritable with constipation and acid reflux, and not being able to sleep without nightmares.

'I had a visitor yesterday,' I began, uncertain of how to broach the topic.

'Hmm,' he nodded, still busy washing his hands and face at the small basin next to the dining table. I noticed the sky outside rumbling, turning dark and threatening, a curious orange-red glow coming from beyond the horizon, beyond where the white-dusted jagged edge of the mountains in the distance pierced the skies. The sun was setting in the west, a strange light was shining orange over the horizon in the east, and it was growing brighter and brighter, until the entire sky was lit up like a flame.

'I should pick up the washing from the line,' I said, rushing out as quick as my feet and my belly would allow me. The *bhootni* followed, hovering behind me, worried that I might trip and cause the baby harm in my undue haste. She was so protective of the baby, she might as well give birth to it, I thought uncharitably.

'Slowly, slowly,' she whispered into my ears. I slowed down, she blew the clothes down towards me so I just needed to gather them without needing to stretch myself. Why had the townsfolk been terrified of her, I wondered, she did nothing except stay on a plane which was no longer hers to stay on, and try to interfere in things which were none of her business. A curious stench floated in on the breeze, riding the orange light. The breeze was no longer soft and pleasant but had whipped itself up into a ferocity that roared in agony, a wail that pierced my ears, the air and the skies that contained it were being cleaved into half. I stood still looking around me, astounded by what I was seeing, something I had never ever seen all my life. Orange hellfire rising from the horizon and blotting out the sky, a crackling sulphurous odour, unmistakable and acrid, invading my nostrils, making me gag. She put her hand into mine, the *bhootni*, a cold clammy sensation of holding icy droplets of fog, and tried to pull me away from the clothesline. She couldn't, so she tried to propel me with all the energy she could summon. I was heavy now. She needed to summon up more energy.

'She will come now, the woman who came earlier to visit you,' the *bhootni* whispered into my ears. 'They have come for her, and she will come barefoot and barehanded. Get indoors, your child should not be out in the open where they can snatch it from you.'

'Who can take my child, who will come, what are you talking about?' She spoke in riddles sometimes, the *bhootni*.

I had forgotten what her name was when she was alive and if she took umbrage to the fact that no one remembered her name any longer but called her a *bhootni*, erasing all memory of her existence as a living breathing human before she had died, the child wedged in her birth canal, waiting to find her baby, to take it with her, little realising the child had gone back to where it had come from. That was motherhood for you. An eternal worrying for the child, when alive, and even when dead. I would know soon enough, I told myself. The air turned rancid in a way I could not explain, the stench of whatever it was suffusing it made me nauseous. The clothes I had gathered fell on the ground. I doubled over, heaving and shaking with the effort. The *bhootni* hovered over me, her feet a little above the ground rather than touching it, that's how I'd first realized she was indeed the *bhootni* who roamed the grounds and not a young girl who had wandered around seemingly without purpose. Strangely, I had never felt frightened of her.

I left the clothes on the ground, and summoned all my strength to rush into the house and pulling the door shut behind me just as the rain began pelting down, angry and insistent. The wind billowed the curtains at the windows. A deep rumbling began under the floor, deep under the floor, the earth itself began shaking, terrified of whatever it was that was now treading its surface. The *bhootni* withdrew in an instant, zooming to the rafters, unequal to confront whatever it was that was arriving. Teja ran upstairs to shut the windows left open there, while I went around the windows on the ground floor. The rumbling intensified until it was so loud it felt like an airplane taking off. The *bhootni* sat on the rafters swinging her backwards turned feet frantically, she was in a panic. The sky outside was orange flames. The gates of hell had opened.

'She's here,' she said. 'They're following her. Don't let them in.'

Then she called. Her voice, trembling with what seemed to be both exhaustion and fear. 'Teja,' she called, panic shredding the syllables into splinters of fear that pierced my ears, 'Open the door. Please.'

A growling came from the distance, sending shivers down my spine. The floor vibrated with the aftershocks of what seemed like footsteps being taken by something huge. Something heavy. Something the earth could not bear on its surface. Whatever was out there, I wanted no part of it.

Dread clutched my heart and squeezed it hard. What if, just what if, it was not her, if it was something pretending to be her. The rapping at the door became a desperate banging with two hands, hands that undoubtedly would be bleeding now.

'Teja, Teja,' she called, over and over.

I put out my hand to stop him, fear taking over me, and a selfishness I could not explain.

'Don't open the door,' I cried, panicking at what we could let into the house if the door opened.

'I can't leave her out there,' he replied quietly, his

eyes anguished and pleading in a way I had never seen them before. I took my hand off his arm and stood aside. Hadn't the *bhootni* warned me she would be here and that I should take her in, and what would I do if I sought refuge somewhere and no one gave me refuge? Sometimes I could surprise myself and be unselfish, this was one of them.

He strode to the door and threw it open. Noor stumbled in, falling down on the wooden flooring, as she pushed the door shut behind her with trembling hands. Her palms were bleeding, her feet were bare and bleeding. She was drenched by the rain, shivering with the cold and fear. The growling outside increased in volume, like the very bowels of hell were being torn apart and all the creatures of the netherworld had emerged slobbering into this world. The skies growled, lightning cut through the darkness at precise intervals with fierce silver stabs that cut through wood and rock, thunder followed swiftly, rolling down the clouds clumsily onto the mountain sides, making the trees quiver and the ground throb. Then there was a sudden silence, a silence so thick that it was not merely the absence of sound, it was the absence of every single thing in the universe that kept it alive. It felt like we had been immersed into a bubble, a vacuum they called it, the absence of air that kept space soundless. Teja brought a bowl of water and a towel and began gently cleaning the mud and blood off Noor's feet with a reverence I had never seen before. There was a knock at the door, a hesitant, gentle knock, one that came perhaps from one who was unsure of the welcome that awaited him or her. The *bhootni* floated down from the rafters and peered out of the windows.

'It's them,' she told me. She looked terrified. It terrified me to see the *bhootni* terrified.

'Who?' I replied. Teja looked at me strangely, he had still not got used to me talking to the *bhootni* since he couldn't see her. Noor could.

She replied to the *bhootni*, her voice lilted liquid music even when she was terrified, 'Yes, it's them. Don't open the door, Teja.'

Teja stood up and went to the window from where he could glimpse the porch. 'Oh no, it is a child, no, it's two little children. We can't send them away, if they get drenched and die from pneumonia, or from an animal attack, it will be a sin on our heads. In this strange weather too.'

Noor stood up, on feet that seemed unable to take the weight of her body. Then she drew herself up, drawing up reserves of strength that she had forgotten existed within her. Was she going to flash her light again, I needed to get Teja's dark glasses if she did.

Her voice, when she finally spoke up, was old and otherworldly. 'They aren't what you think they are and if they enter the house, they will devour all of you, and take me where they have been commanded to take me. This time, when I ran I gave them no sacrifice, I couldn't end the lives of anyone who wasn't waiting to die. They will take your lives as sacrifice. Your unborn child might protect you and me, but I can't guarantee that.'

He looked at her, trying to make sense of what she was saying. 'I can't understand what you're saying, but I can't let those children die out there.'

I couldn't understand it either, but I stood in front of the door, making an ineffectual barricade of my body.

'You can't open it,' I told him, 'For the sake of our child, you must not.'

Noor came up to us, wincing with each step, putting her ear to the door, mumbling something to herself under her breath.

She was now, strangely, larger than all of us, while still of the same height, radiating a living pulsing cocoon of light from her that rippled and pulsed, a soap bubble so huge that it completely enclosed her within, it reached out to me and wrapped itself around my womb. Teja stood his ground, unsure of all that was strange now unfolding around him and of what his response should be.

I could sense all that was within the house emerge from their corners and mass up in front of the door, adding their layer of protection to whatever it was that stood outside. The *bhootni* hovered before me, anxious and protective, something else, it felt like a gust of wind, encircling me, the light from Noor rooting me to one spot. I felt like I was enclosed in a steel capsule, where nothing could touch me. The baby within me sensed my anxiety, it kicked hard, so hard that my breath caught in my throat and bile rose up into my mouth.

The knocks came again and with it a piteous call, a child's voice. 'Please let us in.'

'Whatever it is,' Teja said. 'We can't let these children die because of our selfishness.'

We could see them through the glass panes that framed the main door, their outlines blurry with the frost, and shimmering as though there was heat emanating from them, a heat that sizzled when it touched the cool air outside.

They stood at the doorstep, waiting to be invited in, drenched and shivering. It was then that I noticed it, their eyes had no whites. Their faces were waxen. They were facsimiles of what creatures imagined children were. They were not children.

Noor moved to stand in front of me, her back ramrod straight, her eyes gleaming with a strange light I'd never seen before. She put her hands on my shoulders and spoke in a voice that was high and strong, it bounced off the walls of the room and resounded in my ears.

'These are not children. They are the soul collectors from the seven hells. I have to confront this, I'm tired of running, I've been fleeing them for centuries, and it still won't stop,' she said, her voice firm and resolute.

'Let me open the door, Teja,' she said, turning around to where he was at the door, the *bhootni* and the ghoul already standing in position next to him, not allowing him to budge the latch in order to open it.

'Listen to her, Teja,' I said, 'This is not what you think it is, these are not who you think they are. Let her deal with them.' And I was back to being selfish. My unselfishness could only last so long.

The woman who called herself Noor pushed him inside with one swift jerk, like he was of no strength to her. He was stunned with how easily she flung him to the other end of the room, with just a casual grab of his hand, and lay against the wall, shaken and breathing hard. She threw the door open.

'No matter what happens,' she said loudly to us. 'You will not step beyond this threshold.'

At that exact moment, the skies split open with a thunderclap that threw me to the floor with its force, the brilliance of a thousand suns bleached out the red skies into a white so painfully bright I could not look into it. I saw an old woman walking straight down from a beam of light into Noor, an old woman, unclothed and wrinkled, her white hair down to her knees, her breasts hanging, her skin crumpled like a set of clothes removed and flung onto the bed, a hooked blade in her hand and her eyes brilliant and sparkling blue like the stars of the universe had settled within them. I blinked. There was nothing. Then I saw Noor put her palms out upward and stand within the threshold of the house, blocking us from them with her body which slowly began to grow taller and wider until she blocked the entire doorway with her presence. Both her hands were raised, palms facing upwards, a shimmering pale light streaming from her fingertips towards the two shivering children who stood there, looking perplexed.

'Go,' she said, her voice suddenly a million years old, the weight of the stars in them, imperious and commanding, her language alien to me, but somehow words that made sense as they hit my eardrum. 'You cannot take me with you. I refuse to come. You have no entry to this house that has offered me shelter, the ones who live here have not invited you in, and will not invite you in.'

The children outside looked confused and dazed as the light poured over them and then they began screaming, piteous screams of terror.

'What is wrong with you?' Teja yelled. 'They're children.'

She extended her hands towards the children and the light from her body poured out towards them, they stepped back, changing, morphing, right in front of our eyes, elongating, growing, becoming something grotesque, snarling, slobbering, with jaws that opened to reveal sharp fangs that were longer than our arms and a vile acridity that suddenly fouled the air we were breathing in, suffocating us with an unbearable noxiousness.

'Bring out your souls, boy,' she told Teja without looking at him. 'Open the bag in their faces.' Her voice was the voice of the crone at the railway station, Bilkis Bi.

He gasped in horror, and then decided not to question what was being asked of him. He ran into the bedroom, returning with a faded blue duffel bag that he unzipped at the door, and fizzy pops of light zipped out of it only to be gobbled up by the cavernous maws of the creatures at the door. All of them, all the souls he had collected all these years, offered to these harvesters of the evil and the fallen.

'Go,' she repeated, her voice high and clear and deep and

resonant and old and young all at the same time. 'We have given you souls to take back.'

Go, she commanded them by their names, names that were as ancient as creation itself, names that would not be repeated dare one try, names that the human tongue could not call out for fear of atrophying and falling off, names that could make those who owned them be under the command of the one who had power to utter them. They winced as though a blow had struck them. Names only a goddess could speak without being overpowered by the power they contained.

She pulled her hands back with great effort and a blade materialized in her right arm, sparks of blue and white fire skittered through it.

There was a flash of intense white light, so intense that everything was bleached into nothingness when it ended. Blackness swarmed in front of my open eyes, a deep, welcoming blackness that I wanted to sink into. I felt myself slammed to the end of the room with the force of what could only be a sonic boom or a blast pushing my still body to the wall and then the entire house shuddering with the impact, trembling with the waves of the aftershock. Then there was nothing, just an inky blackness, a blackness so deep that the entire world was obliterated. And there was nothing, nothing, just me curled up deep within myself, searching for a place in my mind where I could be safe and nothing could ever harm me or my child.

Teja

'I am inhabited by a cry.
Nightly it flaps out
Looking, with its hooks, for something to love...'

– SYLVIA PLATH, *Ariel*

TEJA KNEW SHE WAS HERE IN THIS TOWN WAITING for him – why else did he book tickets to this nowhere town where the foothills straggled up to the mountains, where the sky poured clouds into the land and where the roads touched the skies if one climbed further and further to the north, where the high wall of rock and ice plateaued out to become the roof of the world?

It took a while for him to track her down, but once he did, he kept a constant eye out for her. It was strange how she did not realize he was around her, watching her, waiting for her to reach out to him. For all that he stood out in a crowd when he chose to, Teja knew the art of blending in too, it was essential in his line of work. He lurked, he watched, he saw her go in and out of the huge gates of the school campus when she had time to herself. He saw her sitting on the stone wall that circled the campus, her expression vacant and pensive at the same time, the light from her dim and ragged at times, glowing and pulsing with energy at others. He followed her at a distance when she walked through the main market, going into stores, haggling with the vegetable vendors, picking the freshest fruit on display. He ached to go up to her and take her in his arms, hold her tight against him, to feel her body respond to his and his to hers, to be enveloped with what he could only define as the warmth of her, a warmth that washed over him and erased every fear, every anxiety, every worry he had. Teja saw her picking up strangers in the marketplace and taking them with her where she thought no one would see them, he realized that was how it was with her. It wasn't a lack of morality, it was a physical need and he could have no expectations of her following a moral compass where the body and the partaking of its pleasure was something to be rationed out between human beings, and that too only when socially sanctioned by what they called marriage.

He felt like a newborn when he was with her, nothing mattered except him and her. Would he approach her, would he tell her he had followed her here like a lovelorn pup, or would he keep his distance and wait for fate to bring them together again? Teja had chosen to walk away from her, he had no grounds to approach her again. Having her close at hand, where he could watch her was soothing to him in a way that perhaps even having her in his arms wasn't. He was going to be a father now, and he had to keep his allegiance to the woman who was bearing his child. But the heart, it follows its own beat. The body he could control. The heart he could not.

Noor had come into Teja's life one lazy summer afternoon when he was still in college, going into his final year for a degree in commerce. He had grand plans for himself, as did his father: he was going to graduate, sit for his civil services examination, or move to a big city, work for a couple of years and then do his management degree. He had been preparing for a while, he had the brains and the ambition for it. But then life has its own way of humbling one, of shifting one on to another path far removed from the path that one set for oneself. Two things came his way to shift him on to a path he would have never envisaged for himself.

Teja remembered every moment of that late summer afternoon. He was on his way back home from an intercollegiate football match with his classmates, sweaty and grimy, every muscle in his body sore, forcing himself to trudge through the spiralling crash post the endorphin high of the match. They had been dropped off by the bus at the main chowk and walking towards their respective homes, turning off as each neared their homes; Teja lived the furthest from the college. Soon he was alone, holding the dirty ball under his arm, in his custody for the day since all of them had felt rather lazy to go back to college and put it back in the locker.

As he turned off the main road to go into the warren

of lanes that led to his lane, a woman crossed his path. She was going in the opposite direction, and he barely noticed her till a waft of fragrance hit him, the fragrance of a thousand roses, bittersweet and overwhelming, and he was overcome with an inexplicable need to follow her, to touch her. He found himself walking behind her, much like a roadside Lothario, and paradoxically horrified at himself for following an unknown older woman down familiar streets where people he knew could report back to his family that he had been up to no good. His mother would have hit him with her slipper, his father would have taken the cane to him.

Teja hadn't even seen her face but he was following her like a man possessed. Perhaps he was. She gave him no indication that she had noticed him following her, as her steps neither sped up, nor did she look over her shoulder at him to check if indeed he was following her. Teja followed her through the deserted by-lanes, through the busy marketplace lined with the parked two-wheelers, the fruit stalls, the cyber cafes and the shops selling woollens and rip-offs of branded shoes and bags. He walked behind her for what seemed like hours, past the main chowk where a fenced off podium in the middle of a crossroads had a statue of a freedom fighter who had laid down his life during the independence struggle. He was remembered fondly twice a year during the official flag hoisting ceremony on Independence Day and Republic Day, when he would get a hosing down to remove all the encrusted pigeon droppings and a garland or two put on him by the local MLA. The old squat constructions in the cramped marketplace were being replaced by glass-fronted commercial buildings with study classes for various important examinations being conducted in most. Engineering entrance exams. Medical entrance exams. Railway jobs. Banking jobs. Civil services. Preparatory examinations for the MBA entrance. Training them to ace the examinations and the interviews so they could get the prestigious seats in the institutions they hoped for and jobs with promotions at regular intervals and a pension. The young of the town, including Teja, had hung all their hopes on to entrance examinations to get them out of the town and the rut that living here would invariably crumple them into, making them sun-hardened and soul-cynical. He would enrol in one of these classes too, he had decided, once he completed his graduation. Civil Services he had set his heart upon. He would sit for all the exams he could.

Walking past them, she seemed ordinary enough in her light pink cotton salwar kameez, with nothing to set her apart from the other women around, except a strange radiance that seemed to envelop her and the fragrance of a million roses pulling him behind her. They crossed the old market and turned off into the road approaching it from the other side. She stopped at a stall and chatted with an old woman, who was selling some trinkets with a strange camaraderie that seemed unusual for a woman of her bearing.

She walked down lanes and then to where the old

cemetery was, fringed by a broken wall and a spreading banyan tree. Around him, the late afternoon slipped into dusk as he followed her. The shadows lengthened and then deserted them, night spilled over, vehement in its insistence on erasing all light. The late onset of darkness in the summer had tricked his mind into believing it was still just early evening. It was almost dinner time. His mother would have started making food. She would have kneaded the dough for the *phulka*s, waiting for his father to enter the house, wash his hands and feet, change into home clothes and sit down on his charpoy.

The woman seemed to have a clear idea of where she was headed, and that he was following her wherever she was headed. The wall leading to the cemetery had crumbled in spots, perhaps the work of vagrants and loiterers. She slipped through a gap in the wall. Teja followed, curious. She stood in the niche between two crumbling boundary walls, her face expectant; she knew he had been following her, he had been stupid to assume otherwise. He stood perplexed at a distance, unsure of what his next step should be. She beckoned him and he went up to her. She reached out her hand to his groin and stroked him, no ambiguity, no coyness. Within seconds, he had unzipped himself, her salwar was on the ground and he was thrusting frantically into her while she stood against the wall, one leg raised and wrapped against his buttocks. Who would see them in cemetery except the dead?

It became a regular occurrence. She would be waiting

for him at the wall inside the cemetery, and he would go there at a fixed hour after his lectures. Then she began taking him to a deserted, rundown house down the rough path just beyond the cemetery, where the door was falling off the hinges, where the bed creaked with every movement. The place smelt like the cemetery it faced, as decayed and mouldy as the graves lying within, uncared for, unvisited, the dead within now forgotten and left to decay in peace. But once she entered, it was like a thousand roses bloomed. He would never be able to smell a rose again for years after without his heart constricting painfully at the memory of her.

She shared nothing about herself, except her name. Noor. Light. Radiance. It was an appropriate name, Teja thought, as she emanated a kind of light that at first he thought was a figment of his imagination but soon understood it really existed and enveloped her in a cocoon – and when he touched her, it enveloped him too, a light that was wave upon wave of never-ending bliss, such joy that he fell into it entirely, like falling into a sea of happiness.

It began affecting Teja inexplicably, he began losing weight. His mother noticed it first, his gaunt and hollow-eyed look. She worried, the boys around were known for needles and substances that at first gave you bliss and then sapped the life out of you. She gave him no money, checked his pockets carefully, examined his arms for evidence of needle pinpricks, checked his eyes to see if his pupils were dilated, his lips to see if they were changing colour. When she was convinced Teja wasn't on something she began forcing him to eat more, an extra paratha layered with homemade butter onto his plate at breakfast, added extra paneer bits into his bowl, put cream into his glass of lassi, put ghee on his *phulkas*. Teja's sisters laughed at how she was intent on fattening him whilst simultaneously railing at them to eat less lest they bloated out like buffalos and would be impossible to get married off.

It was one of his college friends who told on Teja; he followed him to the hovel and told his mother, who then told Teja's mother. Teja was sent off to the next town where his paternal uncle lived, with a transfer letter from his college. He stayed with them, a huge *kothi* where he was lucky enough to have a room to himself on the top of the house, but unlucky enough that this meant his comings and goings would be monitored by his grandmother who sat in the middle of the courtyard in the mornings and evenings, running the household with her sharp words and cane. One day, he went back to the marketplace where he knew the old crone had her stall. Could she tell him where Noor lived, he pleaded with her?

She shook her head, looking at Teja with what could be sympathy in her eyes. 'She's gone, I don't know where though.'

'Did she say anything to you before she left?'

'Why would she? She owed me nothing, she used my home, like she used you and all the other boys before you.'

She was talking nonsense, the old crone. Noor had loved

him, of course she had. She had loved him with a passion that was not of this earth. The realisation dawned on Teja like a lump of coal hitting the side of his head. Perhaps she herself was not of this earth.

The old woman saw the realisation hit his eyes and laughed, her eyes suddenly shining like the brilliance of a galaxy of stars, her voice deepening and taking on new authority that she had never displayed before.

'Didn't you realize what she was, young man? All those times you were pouring your seed into her without thinking about why a woman as beautiful as her would sleep with you, an ordinary boy? Did you not wonder who she was, where she came from and why she would never give you more than her first name?'

Teja had no reply, he waited for her to tell him what it was that he hadn't figured out.

'She's not human, son,' she said, the expression in her eyes unchanging. 'She is not a woman you should obsess over. She needed to use young men like you to stay alive. It is not her fault. It is what she needs to do in order to survive. It is what she is, like the lion must kill the deer in order to survive. Perhaps she went away because she wanted to save you. It would have cost her, cost her a lot to detach herself from you before she drained you of life.'

A shiver racked his entire body. Now he knew why he had been wasting away, day after day, over the past couple of months. But even after he had been told what she was, Teja knew that should he come across her again he would not be able to keep himself away from her even if it meant he would die in the process. He would see her in every similar silhouette walking away in the distance, every thick brow, straight nose, undulating hip. He would follow the promise of her, and stop, realising it wasn't her. He would nurse his disappointment with alcohol and get on with the business of living a life where he was never cocooned like he had been with her ever again. And then it happened, what was going to change the trajectory of his life yet again. Teja could never go back to being a student again, he became a hitman, a collector of souls.

Rani

'We are all held in the same captivity, and those who have bound others are themselves in bonds – unless you think perhaps that the left-hand chain is lighter.'

– SENECA

THE UNSEEN FLAME BILKIS BI HAD MADE ME SWALLOW settled in my stomach, spreading its fire through my body, burning me alive day and night. To all outward appearances I was just the same, nothing had changed about me, except that I was now me, just me, nothing stayed attached to me, perhaps just a bit of spectral being. I went back home to my husband, took up the threads of the life I had toyed with, abandoning for a brief moment of abandon, sinking right back into the morass of domesticity like I had never put an arm out desperate to be rescued. If thoughts of what would now happen to Gulab and why Bilkis Bi had told me that I was not completely rid of it haunted me, I swatted them down. I would be abnormal not to worry, the fear haunted my every waking moment, that it would return, that it would enter me again, take me over, toy with me, make me its puppet.

Youth and beauty were what it preyed on. I had no more of youth, and soon I would begin unravelling into the senescence that my body had long been protected against… it would begin with a strand of silver in my hair, skin that fell from the bone.

'Find her, find the trunk, make sure it has taken over her,' Bilkis Bi had told me. 'Your salvation depends upon it. If it hasn't, abandon it on the streets. Throw it into a river. Throw it down a ravine. Put it on the luggage carrier of a bus going in the opposite direction from you. Set it out into the universe and let it find its next victim. If you don't, it could come right back to you.'

This was a task I was unsure if I could carry out to completion. I had no idea where Gulab had gone with the trunk, I had just been happy to see her walk out of the house dragging it behind her like a marionette, her strings being pulled by the unseen entity within the very trunk she trailed behind her. I spent the few days after I had returned asking around where Gulab and her brother had lived. A shopkeeper had seen her hurrying out of my lane carrying a trunk. She had hailed a cycle rickshaw for the bus stand, he told me. At the bus stand I asked around if they had seen a young girl dragging a tin trunk a few days ago. Perhaps she had been accompanied by a man, I didn't know what he looked like. I showed them a photograph I had clicked of her on my phone when she had visited us, a photograph

I had clicked surreptitiously, her head down as she sipped her tea. The tea stall owner next to the ticket counter told me that the older brother had embraced a woman for a long, long while, it was almost indecent, he muttered. That woman left first on the bus going to a small hill town some five hours away. The girl and the man with her had taken a bus going to the same town many hours later. They had sat at his tea stall in grim silence, he recalled. The girl had told the man that she was pregnant, loud enough for the entire bus depot to hear, that's how he remembered them, and then they had sat in silence for hours. Yes, she had been dragging a small tin trunk. Who was the woman who left before them and why had they followed her to the same town I wondered. These were questions I would have to find the answers to myself if I could.

The very next day, I caught a bus to the same town. I had no idea of how I would trace them, but I needed to try. The Professor had begun to be a trifle perplexed about this constant coming and going of mine, but he hadn't asked any questions, thankfully. There was a sense of resignation about him, one that did not probe too deep. Perhaps it was indifference. I did not know. I would not ask. I would do what I needed to. Sometimes I thought I should end it all. Death would be the solution to this lifetime of misery, but then I wondered if death would truly be release or whether it would mean walking into an eternity of even more misery that lurked behind the dark veil of not knowing.

Getting off at the destination I began asking around

again. The tea stall and the taxi drivers outside the ramshackle bus depot looked at me curiously, a lady with no luggage out of an interstate bus, asking around about a young girl with a trunk who had reached the town a month or so ago. One of them came forward; Kishan Singh, he introduced himself.

'They have something of mine I need to get back.'

He eyed me speculatively, perhaps wondering if it was worth his while to help me to get whatever it was back. 'I can take you to where they are right now,' he offered. 'What is in it for me?'

'I can pay you.' I named a sum so exorbitant his eyes almost popped out.

He would have sold his firstborn for the amount I promised to pay him. I gave him some cash as a down payment for his efforts. It made him servile and obsequious. That's what money did, it bought you all that you couldn't hope to get with an honest appeal to reason or emotion.

The taxi driver took me through a long and narrow road which crossed the main part of town, went away from the thicket of homes piled one on top of the other, then thinning out and scattering across the edges of the mountains, and then turned off upwards into the higher reaches of the mountains. He finally turned off the main road, and the circuitous offshoot of the road ended at what looked like a path, and the thicket obscured what was at the end of the path. A young girl stood where the path turned off, her arms on her hips, staring curiously at me, her expression bemused. Her clothes were ordinary, a faded salwar kameez, a hand-knitted woollen vest that was more darned than of the original wool it was made of. She couldn't have been more than eighteen, poised at the threshold between burgeoning adolescence and the self-awareness adulthood. She smiled at me all of a sudden, a smile that was radiant with beauty, a beauty that was otherworldly and surreal. Her eyes piercing and dark, her skin pale and milky in contrast with none of the freckles that characterized most faces in these parts. I stopped in my tracks.

'Who is that girl?' I asked Kishan Singh, who looked at the path with a blank expression, not registering anything.

'There's no one there, madam, you must be mistaken.'

'Of course, there is,' I replied, raising my hand to point. 'There's this young girl standing right there looking at us.' I turned to look, but there was no one there now.

'Anyway,' he said. 'The house is right there, you have to walk up the path. I'll go and eat some lunch at home and come back in an hour for you. An hour will be enough, won't it?'

It would, I assured him, and thanked him for getting me here, telling him I would be waiting there for him at the spot where the road branched out into the steep uphill forked path, a path that no vehicle could climb. My handbag, a brown branded leather one, clung precariously to my shoulder as I navigated the steep climb on slippers that were unsuited for the slippery path, damp with residual fog and rain on a day that was not quite sunny and not quite rainy.

The girl was nowhere to be seen, the girl with skin like milk and the smile that was insolence. I walked past where she had been standing, wondering whether I would slip, which would mean a broken ankle. I felt I was walking through something, something that was a block of ice and yet air. I hadn't carried along warm clothes, and what I was wearing was inadequate. Only the heat from the lump of coal I had swallowed, which had lodged itself in my chest, kept me alive. I found my body stopping of its own volition as the iciness seeped in through my ears, my nostrils, my mouth, encountering the blaze within my chest and then blazing into steam that emanated through my nose.

'Do you think it will let you reach the house?' a voice asked me. I looked up and she was standing there, arms on her waist, strangely intimidating.

'How do you know about it?' I replied.

'I know about it from it,' she replied, suddenly leaping up from the path into the branches of the huge spreading oak. She sat there, looking down at me, swinging her feet. Her ankles were turned backward. I felt the bile rise in my throat.

'It will stop you. It knows you're here.'

I clutched my neck where the pendant had been, then realized I had returned it to Bilkis Bi. I had nothing now that would protect me. I had what burned within me. Perhaps I was still safe. I heard his voice in my ear.

'Did you think you could get rid of me so easily, Rani, after all I've done for you, all the time I spent with you, a lowly human?'

I closed my eyes, took a deep breath, and then I felt him all around me, searingly hot, a gust of wind that whipped itself around me, singeing my skin, the acridity of burnt leaves and wood entering my nose, the weight of his ownership pressing down on my shoulders. I was not free. I had never quite been free of him.

He was here, roaming around outside the trunk in a complete fury, unable to enter me because of what Bilkis Bi had put into me. Unable to enter Gulab because of the child in her womb. He was angry, very angry. I had to get to the trunk.

I took another step, my feet strangely and suddenly leaden, the sheer effort of just lifting them off the ground making me wince. The ground below my feet itself changed, becoming sludge and molasses, the mud a swamp, sucking me in. I felt myself sinking in, deeper, deeper and I saw myself walking past me, over the me sinking into the ground, unaware that I was sinking, sinking, sinking into something I could not extricate myself from, a quagmire that was fetid with the sulphurous stench of something that was beyond anything I had ever experienced before. The path closed over me. There was pitch darkness and a heat that seared me. My knees sagged with the weight of the fetid air, I fell to the soft floor of whatever this was that I was entombed within, gasping for breath. Around me everything bubbled with the heat and I could see pinpricks of redness glowing all around. Millions of eyes waiting, watching, eyes belonging to creatures I could not see in the darkness.

Noor

> *'You're trying to escape from your difficulties, and there never is any escape from difficulties, never. They have to be faced and fought.'*
>
> – ENID BLYTON

I NEVER KNEW I HAD THE STRENGTH IN ME UNTIL I summoned it up. All it boiled down to was the strength to resist what I had always assumed had been fated for me, an inescapable fate that I would need to keep constantly running from in order to survive. But that moment standing in the front room of that little cottage, a terrified young girl heavy with child standing next to me, carrying the child of a man I had once, many years ago, used as fodder to keep me alive, to keep me human, I knew that this was not what I wanted when I'd decided to turn to flesh from light. This was not the destiny I had moved towards, this was not what those who found themselves unwittingly in my path should suffer for being with me. I could not throw them as bait to assuage those who had come to claim me, the unborn she was carrying was the biggest trump card I could offer those who chased me down.

The purity of the child in her womb had saved me, it had sent out its light to protect me when I had gone forth. There was no denying it, I had been protected by strengths that were not mine and this came from a ball of flesh within a human uterus, yet to be born, perhaps just having welcomed a soul into it.

And there were the other strengths that had rallied behind me, the *bhootni* who was now happily swinging from the rafters in a jubilant frenzy, delighted to be a part of this… excitement. And there was Bilkis Bi, no one saw her but me, no one understood what she was but me. She was when the light began and ended and when the light filled me up, when it suffused me with its strength and when it poured out of me, when it eviscerated all that pursued me, blowing the light into the faces of those creatures, peeling away their guises of being young children, drenched and piteously, revealing them for what they really were, slavering, huge monstrous, creatures, fetid and putrid, maggot infested, their fangs dripping acid on the porch, burning up the wood with a hiss and a sizzle, when she sent them back into the dimensions they had come from. The beginning and the end of all things, the alpha and the omega, the creator and the destroyer, the god of us all, the goddess who ruled us all, the divine force, the mother of all creation, the progenitor of all destruction, she had saved me, saved us all. She had blazed in through the turbulent skies, dancing in a tumultuous rage on a shimmering beam of light, her small crescent-shaped scythe with its flat blue iron blade slashing through the necks of the howling hounds, laughing manically as she did so, a laughter that resounded through the three worlds. Only I could hear it here, on this plane, on this temporal level of the earthly, where human ears were not meant to hear the voices of the divine. She had called them by their names, names that would have torn apart the human ear had they been able to hear them, and commanded to return to their dimensions, to never come for me again. And thus commanded, they had no other option but to return to the pits of the hells they had emerged from, chastised by the one who ruled over all that had been created and destroyed. She left, as she had arrived, dancing on a ray of sunlight, a sonic boom and a blinding flash, and no human eye having registered her presence or absence.

Bilkis Bi had not forsaken me. All she had been waiting was for me to find my own strength to resist what was claiming me for their own. I was never meant for them, I wasn't meant for anything or anyplace that I didn't want to be. I understood that now. I was right where I needed to be. Here, on the surface, feeling the solidity of the ground under my feet and the light of the sun in my eyes, the wind ruffling my hair and the air in my lungs, this was what it was all about. Being mortal, being alive, in this flesh and blood body, tasting, smelling, feeling, sensing. Humans didn't realize what they so took for granted when they lived, that they rued getting older and dying, not realizing that this too was a blessing.

How long would I have this unending skin? Immortality was burdensome to those who had it, humans hankered for it, not knowing that the tick of passing mortality was that which infused sweetness into the day-to-day. Humans had too little of life and too much of want to be contained within the littleness they had been allocated. If only humans realized that they lived forever in the churn of the souls that lived on and on, and on, they would stop chasing their dreams of momentary immortality.

The light clap faded and the clouds rolled back, I saw Gulab lying on the floor groaning in acute pain. Teja was slumped in a corner, dazed and disoriented. The beam of light and the dancing deity balanced precariously on it had withdrawn to the path just outside the house leading down to the road, and had, through a majestic gesture too quick for the human eye to follow, slashed it open with a swift movement of her hand wielding the blade. I ran out, a hollow pit had been excavated in the path, fumes emanated from it, fumes that uncoiled from the depths like spring coils and reached out to dance lovingly into the unwary sky. I ran out, wondering what on earth was happening. I could hear Bilkis Bi's voice in my head, even though I couldn't see her anywhere, the beam of light that had carried her had receded into the vault of the heavens, far beyond anything my human eyes could discern.

'Take her out of the earth and bring her into the house,

tend to her wounds. She is my daughter too, like you are.'

The gaping hole in the earth was like a meteorite had struck the path. The smoke rose high into the air, black and virulent. The pit that had been revealed was deep, I stood over the edge and peered within, there was only slush and fumes there. In the sludge I saw something move. I called out, 'Is anyone inside?'

I could sense a consciousness within, I realized then at this point that I no longer had the gift of the light, I had exhausted what I had, I had to refuel. I could not send it down to reach what was within. It could be a person, it could be an animal, it could be something I couldn't define, and had no desire to have a close encounter with such a creature. But Bilkis Bi had told me to bring her out of the sludge and to take her home, that whoever was within was her daughter, just like I was. Whatever was within would not harm me, I was sure of that. It stirred at the sound of my voice, and then rose, drawing itself to its full height. Covered with sludge and slime, it seemed like it was a human, and as the sludge dripped off, draining away, I could make out it was a woman. I rushed back to the house, to the back where I knew a ladder had been placed against the small outhouse and carried it to the pit with all the strength I could muster. I lowered myself within, trying hard to push the muck away from me as I descended. It withdrew by itself, almost as if it were terrified of my light. It seemed like I was climbing down for an eternity, miles down into the bowels of the earth, longer than the ladder had ever been or could be.

The rungs kept extending below me and then more so that the sky above receded and I realized I had climbed into utter darkness, where I could make out not even my shadow, where sulphur and noxious fumes and where my light began withdrawing into me, terrified by whatever it was that lay beyond those boundaries of whatever it was that enclosed us.

The woman was standing up, albeit in what seemed like a stupor. I climbed down into the noxious sludge that made up the cesspit she was in, took her by the hand and led her up the ladder. She moved with the jerkiness of one whose limbs had not moved for a while, disoriented and shaky. I hauled her up with all the strength at my disposal, at the disposal of this body. She made it up the ladder, her limbs jerky and disoriented, and collapsed again when she was on firm ground. I climbed up after her, leaving the ladder where it was, in the suddenness of the hole in the ground, the sinkhole to hell's doorway. The ground closed over us as we exited, devouring the ladder with it. The fumes that had been emanating from the ground withdrew back into it, and the fresh breeze of the mountains blew in to erase any lingering odours. I found a bucket near the outhouse and filled it with water, throwing it over her to wash off whatever it was that covered her. It took two or three buckets, and by the end of it, she was shivering with the chill of the evening air on her wet body. The orange heat of the skies had given out and now a powdery snow began descending upon the earth, a snow that settled on the surface like a benediction, like a curse, like a whitewashing of all that was putrid and evil that had just walked the earth.

'She is a daughter to me, like you are,' Bilkis Bi's words resounded in my head. What did she mean by them? How was I her daughter? She had always taken care of me though, my need for light, she'd kept me supplied in life force whenever I needed it, she'd warned me through distances of time and space of the hounds being unleashed, and now she had finally, when I'd decided to confront them and not run from them, helped me to do so. I lifted the woman to her feet and helped her down the short way into the house. The porch, I noticed as I passed it, was scorched, the timbers burnt like blobs of acid had fallen upon it. The acrid stench still lingered, whatever they were, they that were periodically released from the gates of hell to hunt me down. But they were gone now, hopefully never to return and I was here, in this small town in the cradle of the mountains, hoping to live with this strange couple I was connected with in the strangest way, a connection that had been initiated first by lust and now my flesh body's need to survive, a need I would now hopefully have done away with. I would live a life of mortality, of senescence, I would decay, I would disintegrate, I would die. I could hope.

A while later, when I had managed to dry her off and get her in front of the heater, she emitted the first sound she had since the time I had got her out of the pit. She groaned. Her face was obscured with a layer of mud that had not been completely washed off when I'd doused her with the buckets of water, now dried. Who was she, how had she reached within that strange pit, who or what had trapped her there, how had they managed to seal the pit so hermetically with absolutely no indication on the surface of the path that a cavity like this lay below? I had myself crossed this path just some hours ago! How long had she been confined there, what were those fumes within the pit, these were questions that would have to wait until she was able to answer coherently.

In the house, Gulab had taken to her bed, exhausted and drained. Teja was disoriented and sitting at the dining table with his head between his hands. In the attic something was rattling ferociously in what seemed like a metal container. I handed the woman a set of clothes I had in the small bag I had been carrying with me, and helped her to the bathroom where she could wash herself and change out of the wet, mucky clothes she had on. I waited outside, ready to be of assistance if needed. I knocked and asked if she needed help. She replied that she didn't. She was okay. Her voice was firm and strong, she was alright. She was familiar in a distant kind of way, I felt my light reach out to her, we had met at some point, we had touched, we had exchanged fluids, I was sure of it.

Teja was still at the dining table, he looked up as I passed by going up to where the infernal racket was coming from in the attic.

'What happened? I can't remember a thing, except a flash of light and then everything went black.'

Perhaps that was for the best, it helped humans, this ability of theirs to tune out experiences that were disorienting to comprehend or assimilate within what they understood of their world. That there were worlds within worlds, bubbles of existences, foam in the cosmos so to speak, where the material and the immaterial collide and withdraw, exist and don't exist, create and dissipate, beyond the ken of what human sense organs could comprehend and interpret for the human mind, fragile as it was.

'I don't know what happened,' I replied as honestly as I could, 'But whatever it was, it is over now.'

'Who is she?'

'I don't know, she was outside, I brought her in. I hope you don't mind.'

'Is she injured? Do we need to call a doctor?'

'She seems fine, just perhaps in a state of shock.'

'Where did you find her?'

'Inside the ground. In a pit just outside your gate.'

He looked up in shock, his expression disbelieving. 'How is that even possible, there's nothing outside the gate, only the path to the main road.'

It would perhaps be easier to tell him that a goddess dancing on a beam of light had saved us all and opened the pit to reveal this woman encased within, in a state of suspension. But I had a feeling he wouldn't quite swallow this explanation. It was too implausible to be true.

'How did you find me?' he asked.

I smiled. 'The same way you found me.'

'I couldn't reach out to you,' he replied, his face grave and serious. All traces of the boy he had been when I'd first met him had been erased by the world and the sandpaper of living in it. 'Gulab is carrying my child. I had to make my choice.'

I knew he had made a choice, and stayed true to it. It didn't rankle me. I didn't love him in the puerile way humans assumed love to be an all-consuming emotion that excluded all others. For me, love was all encompassing, I could take in more than one person to love. The body too I could share with as many desired it, but only if I desired them back, but I felt nothing about it, none of the emotions that plagued humans about fidelity and love and moral compass. It was a blessing, it left me free to pursue survival in the human body without actually getting emotionally attached to any human. I could leave when I chose.

'You did the right thing,' I replied, for he seemed to need reassurance. I would not allow him to enter my body anymore. That I was clear about, I felt absolutely no desire for him, and hoped that perhaps now I wouldn't need the seed of the human male to energize me, or the awakened light from any human to fuel my own light. Perhaps I should just let the light dim, see if that ended me and my journey here on the surface.

I heard a step behind me. It was the woman from the pit. She was wearing the clothes I had given her, which were just a little tight for her. She was taller, heavier, her face sharp-featured and radiant now that the slime and muck had been washed away. She was familiar, I put my hand out to her cheek and her eyes filled with tears. Now I knew. The brash young thing who had thrown down Bilkis Bi's stall in a froth of rage, who had been so glorious that my light had reached out to her without my consent and enveloped her with desire and want, who had been cursed to live out her life in torment by an irate Bilkis Bi who had immediately regretted her decision but had been too angry to take it back.

'Rani.'

From all those years ago, so many decades. She was exactly the same as she had been, just a bit older than when I had last seen her, a few years perhaps. Something had stopped her from ageing. She was as glorious as she had been then, even more so if that were possible.

'I never thought I would see you again,' she replied, her voice heavy with an emotion that made each word pull itself back into the comfort of her throat, from where it would sink down further to the heart.

There was a gentleness about her that brought tears to my eyes, a suffering that most humans would not know nor even be able to comprehend even if she told them what she had been through. The gentleness about her coexisted with an imperialism that made her almost regal. I looked at her and I knew, I knew exactly what it was, and it was not of this world. She had been touched by the other, and she had emerged from it and not quite emerged from it. Now she was here because she had to reclaim it or do away with it, as she might. It was a task only she could do, and the consequences of succeeding or not, she would have to bear. And perhaps Gulab, that I knew without her telling me.

'Professorni!'

Rani blinked, as though emerging from a dream, she looked at Gulab again, taking in her belly, ripe with child. 'What date is it?' she asked, looking with a perplexed expression towards a calendar on the wall. I told her, she gasped.

'How can that be?'

I looked at her, confused.

'I last remember walking up that path months ago. I've been entombed in that pit for months!'

'How did you stay alive if that was the case?'

'I have no idea.' She looked disoriented.

'I was stuck in a strange place, deep inside the earth. It wasn't even in the earth, it was somewhere else. I can't even explain what happened and how I got into the earth, it just...'

'Didn't anyone come looking for you? Wasn't your family worried, there must have been a missing person's complaint,' I replied.

'I think my husband thought I left him. And perhaps he was too embarrassed to file a complaint. I'd left him before, many years ago, and come back after ten years. Maybe, he's just waiting for me to come back.'

'But surely your children, your parents, someone...'

'I have no one,' she said, her voice suddenly stone. 'I have no one to call my own...'

A loud crash from above drowned the rest of her sentence. We all looked upwards instinctively, expecting the ceiling to come falling down on us. A hissing that had begun some time ago suddenly intensified. Somewhere in some distant recess of the house, an infernal racket was on, that of wood colliding angrily against metal over and over again, a rattling that echoed through the rooms and pierced our ears, getting louder and louder until it became a howling that made everything in the place vibrate, making us wince at whatever unearthly thing was howling through the rattling. Whatever she had sought, whatever had confined her in the hope that she would stay within the earth long enough so that the child would be born and Gulab would no longer be inviolate, was swirling angrily above us now that it realized she had been released from the place he had trapped her within in the hope that she would never be found, never be let out.

Rani looked up at the ceiling which was where the rattling and howling was coming from.

'The trunk.' She turned to me with agony in her expression. 'Please, please, help me to throw it into a river, the ravine, anywhere, where no one can ever wake it again.'

'The only sin is the sin of being born.'

– SAMUEL BECKETT

Noor

GULAB CLUTCHED HER BELLY, WINCING AND groaning in the midst of the infernal chaos erupting in the room over our heads. Teja went up to her, putting his arms around her, a gentleness that was completely at odds with what his appearance would suggest. It was a side to him I had never seen before, but then what had I seen of him apart from an adolescent obsession with my body? She was, I realized now, more important than I could ever have been to him, she was bearing him a child.

She looked like she was about to break, her stomach straining, her back arched with the pressure of staying on her feet. There were beads of sweat on her forehead and she clutched the door jamb.

'I think the pains have begun,' she whimpered. Where she had been flung against the wall was a pool of wetness. Her kurta and salwar were drenched down the front and the back. Her water had broken. Her uterus had begun its contractions. The baby in the womb flexed angrily, upset at being dislodged by the very body that had nurtured it all these months. A contraction ripped her body into two and she screamed, a scream that for a brief moment drowned out the noise coming from the attic.

She clutched my hand, the desperation of a woman, of every woman who had ever given birth on this earth, who knew that she must first walk through the valley of death in order to be the harbinger of life. The *bhootni* hovered next to her, trying to soothe her with words and love.

'Whatever it is that you do with this light you spread, you make the pain go away,' she said, her voice raspy on the edge of a pain that was new to her, to every first-time mother, who had only heard whispers of how terrible it could be and that a woman was born to endure it, and now having experienced it, was despairing of getting through onto the other side of childbirth.

'Do you know how to deliver a baby?' I asked the Professorni.

'I've never given birth or watched one,' she replied. A crash resounded from upstairs, something small and metallic was repeatedly throwing itself against the timbers, trying to get the attention of those on the floors below or trying to escape what confined it. Gulab whimpered, her hand on her belly which was quivering unbearably with a force within that refused to be contained. And then it went still, Gulab groaned and hauled herself to her feet. The Professorni looked up towards where the sounds were coming from and trembled. Fear emanated from her in waves, fear that was. She shivered, a nameless terror I could not help assuage, I no longer had the light, I couldn't console her the only way I had known how to all these centuries, without my light, I was nothing I realized, just an ordinary woman who would now learn what it really meant to be human, to not have people and things bow to your command.

'Call for the doctor or take her to the clinic, we don't know how long it will take. Perhaps, it would be safer to take her to the clinic while she can still walk, we don't know when the doctor or the midwife will arrive.'

For all that he was to be a father now, he seemed more like a confused adolescent, uncertain about what he needed to do, what was expected of him. I helped Gulab walk down the stairs to where the old beat-up Mahindra Jeep was parked just outside the gate, on the same path where I had found Rani deep, deep within the bowels of the earth. Teja ran in to collect his wallet and the keys and ran out again, tripping over his own feet in his haste. I saw him drive off, his control over the vehicle made jerky by his panic.

By the time I reached the house again, the timbers of the upper part of the house had been ripped, a crashing of wooden beams and plaster had cascaded through the floors, an incessant infernal din that echoed relentlessly through the entire cottage, rattling through the walls, the floors, the ceilings, a din that had now become a physical ache because it had entered through the ears into the brain and was slowly seeping into the blood. Rani was standing where I had left her, transfixed to the spot, as if she was listening to someone speaking to her, her lips moved soundlessly, a conversation I was not privy to. She then turned to the stairs, her movements jerky and agonized, like a marionette.

I went up to her and shook her shoulder, 'Are you all right? Who are you speaking with?'

Her eyes, when I looked into them, were glazed and disoriented.

'Help me,' Rani pleaded, her voice a low monotone. 'It will take me again.'

I ran up the stairs ahead of her as fast as I could. I realized I was feeling a very human emotion, one that I had never felt before this moment. I was experiencing what humans called fear. I was terrified of what might be in that casket, that which was bouncing around in such a rage. The *bhootni* floated down from the rafter, where she had been languidly curled around one central one surveying the chaos unfolding below and moved with me up the stairs.

'He's angry,' she informed me, evidently in a chatty mood.

'Who is angry?'

'Him. Whatever it is. The thing in the trunk. The thing that owns this woman.'

'Owns?'

'Whatever you may call it. Possesses. Stakes claim to. She's his, basically. And she managed to fool him into shifting his claim to Gulab. But he couldn't stake his claim on Gulab because Gulab had one more life within her. So now he's confined in that trunk.'

'What is he?'

'I don't know. But he is scary and angry. And if we let him out, he will take her again.'

Behind us, dragging herself up with leaden feet that seemed to be obeying a command not emanating from her mind, was Rani. Her face had lost all colour, her eyes were glazed and unresponsive. As she took more steps up the stairway, she became more of an automaton, as though being propelled up by a force that she found impossible to resist. I pushed open the tiny door leading to the room where the noise was emanating from and found the strangest scene playing out in front of my eyes. The trunk, tiny as it was, was sitting calmly in the centre of the room, and coiled on top of it, was what I could only describe as a wisp of smoke, or the remnants of a flame, a red wind perhaps that had contained itself in a single spot. It was waiting, calm now, waiting for whatever it desired to come to it. I recognized it at once and unfurled my light around myself and reached out to Rani, wrapping her within it.

It spoke to me, a male voice, smooth and polished, a refined cadence and diction that came from times of yore, unknown to humans of the here and now. I recognized it, I spoke the same way. We spoke in tongues that humankind had never learnt, never heard.

'Welcome,' he said, to me, the *bhootni*, or to Rani who had laboured up the stairs and was now standing at the doorway to the room, right behind us, the fear wafting off her in waves, I did not know. Perhaps the welcome was for all of us, a welcome that had me wary.

'Why are you claiming this woman?'

'Do you really not know? You who consort with multiple humans think you can look down on me and my kind who choose but one human to make our own for as long as they are alive,' the voice replied. The flame coagulated into a faint human shape, that of a young man, dressed in loose tunic and trousers. He was seated on the trunk with his legs crossed at the knee, his hands resting by his sides.

'We are one of a kind. Malakha, or should I call you irin, chose to be flesh in order to consort with flesh. I chose to stay the way I was created but I consort with flesh when I choose to. I am loyal to the one I choose, and I have chosen her, this woman to be my consort. And now she, the one who bid her to cast me into another. I have no one now, the one I was cast into bears new life. I will return into this one.'

We had all been created together, our kind, their kind. We were the beginning of all creation, before man, before the earth, before the sun, before the stars. This was one of those who were created from the smokeless fire, one of those who had a beginning before the creator made humans but no known end, those who lived on the intersection between the human and the otherworldly and were fire and smoke, and who envied humans their existence. This was one who had claimed a human woman for himself and had attached himself to her, to the exclusion of the human male she had wanted to attach herself to. He would not release her until she had atoned for trying to cast him away.

'She does not wish to consort with you. Release her from the bond. Nor does the other. Find a willing consort.'

'Her consent is immaterial. I have chosen her, and for the duration of the life that has been written for her, I will keep her as mine. She may try as much as she can to dislodge me, but until her days end, she will not be rid of me.'

Rani stood behind me, rigid with a dispossession of herself and all her human faculties. Her eyes were blank slates, her face drained of all colour, her beauty, ethereal when she was in control of her body, now ghastly and ghoulish, as the blood stopped flowing to all her extremities and congealed where it was.

The power that had severed the bond between the two of them was no longer here to protect her completely. I had placed myself between the two of them, I had but little of my strength left right now. But I needed to do what I had to do to protect her, after all it was the one who protected her who had also protected me from being dragged down into the pits of everlasting darkness, deep within the bowels of the earth, where the fumes and the vapours corroded both skin and one's entrails, eating away at the body till the spirit left it and the carcass dissolved into sludge.

He smiled and reached out a hand that grew longer and longer until it passed through me and caressed the cheek of Rani, standing petrified behind me. I realized, with a start, that I was no longer any defence, no bulwark, I had been drained of all the light within me. Right now, I was just flesh, sodden, base flesh.

He sighed and stood up, in as much as he could stand up if that term could be used for something, someone, that was air and breath and smoke and wind. His voice, if it could be called a voice, was a susurration that rustled in the air as it entered one's mind. I could hear him, as could she.

'Rani. I made you my queen and this is how you tried to deceive me. I hate to punish you but you leave me with no option but to do so, over and over again. Do you not realize that I cannot be killed, I cannot be ended, and I will not leave you unless I choose to, no matter how you try to deceive me, by mingling your blood with another's?'

I could feel the fear coming off her as his voice shifted the air, and made the light streaming in from the dusty skylight above us, shimmer and dance with a million untethered motes of dust.

'I've missed you, Rani. Did you really think you'd rid yourself of me by putting me in a stupid bottle in a tin trunk? She was not for me, the only one for me, is you, Rani. You. You know that. You know there is no escape.'

His words dissolved into a smoky nothingness as did he and, the dust and smoke whirred through me and slammed right into her with an impact that made her stagger and gag. And then she fell hard and heavy to the ground, a dead slump from which all my shaking refused to rouse her, her body burning to the touch, as hot as glowing red coals in a furnace, singeing my fingers. There was no breath, no life, no response. And then she sat up, eyes blazing.

Rani

I could feel him sifting his fingers back again through my mind, as he had the first time that evening by the fort all those years ago, that very moment when I had bent to take an errant pebble out of my *jutti* and the bending forward had caused my hair to tumble down loose from my carelessly knotted bun. I had tied it up, quickly enough I thought, but not quick enough as I learnt later. They always told us to keep our hair tied up, and we laughed at them. Old crones, we said dismissively, jealous of our youth, our beauty, our glory. Their scalps shine through the few strands of hair they preciously have left of their once glorious manes, so they must deny us the magnificence of displaying ours for the world to admire. But they knew, they did, the old crones, of the unspeakable terror that beauty attracted. Of what might come drawn by the glorious beauty of our youth, of what could be too unbearable for the world to accept or admit, of the denizens that sniffed us out between the corporeal and the temporal and swooped in to stake their claim on us, in one swift unwary moment. I had learnt my lesson, I knew now even as I suffered that to tell a young woman to shrink her radiance was an exercise in futility. She would shine, come what may.

He had slammed into me like a breath of hot air, burning

through every synapse, every dendrite, taking over my physical body in a manner I could neither understand nor explain. The fever that took over me racked my body for days, sending me into delirium and a world where I wandered in the realm where those of fire and smoke lived and was then betrothed to the one who had taken me. But I could not stay there forever, I was of the flesh, I had to return to this world. When I emerged from the fever, I was not me, I was me. I was still Rani, I was still the same physical person, but something within me had intrinsically changed. I was hosting within me and about me, another being, one who now controlled me, who took me as he pleased, who owned me and had now claimed complete dominion over me. A creature of fire and smoke and ash, a creature from another realm who had claimed me and kept me as I had been when he had first seen me, young and radiant, even as the years climbed on their dreary tread towards senescence. I had tried unsuccessfully for years to rid myself of him and never succeeded. And then I'd returned to where it all began, the curse, and found myself a way out.

And now he was back. Bilkis Bi had been unsuccessful in her attempts to help me, she had failed. And he had confined me into the pits of the netherworld. Had he ever intended to release me, I didn't know.

I had been a fool to come here in search of the trunk. The original trunk had long gone, the trunk in this room was an imposter. It was not made of the sky metal that could confine this being, it was a dross alloy, hacked in a round foundry, manufactured off an assembly line in a small town workshop. Tin trunks were manufactured for those who hadn't yet elevated themselves to suitcases or duffel bags, people who were content with what they were always familiar with, the solidity of a lock and a key, and a latch to hold it all together, a sturdy metal box that would protect whatever they chose to entrust to its care. Someone had recognized the original trunk for the precious metal it was and had replaced it with this one. It was the owner of the lodge that Gulab and Teja had stayed in for a few days before the keys and the papers to this house were sorted with the caretaker and handed to them. He had taken the original trunk and replaced it with this counterfeit one. He had merely puzzled over the empty bottle within and then bunged it in before locking it. Gulab and Teja had known no better. The original trunk had been opened before I had even reached here, he had been released, he had been waiting for me to come to him. What was within the trunk was nothing, just wind, ether.

He caressed me, breathing my name into my ears with the wind. 'Rani,' he whispered, a formless voice that ran through my thoughts, entangling with my own, so I couldn't fathom where mine ended and his began. 'I've been waiting.'

Earthly time meant nothing to him, months were less than seconds to him, the lifetime I had spent being his plaything was but a blink in his entire existence in his realm, a realm parallel to but removed from ours by the laws that governed all the realms and dimensions as deemed by that which created us.

Majnu, I had called him. He was that. An obsessed lover with no shape or form except when he chose to take it so I could see him. And now he had taken form again in front of another to see him, to know what he was, and this woman was not afraid of what she saw, so he could not affect her even when he passed right through her and reached into me. I was powerless to defend myself, she was powerless to defend me. Whatever power she thought she had to protect me was nothing in the face of this, this entity that toyed with me like a cat toyed with a dead rat. Majnu. The obsessed lover. Perhaps lover was too simple a term for what he was.

'Let me die,' I pleaded. 'I don't wish to live.' This time I knew I would kill myself before I let him take me over again.

'I won't let you kill yourself, you know that. I won't let you grow old, I won't let you die. As long as I am with you, I will stretch out your life so you will live forever. Think of all that I can give you. A life that is forever youthful. All the riches you desire.'

I didn't want it. All that he offered me was meaningless. I had lived sixty years on the earth and looked like a twenty-year-old. My husband had aged and shrunk, as he would, and I was the ghastly abomination right next to him that he couldn't explain, was embarrassed to be seen in public with. They thought me to be his daughter, and while it had not bothered him in the years when he was middle-aged and I looked youthful enough to be in my early twenties, it did now. He sought his pleasure elsewhere all his life, because I had never given him any. I could never give him any, or risk him dying.

'I want to die,' I hissed. 'I'm not going to let you take me over again.' I had given back the talisman Bilkis Bi had given me, I had nothing with me any more to give me anything that I could use against him. I was powerless against him. He could take me as his will and do what he pleased with me, twist me and turn me, fill every cell of my body with the awareness of his presence, controlling my every breath, watching in amusement as I fought him, tried valiantly to resist him taking me over. I fought with him as fiercely as I could and felt within me something else fighting with me. It recoiled at the unexpected resistance it encountered.

Perhaps the only way out was death and I should have done it years ago. I had always been a coward. I could feel him pulsing in my thoughts. I struggled to take control of myself, I needed to move down to where the kitchen was, there had to be knives there, knives I could use. It was then that I realized what it was that had been pushing it out of me, it was the light, it was Noor. I opened my eyes to blankness and then saw her standing in front of me, her palms spread open and supplicating, streaming from them a light that bathed me in its glow. It was Noor. It was not Noor.

'Run,' she commanded, Noor, singing out words in a language that was as old as creation and that humankind could not comprehend. Her voice was silvery and high, and I was filled with light and brightness, a filling that left no space for anything else to intrude into me. I felt a jerking, and flash of pain, like a flame had singed me from the inside. He shuddered excruciatingly out of my body, unable to find a spot where his darkness could exist because her light now filled me. He could no longer take me over, until he was me and I was him and there was no divide between the two of us, body and mind. I ran. I didn't know where I was running to but I ran. Down the stairs, to the door, hearing the terrifying crashing sounds from above my head, that echoed to the four corners of the earth, and had the earth and the skies roil and roar in response. Storm clouds began gathering quickly in the distance and closed in on the house, I could see them swirling and growling in rage, a rage I couldn't comprehend what I had done to deserve. But it was not coming for me, and so I ran, as fast as I could, running away from what had awaited me, to what I did not know, I ran recklessly, careening down the path, running down, slipping and stumbling down the wet road, uncaring of the vehicles that were passing, honking musically as they navigated the treacherous bends and turns. The night had fallen, the road was dark, the shrubbery fringing the road stung my face as I ran through it and then the ground slipped away from under my feet and I fell. It was a fall that was never-ending, twigs snapping as I fell through the tree cover of the steep slope, until I landed on something soft and welcoming. I was too exhausted to open my eyes and figure out where I was. I felt the welcome emptiness of being just me in my body. No one else. Nothing else. And when I opened my eyes, I was floating on nothingness and sitting next to me on a wisp of cloud, smoking her bidi was Bilkis Bi, looking unconcernedly into the distance, while the earth fell away into the darkness from below us.

'Rani,' she said, between puffs, 'Do you want to help a baby be born?'

'What about… *it*?'

'It is gone. Noor has dispatched it back to its dimensions. I helped her a bit, of course.'

'Gone?'

She smiled, the smile of one who was regretful and powerful, all at the same time. 'Gone forever. Or at least imprisoned in human skin for a lifetime. A punishment for it, to know the limitations of skin. You are free now, Rani, go age and live a normal life.'

Gulab

I had never seen Teja drive so recklessly as he drove right now, swerving and screeching, honking crazily as we approached corners. I was torn between panicking over the pains and panicking about a truck bearing down on us at a blind turn. 'Slow down,' I panted as yet another contraction hit me. 'We'll die from an accident before I die of childbirth.'

He laughed. 'We're not going to die, we're going to have a child.' He could laugh. His insides were not being ripped apart. I could have committed my second murder at this point, but I needed him to get me to hospital.

Each contraction was unbearable pain that only one who has crossed this river could hope to understand. This was my punishment for sleeping with a man without being married to him. My body was a traitor, it had always been one, I had enjoyed the pleasures of the body, I had sinned. The child within me was the fruit of all my sins over all these years. It had been conceived in order to kill me, that I knew. I was being punished for being a sinner. Okay, enough with the self-flagellation, time to push this kid out of me. Narrow birth canal, the lady doctor had said.

Another contraction ripped through me. I could feel the child begin its descent, its head pushing through my cervix. It was coming, it was time, it would be here any moment now. I opened my legs and screamed, a scream that echoed in the skies and was absorbed by the snow falling soft as talcum powder. Here I was in a pickup that was swerving through the narrow roads at breakneck speed, a child bearing down through my womb, thoughts of death flooding my brain. The jalopy shuddered to a sudden stop, so sudden that my head hit the dashboard as I bent over in pain.

'It will snow,' she had said, the memory came to me.

'You're really intent on killing us, aren't you?' I muttered.

'There's no road,' he said, his voice puzzled. 'The road has just ended. It's sunk in a huge hole. Must have been a slip when the storm came.'

I opened my eyes and looked out, there was a sinkhole

in front, it was obviously newly formed, the mud and stones were still falling into it as we watched. Where the road had been there was now nothing. We were still on the outskirts, we hadn't yet reached where the fringes of the town began. There weren't houses for kilometres here, I was in no condition to walk to town. The jeep wouldn't pass, and we didn't dare walk around the periphery of what remained, it was loose soil and rocks that would give way at the touch of a foot. The snow that had begun drifting down when the creatures had disappeared through the sky was now a steady pelt that would soon become slurry, slippery and treacherous to walk on.

'Let's go back home, if I can manage to turn the jeep around.'

I whimpered; the child was straining to emerge. I could feel it pushing and demanding to be let out, an alien creature I was bearing within me, mine and yet with a life of its own. He struggled and reversed the vehicle with precise, intricate manoeuvres on the narrow road while I moaned with pain. We drove for around five minutes before he slammed on the brakes again. My head hit the dashboard again. I kicked him in rage.

'Just kill me once and be done with it.'

'It's collapsed again. What is happening? Why is the road sinking here too?'

Darkness crowded around us, a cacophony of voices and susurrations that were questioning and probing. It undulated with a life of its own, a raw power that throbbed with the metallic acridity of electricity and then a sudden flash of light that split the skies open into two halves, a woman stood on a beam of light coming down from the skies right in front of the jeep. She was wearing a ghagra and a blouse, both faded, a dupatta tied around her head, torn and much mended but had the stars shining through it, her face was a hundred years old or a million years old, I could not tell. All I knew was that I couldn't bear to look upon her without shielding my eyes, so bright and glorious was she.

Next to her on that beam of light was the Professorni, looking about her with as much confusion as I had felt when I saw what was unfolding before us.

Teja gasped and stepped out of the car. I gasped too, but it was impossible for me to step out anywhere.

The old woman stepped off the beam of light as one might descend the last step of a stairway and beckoned to the Professorni to follow her. I had met her before. I recognized her now that the light wasn't blinding me. I had bought trinkets from her stall at the marketplace in a town not so far away from the Professorni's town, where we had lived for a couple of months before we moved to the Professorni's town. She had carefully helped me put the bangles on, and the chain and pendant, made of dross metal, and then told me to take them without accepting any payment. I'd gone back again the next day with a bag full of apples for her. We'd chatted for a while, she'd insisted I wear the chain and pendant always. It was a pretty one, a rose on a silver chain. Gulab, she had said while searching for it in her jumbled stash under the counter, for a Gulab, when she'd asked me my name. She was her but she was not quite her, in the way you know someone who had been playing out a role but was not quite the person they pretended to be, I realized this now. I had met her earlier too, at the railway station, the crone who sent Teja my way. This was who she was, this woman who was sparkling with blue iridescent light all over, this woman who was older than anyone or anything I'd known, including the mountain and the seas, the earth and the skies, the suns and the moons of all creation. In her hand, she held a small curved knife and she smiled beatifically at me, a smile that immediately quelled the violence of the contractions that were breaking me in half.

'Bilkis Bi,' Teja gasped. She smiled at him and then turned to me, putting a hand on my stomach, calming down the waves of pain.

'We meet again, my little rose,' she said, her voice the voice of ancient deities carved from primeval rock, waves crashing against shores, magma rising through from the depths of the earth, starlight twinkling through the vastness of the vacuum and the warmth of the sunlight on bare skin all at once.

'You're still wearing this,' she said, smiling, reaching out to touch the pendant that still hung around my neck. 'It kept you safe, didn't it? From all that had come searching for you, that would come searching for you. Foolish child, did you never realize you had the light in you. You got it from your mother, my daughter, you attracted these to yourself, those that needed the light. Teja. Rani. The *bhootni*. The thing in the bottle in the trunk.' My mother was her daughter, that would be strange because she looked like she was definitely over a hundred years old. I would calculate that later, right now I hoped she had a plan to help this baby get out of me. Could we have this discussion later, I thought to myself, with all due respect, I had a baby emerging from me and I couldn't care less about the light and those who needed it at this point. I would never have sex again in my life, I swore, if only I could get through this alive. If I died, of course, I would never have sex again.

I put a hand up and touched that tiny pendant with newfound respect, I had never thought twice about it all this time, I had just kept it on because it was pretty and never stopped to wonder as to why it never got tarnished. Perhaps this was why we had been safe in that house, the house with the *bhootni* and the strange thing in that tin trunk which I had opened, little knowing that the bottle within was never to be opened without a plan B to keep me safe from what it contained. I hadn't realized I was losing time because it had been slowly trying to test bits of time when it could take me over.

The Professorni clambered down clumsily from the beam of light, perhaps she hadn't the kind of experience balancing on beams of light that the woman from the marketplace had. Beams of light were tricky for mortal flesh, I mean you couldn't really watch your step, could you? I didn't know her name, the woman from the marketplace who was standing in front of me with a sharp curved knife in her hand and an expression of calm waiting on her countenance, she had just been Biji to me, a catch-all term for all women above a certain age. She was not, I realized now, just another old woman selling pendants, rings and earrings on a rickety plank under a sprawling banyan tree at the entrance to the old market. Or at the steps to the railway station. She was so much more, so much I could neither understand nor explain, nor had the desire to do so right now, while my uterus roiled with rage trying to expel the child within, eager to rid them of their imperviousness. I would offer coconuts at every temple in town if I emerged from this alive, I promised. Another contraction hit me and I wished for death. Coconuts be damned.

'Go lie down in the back,' Bi told me, indicating to me that I should clamber into the back of the jeep and lie down. There was enough light from the beam to brighten the place up. Teja helped me up unquestioningly, carrying me like I was a doll. He had seen enough strange things through this day to not question anymore. Neither did I question things now. After all, I had lived in a world of people who had tried to dim my light every chance they got. The snow stopped falling, suspended in the air, a shimmering veil that no longer felt cold as it touched one.

'Now,' commanded Bi, 'open your legs wide.' I did as she said, without question. I could feel a presence, a warmth, go through my canal and caress the baby struggling to emerge.

There was no pain anymore, only a blessed euphoria like I'd smoked up too much ganja. Slowly, the passage opened and the baby slid out, and I could feel my womb contracting, over and over, to give it the momentum it needed to slide out. And then a ripping that felt it was tearing me into half, and it was out.

I floated on a deep velvety blackness that let nothing come within me, not even thoughts. A wail rang through the air, a piercing rending wail that was a newborn's and as old as the hills. I tried to open my eyes but could not. Bi laughed.

'Here he is,' she said. 'A healthy boy.'

Teja clutched my hand tight, so tight that he threatened to cut off the blood circulation to my fingers. I screamed and he released my fingers without apology. When had he ever apologized to me, perhaps he believed his penis would fall off if he ever did. There was no sound from him. No sigh of relief, no cry of joy. Sometimes even silence contains words, words that are too heavy to be articulated.

'Is everything all right with the baby?' I asked, wondering about the silence from the Professorni and Teja.

'Gulab,' he said, like he was beginning to tell me something and then stopped. Bi grunted, raising a hand to stop him, her head and the Professorni's head were bowed, as they cleaned up the mess of the afterbirth. A rough shawl lying discarded in the vehicle was turned into a swaddling cloth and the baby handed over to Teja who stared at it unblinkingly, a strange expression on his face, an expression that was reverential and yet disbelieving.

'Why are his…' he began, his voice puzzled. When had he become incapable of completing a sentence coherently? Or had I just lost my patience with him, in the manner most couples do with each other after a few years?

'I want to see my child,' I said. 'Show me my baby.' I could feel my voice rising in pitch and tone – it happened when I panicked.

Biji took the swaddled child from Teja's arms and the Professorni helped me sit up. She placed the baby gently in my arms. The child was light, weightless, like air, hot like an ember. I looked at the face before me, a squished face, crumpled and creased like the earth seen from the sky. All would be well now, I knew, all would be fine. All the strange incidents and occurrences of the past few days would be put to rest, and I would live out my life peacefully with my man and my child.

The road up ahead towards the house rose up again and became whole.

Bilkis Bi stroked my head. 'The child, raise him well. He can save you or destroy you. He carries both the light and the blackness.'

The beam of light rolled down and lifted Bilkis Bi off the ground, and in a flash of intense radiance, she was gone. The Professorni, Teja and I looked on, for a long moment where the light beam disappeared beyond where the atmosphere ended and the vacuum of space time began.

I smiled through my tears at my child, still sticky with afterbirth, flailing his limbs helplessly and mewling, his breaths little gusts of hot vapour that sizzled as they hit the cold air, his eyes crumpled and screwed shut. Beneath his skin was a faint glow that grew as we watched, the moon shining through his skin, lighting up the veins and arteries running through him with an unearthly brilliance, a riverine map of light, a brilliance that lit us all. And then, he opened his eyes and looked at me, a helpless newborn, his irises little candle flames, blinking and myopic in human skin.

Acknowledgements

There are always thank yous. And then some more. But these are mine. Not too many. But all too important and integral, and I would be remiss to not include them.

The first to Shinie Antony who has more confidence in my work than I do.

To Anupama Manral at Hachette India, who took this very strange book on.

To Rupal Vyas who went through the manuscript with the proverbial eagle eye.

For the lovely cover, Sahitya Rani.

To my mother, the fiercest woman I know. To Krish, for the love and light he brought into my life.

And finally, to Kirit. May our lights always reach out to each other, wherever in the universe we are.